Tomorrow, the truth is waiting for you…

I0658576

Death Before Revenge

A Cal Lynch Thriller

Seamus Connolly

For Sal

Accuse me not, inconstant fair,
Of being false to thee,
For I was true, would still been so,
Had'st thou been true to me.

Robert Tannahill

Chapter One

Paisley, 1985

'SO WHO IS SHE, Son? And why was she following me?'

'Mum. It's six in the morning. Can you not call at an earthly hour? Anyway, how are you keeping?'

'Och. Don't try that how are ye shite on with me. Ah phoned the now cause ye never answer ma calls when ah phone yer fancy office during the day. And ye never seem tae be in at night either.'

Cal Lynch pictured his mother standing with a stern face, her right arm rigidly tucked under the left elbow, the phone receiver pressed tightly against her ear. Her right foot would be tapping continuously as she irritably awaited his response. Immediately she would be tightening her lips, adding the customary frown that she had worked on and perfected in her previous seventy-four years, revealing the deep lines on her forehead and a fearsome anger in her eyes. She would have then started to move the small animal figurines around the melamine dresser, tucked neatly under the stairs of the narrow hall.

'Two fuckin hours, son.'

She would have nodded for forgiveness to the Sacred Heart picture hanging above the two-tone green phone. The good Lord's affectionate expression and sorrowful eyes looking down sympathetically, His open, wounded palms framing His exposed heart.

Despite living in London for over three decades and being relaxed in her surroundings, Cathy Lynch had never fully assimilated or felt the need to do so. Her distinctive Scottish accent remained completely intact and, just as importantly, her fiery, no-nonsense Gorbals attitude and sharp tongue had also travelled the road with her.

The framed photograph hanging below the Sacred Heart, on a backdrop of woodchip wallpaper which was encased in layers of magnolia paint, was the only one she possessed of her wedding day.

* * *

Having to leave their Glasgow home at a moment's notice had put paid to any opportunity to pack even a few of the treasured possessions she and her late husband Peter had accumulated during their all too fleeting time together.

Cathy was nervous to the bone the day prior to the wedding ceremony. She had a worrying gut feeling that all would not turn out as she hoped. Her sister, Agnes, picked up on her fretting and her constant glances out of the window of the family home on Caledonia Road in the Gorbals.

'Yer no scared or having second thoughts, are ye? Whit's wrong with ye, Cathy?'

'Ach, it's nothing, nothing. Ah'll be glad when it's done, that's aw,' Cathy replied, pacing the living room as she tried to curtail her fears.

As she stood with her new husband outside St Francis' chapel, the large imposing doors framed with discoloured sandstone in the background, she beamed radiantly, a life of dreams ahead of her. Peter was resplendent in a dark suit and light green tie, both items borrowed from his brother, while Cathy lit the scene with her piercing blue eyes, high cheekbones and a bright smile that was enhanced by a flipped bob hairstyle. Her wedding dress was homemade, created by her own hand from yards of white silk and lace she had bought at the Barras market just four weeks previously. They had enough money to treat their close family to a celebratory tea at Coia's luxurious restaurant in Denniston, the staff going out of their way to spoil the couple and make their day extra special. It was then back to reality and their single end flat as they awaited completion of their shiny new council house which had been acquired at Queen Elizabeth Square.

Basil Spence, a renowned architect and visionary of new innovative housing projects, designed the new estate. The Glasgow Corporation fully embraced his brutalist designs in an attempt to find a solution to the overcrowded living conditions experienced by residents. Hutchesontown A, B, C was a dream move for families anticipating a whole new life of luxury. 'The future of city living,' an excited housing officer remarked, while showing them round the premises. The natives soon christened it Alcatraz, Barlinnie and Colditz.

She had wanted nothing more than to be married to Peter, to build their future together. She thanked the Lord every day for her good fortune at finding a man who respected her and vowed to be her protector. Always to be there for her. The correct decision was made; she was completely clear in her own mind of that. It was undisputable, she was sure.

He was different from the other local men: kind, thoughtful, aware of his surroundings, and one who would take seriously his role as her husband. She listened as her mates at the rope factory moaned every Monday morning about their other halves and their inadequacies. A few sporting faces that seemed to constantly walk into doors. Peter would come home from work every night, avoiding the heavy drinking culture of the day, and hand over his pay packet from the Forge Ironworks. He didn't hang about waiting for beer money or, importantly, attempt to be a scheme gangster. She had had enough of them, as they tried to achieve some sort of artificial status or peer recognition within their area.

Their life was made complete a year later with the birth of Cal. Peter chose the unusual name, remembering an old Irish clan from his forefathers' homeplace in County Monaghan. *A young battle chief. He'll be a leader. And have a better life than us, Cathy*, he'd say, putting down his book and pointing towards the Moses basket in the corner of the increasingly unliveable room.

The bright floral wallpaper, on the walls for little more than a year, was beginning to slide from the damp surfaces. The streets and villages in the sky. The great new concept in social housing had quickly turned into a living nightmare with condensation continuously running down the prefabricated concrete walls, ill-fitting windows allowing the ice-cold winds to flow freely into their ten-storey-high flat, and the black mould which became embedded within and ruined the small amount of decent clothes they possessed.

The new baby was the saving grace, the future, and their focus. *We'll get out of here soon enough. And am tellin' ye, Cathy, no Ironworks for him.*

The move to London had been traumatic but necessary after Peter's brutal murder. She was determined that their son would fulfil the dreams and aspirations his father had mapped out for him. She now saw it as her role in life to ensure the prophecy of her dead husband came to fruition.

She fought relentlessly to ensure their only son had the best education available to him. She confronted teachers, headteachers and priests to improve standards, eventually securing a placement within a fee-paying establishment, something she worked round the clock to pay for.

Cal was challenged to push the boundaries with his learning, his career ambitions and how he could influence the world with an aptitude built on a sound footing of basic hard work, just as his father had done.

Cathy was not slow to share her fiery temper with anyone on their Camden Town estate who dared mock her boy's accent or eccentric ways. She'd fight his corner until he was ready to do so himself.

* * *

'Mum, that's another two Hail Marys. Father Tom will be deeply disappointed. Do you still help with the flowers for the altar?' Cal responded, in another vain attempt to divert the conversation.

'Don't you worry about Father Tom. And remember just cause yer a big knob now doesn't mean you'll no get a slap. Two hours wandering about Camden Road waiting for her to piss the fuck off.'

Another nod, a double, towards the Big Man, he thought.

'Do ye know who it is or do a need to go to the Polis? Ye know what we were told years ago, to always be on alert. To be on our guard. To keep an eye out for anyone following us, anything unusual. She was slim build, bout five foot four inches. Natural blonde. Well dressed. Very pretty.'

Cal took a deep breath, 'Mum, look, don't worry. It's fine. It was a friend of mine who happened to be back down in London for work. I've not seen you in a while and with all the carryon that's being going on up here, I just wanted to be sure you were OK. I asked her to check in on you for my peace of mind. That's all, Mum. She said you looked to be in fine form.'

Cal ran his hand through the fine, silky blonde hair of the head which was resting on his muscular chest. She tightened her grip around his waist, awakening gradually due to the voice booming through the phone and the morning brightness piercing her eyelids.

'Aye, fine form right enough. Ah spent at least an hour in that jumble-sale clothes shop on Camden Square, where Denise Clinton works. The smell ah stale pish in there would honestly knock ye clean out. Is this lassie Polis?'

'Yes, Mum, she's a serving police officer. A senior officer.'

'Well, tell her she's no very good at following folk around and mibbae tae cut back on the blusher. She dosnae need it.' The line went dead, and Cal let out a worrying sigh.

'Your wee mum doesn't rate my surveillance techniques then? I should have just said hello.' Nicki Henshaw stirred, sleepily stretching in the large bed. She tucked the white sheet under her arm and shook her head in frustration at the bright natural light beaming in through the windows. Cal's preference for having the curtains opened to greet each day, rain or shine, irked her, though being a penthouse apartment, their privacy was protected.

The large windows overlooked the ever-changing Gleniffer Braes. As the sun lit up the hills, the mixed palette of greens fluctuated in colour as the clouds predictably rolled in, darkening and casting shadows across the grassland and mature woodlands.

'She's sharp as a tack. Always has been. The day my dad was murdered, she seemed to switch on some sort of survival mode, which took over her. I don't think it ever left her, to be honest.' He let out a slow, drawn-out sigh, his mind arousing memories of his childhood.

Henshaw sat up on the bed and entwined her fingers in Cal's. They had become close when going over the case files, notes and detailed confession, and the eventual fall of Eddie Quinn in the aftermath of his premeditated murder in Barlinnie Prison. She had nursed Cal as he recovered from life-threatening injuries in addition to assisting him with his mental recovery, helping him to rebuild his resilience. They were now inseparable.

Detective Chief Inspector Nicki Henshaw was consumed by work and her personal relationships suffered and were, consequently, sacrificed. Chasing down and jailing criminals provided a buzz and surge of energy which she constantly sought.

The romance with Cal had arrived unexpectedly, caught her off guard and at times left her feeling uncomfortable and vulnerable, as she was giving up some of the control that she had held so closely and fiercely protected. Now someone else mattered, dominated and consumed her thoughts. She still held a deep passion to hunt down the big players in the criminal underworld, though maybe more local, maybe in Scotland, not all over Europe, would be the best policy. She could create a life away from this, with Cal. Who knows what the future would hold for them? Their mutual growing love for each other was a solid foundation to build on, was it not?

Eddie Quinn's confession, which proved to be his own death warrant, provided her with the opportunity to justify to her London-based gaffers that a prolonged stay in Scotland was required to follow up on the long trail of evidence he had revealed. Time had to be spent checking the detail, chasing the leads, and remaining in the shadows, to allow the investigation to take its course, not to spook the targets.

Nothing would be off limits with names and leads linked to criminal activity reaching to the highest echelons of Scottish society, with judges, senior politicians and established businessmen, as well as serving police officers, being exposed as part of a network which protected and benefitted those who were hellbent on making money regardless of the misery their activities would place on others. No doubt some had succumbed to extortion after being caught in compromising situations that exposed them to the Quinn crime syndicate, which was all too ready to exploit them to the maximum.

It was becoming apparent that the organisation with the ruthless Jimmy Junior Quinn at its head, ably supported by his, until recently, inconspicuous daughter, who ran their operations shrewdly with an increasingly iron fist, was a formidable and well-established opponent. One that touched on and manipulated so many aspects of people's everyday lives that to disentangle it, to unpick it, would require a concerted effort by all those who were determined to smash it.

What wasn't clear, she thought, was how the crime gang had allowed Cal to get so close without dealing with him earlier. Had Eddie Quinn's confession to her accelerated matters beyond their usual, customary control?

Their flourishing relationship remained a secret with only a few trusted close friends being aware of its existence. They spent their time holed up in Cal's large, plush flat, getting to know each other intimately, shaping their potential future, or pouring over the documents Henshaw had acquired around their joint targets. Occasionally it would be a romantic meal out in Glasgow or, much to Nicki's dismay, early mornings travelling further east for regular fitness runs around Strathclyde Park. The mutual inbuilt competitive edge they both possessed was never far from the surface. They were seldom seen together in Paisley, the epicentre of Quinn's business portfolio and where Cal ran his ever popular and growing criminal lawyers' firm.

'Babe, I've got some stipulations if we are to create this wonderfully romantic utopia together.'

Cal raised his eyebrows, fearing the worst. He was a sucker for beautiful, ambitious women, though his choices hadn't resulted in positive experiences of late. He hoped Nicki was the exception. She nodded her head towards three large bay windows.

'The curtains are closed at night. I know you love to watch the flea-bitten pigeons and magpies flying about, but a five o'clock start – that's not on. Next, once my transfer is approved and I work up here full time and after the Quinn syndicate is smashed, we keep our work lives separate. And we eventually move somewhere else. This is a lovely flat, but it's yours, not ours.'

'That all sounds reasonable, darling. We can start looking at houses on the outskirts of Glasgow; a swanky place in Milngavie or Newton Mearns would suit us nicely. It would be very posh circles for us to move in. I think you've cramped my style in the penthouse anyway.' He laughed as she grabbed the sheet and made her way to the bathroom.

'Maybe not swanky or posh,' she called from the bathroom. 'That's usually where all the crims stay.'

'We can talk more tonight,' he replied, quickly changing into his running gear. He stuck his head inside the bathroom door as Nicki climbed into the shower. 'Right, I'm going for a run. Can we go over those final files with a glass of wine this evening?'

'Beat it, you perv.' She grinned. 'I shouldn't be letting you look at the files. They're confidential.'

'You trust me, don't you? We're after the same thing – finishing Quinn. Then I'll go back to defending the likes of them in court,' he responded, quickly brushing his teeth and heading for the door. 'I've got at least half a dozen clients in jail who are innocent. I need to work on those cases at some point also.'

'Yeah, whatever,' Henshaw shouted from behind the frosted shower screen.

Chapter Two

CAL'S MUSCLES WARMED AS his strides began to loosen. The early morning run generated the only sound present as he pounded the damp, hard granite of the Paisley pavements. The air was cold and fresh with the expected summer sun not wanting to crack itself open despite it being early June. Inhaling large gulps of air, he had pushed on. *Concentrate on your breathing,* he thought. *Lose that and everything else goes to pieces. Your brain starts to enter panic mode and forgets to tell your lungs and muscles that all is under control.*

He was determined to return to full fitness and banish the residual pain lingering in his body from the brutal attack that nearly ended him. Having an inbuilt confidence in his own strength, endurance and willpower also helped with the mental scars he carried, the flashbacks, the blackouts that were hard to explain and he discussed with no one with the exception of Nicki, who listened attentively and offered words of advice and comfort.

Businesses slowly set themselves up for another day as graffiti-laden shutters were being noisily lifted as the shopkeepers placed their wares at front doors to entice customers with their produce and bring the streets to life.

He ran on, following his favoured route heading east past Hawkhead Cemetery, the headstones standing upright to attention, stretching out endlessly across the steep hill and rising and blending with the grey skyline. Over the humped bridge, its walls emblazoned defiantly with white emulsion paint – 'End English Rule!' Onwards to the green expanse of Barshaw Park, over the manicured grass hill and past the derelict hospital, its sandstone walls showing its age due to decades of neglect. Reversing his route, he picked up his pace through the mature woodland and the lime-tree-lined road which had previously been the track for the park's illustrious owner's horse drawn carriage, down past the pond, the resident swans gawking and expecting the usual offering of a stale pan loaf from a visitor. Pushing himself on, he returned along the Glasgow Road, the town centre and towards the West End.

He observed the stark contrasts in affluence and social status evident in the properties set out in front of him. Plush, well-kept bungalows and large detached houses mixed with tenements which were in dire need of repair and loving owners, all living in close proximity to each other. Derelict shop doorways and windows were encased in posters advertising the latest circus or fairground to land in town.

Local pubs were also in on the act, promoting their deals for the forthcoming and much anticipated Live Aid concert. Newly pasted flyers featuring an emaciated Ethiopian child, her large, captivating eyes staring out from a stricken face almost certainly in the final weeks of her short life, were being used to hawk a full day of music on their premises, which they aimed to exploit and fill their tills with much-needed profit.

His lungs were working frantically as he challenged his body to do more, beyond his own expectations. Pushing himself on his goal was to climb the steep hill of West Brae at Oakshaw with the grounds and plateau of the imposing, vacant Porridge Bowl being the target. His finishing line. His long muscular legs began to buckle as he tackled the gradient. The grey domed roof of the iconic bowl seemed to move further away, becoming ever distant. His breathing was becoming laboured, calf muscles burned, and every part of his body ached. His mind blurred. He stopped and submitted to the restraints his mind was telling him were ever present. Frustrated at his pitiful effort, he despondently rested on a low, white-washed wall.

'Hawl, get aff the fuckin wall. Ye think ah spent aw last week building and painting that fuckin hing fur you tae plank yer sweaty arse oan it. C'mon, get tae.'

Cal turned his body slightly, his face a deeper shade of crimson. His shoulders were rapidly moving up and down as his lungs fought to consume as much air as possible. Raising an open palm, he waved apologetically to a large, imposing figure that was filling the width of a porch door of a pristine cottage.

Dressed in an off-white vest and a pair of faded navy Scotland football shorts, the man's burly build and thick neck were framed by a mass of unkempt white hair and a long wiry beard. Homemade Indian ink tattoos used his muscular arms and large shovel-like hands as a canvas. His red-rimmed eyes bulged as he swaggered towards Cal, his feet crunching on the golden gravel path.

A steady stream of cheerful polytechnic students making their way down the hill on the narrow, cobbled pavement squeezed by.

'What a grump. Where's your community spirit, Mister? Can you not see that this man needs to rest? He's exhausted,' an inquisitive student interjected as she passed with her colleagues, her friends providing moral support with loud tutting.

'Keep oot ae it, ya nosey wee fucker,' the man responded sharply, moving purposefully towards the garden gate. The student stood her ground, her files held tightly across her chest.

'I'm moving, I'm moving,' Cal whispered under his breath. He had that feeling again that he had blanked out for a second. The last conversation was not clear in his mind. He stood up, gingerly leaning on his thighs to gain some traction. Smiling towards the angry resident and the small band of students, he raised both arms in submission.

'Aye, make sure ye do. Next time, Ah'll roll ye down that fuckin hill.' The householder's aggressive attitude was at odds with the homely artefacts of gnomes and crafted wooden bird baths scattered throughout the well-kept garden. A collection of wind chimes hanging in front of the patio door caught the breeze and broke the tense atmosphere with an unscripted tune. Cal laughed. Looking over his shoulder, he left the early morning confrontation as he slowly meandered down the hill to his office.

'What a horrible, mean person you are. I've a good mind to report you to the police for threatening behaviour,' the student smarted.

'Aye, nae bother, hen, you dae that. The names Ger Johnson. That's wae oot the T.' He laughed, raising his voice intentionally and pointing his thick index finger at the student's files, and winking slyly at Cal as he retreated towards the house. 'In fact, write it in yer wee flowery jotter there, fur future fuckin reference.'

The bearded man continued to mutter to himself and flicked the wind chimes further into life as he slammed the patio door shut behind him.

'Well…is it him?' a woman's voice asked from behind an adjoining closed door.

'Aye, it's him, awright. Nae question,' the man replied. Smiling he lifted a faded picture of two individuals posing with a bouquet outside a church, which was placed against a gilt carriage clock on the stone mantelpiece. He threw himself down on the worn couch in a living room cluttered with a mishmash of furniture, a place that looked staged or just unfinished. He quickly built himself a roll-up from a rusting old Holborn tin.

'Looks the complete double of his da now. It's him, awright. Ah'm in the right place. Don't worry.'

'Good,' the voice replied.

* * *

Cal sluggishly entered his office, sweat wrapping his loose training top tightly to his body. Grace, his dedicated secretary, was already darting round the premises, watering the large newly installed foliage plants.

'Morning, boss.' She smiled. 'These poor things don't get a drink when we're no here. Ah always think they're glad tae see us oan a Monday morning, don't ye think?' She took a second glance at Cal, her long red ponytail flicking back and forward. 'You awright, boss? Ye sure this running lark is good fur yer health? Ye look, err, a bit…gubbed.'

'No pain, no gain. I'm away for a shower,' he replied quietly.

Grace shook her head. *Are ye no meant tae feel fresh as a daisy after dain that, huv mair energy*, she thought. *He looks goosed. I'll stick tae ma Club King Size.* 'You dae that, boss. Get yersel smelling nice again. First appointment is in twenty minutes. Yer pot of coffee will be waiting.'

He had settled well into his busy criminal lawyer business, taking on new cases, of which there was no shortage, researching potential wrongful convictions, representing clients within the courts, and achieving favourable results. The local celebrity status he was now lumbered with was tiresome. He was tagged as the man who arrived in Paisley's West End in 1984, an unknown entity, and singlehandedly brought about the collapse of the insidious, powerful Quinn empire. The urban myth continued to grow arms and legs from "legal warrior" to the "voice of the *wee* guy." He wasn't even something in between. Nonetheless, he couldn't influence what people thought, so he tried to pay it little attention.

What would happen next could only be guessed at. How would it play out? How many may fall along the way? Could Cal control it, influence the outcome?

He always had a plan.

Chapter Three

'IT'S JUST A COUPLA non-uniform, keeping their distance and watching yer back. That's it, Cal,' Lawrie pleaded, tapping his thick knuckles on the roof of the car as he caught up with the lawyer as he left the Sheriff Court after his late morning court case. Fully refreshed from his exercise routine, Cal greeted him with a wide smile as he rolled his black gown over his forearm and attempted to balance a pile of client files in his opposite arm.

Lawrie leaned on his old car, shading his eyes from the glare of the sun, the customary smoke billowing from the cigarette nestled between his tar-stained fingers, the blue haze disappearing above him. The frustration was clear on his weather-beaten, war-weary face. Frown lines ran across his forehead and displayed a toughness which was due to environmental conditioning, as they called it, from years of frontline interaction with criminal fraternities and small-time scrouts.

His cold, glowering eyes coming to the fore as he awaited a response.

Quinn and the organised crime gang he ran preyed on the vulnerable, the desperate and those wishing to block out their mundane existence. There were plenty of people to exploit thanks to the wilful decimation of the town's economy by a harsh, profiteering government with the cold-as-stone chief architect, Thatcher, as its ringleader. The gang flooded the town, previously an industrial, prosperous powerhouse, with drugs and created a residual, incessant fear of reprisal for any interference with their illicit trading. This was backed up by a justifiable reputation for torture and murderous actions when and where they saw fit.

Cal was aware of the undoubted benefits from his newfound status, which helped to develop a mutual trust and respect with certain police officers, allowing him to continue to work without hindrance.

Strathclyde Police, K Division, or 'the Crazy K' as it was lovingly referred to, had no shortage of challenges for the resident police cohort. Any support, advice or legal ear that they could access from an established lawyer not tarnished by any connections with criminal outfits was welcomed with open arms.

Detective Sergeant Frank Lawrie was a regular visitor to his office and a trusted friend. Suzie McGrath was still on the run months after being sought on a murder charge, and Lawrie continued to dig out further links and evidence pertaining to her key role in the protection rackets, drug dealing and vice-like grip the Quinn syndicate had on the local community and beyond. Thrown into the mix was her father Jimmy Junior Quinn's impending extradition from his palatial villa and previous safe haven in Spain, on a host of charges as head of the biggest crime organisation to operate in Scotland, with tentacles and links across Europe and South America. Lawrie was justifiably concerned on how this may play out.

'Cal, this isnae some cardboard gangster fae the scheme punting a few porno videos fae an ice cream van. This guy's a fuckin certified lunatic and he has other professional, dedicated, gold-plated lunatics behind him who'll be more than happy, will take great pride in fact, tae claim it as a badge of honour as being the wan that took ye out. Ye honestly think Quinn's gonnae give up all his ill-gotten gains, his fancy life, his power and status without a fight? For a wee plum like you? Catch yersel' oan, man.' Lawrie's exasperation was evident as he tried once more to convince the man he had begun to admire that he required round-the-clock protection.

Cal had complete trust in Frank Lawrie; the man had saved his life. He wouldn't forget what he had done for him. But having cops following him at every turn would affect how he operated. His intentions and plans could inadvertently be exposed as he became accustomed to their presence, as they blended into the background of his everyday life. That wouldn't do, not a chance.

Lawrie had also sussed out his past and put all the pieces together. Using his wily detective skills, he discreetly worked out the planning and research Cal had undertaken prior to landing in Scotland's biggest town. Cal may have sought revenge and not followed conventional lawful means, he thought, but sometimes when pitching yourself against a vast criminal empire dressed up as legitimate, thriving businesses, you had to be inventive, cunning. You had to bend the rules. He had bent a fair few himself to get the results he wanted, and he would do so again, without a second thought.

'Thanks. I've not been called a wee plum since I was nine and was the last pick, as always, for the football in the school playground. "Right, Cal, ya wee plum, we'll take ye," were the exact words said by Shug Pearson, who was a fantastic football player as well as being a complete maniac in the making. I still carry those with me today, burned into my brain,' he replied flippantly. 'There's no need for security, Frank. I'm stuck in the public eye after what happened last November. They would be insane, totally insane, to try anything that may help sway a jury if the evidence bundle is in any way debatable once they are eventually sitting in the dock. You've still to track down and arrest Suzie McGrath – how is that going?' Cal responded, attempting to alter the course of the conversation with a hint of sarcasm.

Suzie had played Cal, showing him love and affection – which was all part of the gang's strategy to get close to the new lawyer with a family history connected to Eddie Quinn and his psycho brother Jimmy Junior.

Cal had been working to his own assiduous plan after years of study and research into the workings of the crime gang and their role in the brutal death of his father in the sixties. This led to his life and that of his loving mother being turned upside down. The repercussions of which they still felt and lived with decades later. He had lost focus, he realised, due to being partially smitten for a time by Suzie's beauty and charming personality. That wouldn't happen again – there was still work to be done, final stages to be completed and a conclusion which would finally close the devastation inflicted on his family all those years ago.

Lawrie flicked the remnants of his cigarette towards the kerb, climbed into his beaten Ford Escort and glanced up at Cal. 'They. Are. Insane. That's what I'm trying tae tell ye. Yer a dead man walking. Fucksake.'

* * *

Settling into her office chair, Grace slowly rubbed her fingers over the address on the white envelope. She imagined her boy, his hand almost turning back on itself, the fingers white, gripping the pen tightly as he wrote. The handwriting and foreign stamp made her smile as she returned it to the safety of her bag. She'd read over it again, and again, tonight in the solitude of the living room with a coffee and a fag. Then she'd scribble a response and rip it up numerous times before settling on her final words.

Terence wasn't the neatest of writers. His schoolwork was always complete though untidy and at times, if rushed, illegible. An overzealous teacher in primary school had forced him to use his right hand rather than his natural left – 'using *that* hand is the devil's work,' she scolded him, rapping a wooden ruler across his knuckles. Grace hadn't found out until years later, having skipped parents' evenings due to working nights cleaning offices to subsidise the periods when Dixie wasn't earning from his maintenance business.

She scanned through today's appointments. *10am, Mr R Sanders.* The name seemed familiar. *I booked it – you'd think I'd remember.* She wracked her brain. *Oh well, I'll soon find out*, she thought, arranging the mail into the relevant neat piles.

The job at the lawyers provided her with independence and an opportunity to keep her mind busy during the quiet hours when the boys were at school. She had made it her own and dominated the office, her office, with a friendly face, empathy, and built-in quick wit. Immersing herself, she had renovated the previously bleak surroundings, creating a modern, relaxed ambience where visitors were put at ease, while ensuring the professional outlook Cal had insisted upon. As well as adding a shower room for his late shifts and now a fitness health kick, the old, broken furniture, damp walls and random faded pictures of Scottish scenery had been replaced with uniformity, inspiring quotes and prints of the world's most iconic cities.

The last six months had been a living nightmare with the murder of her husband, Dixie, and her oldest son, Terence, moving to Berlin to study music at the prestigious Orchester-Akademie der Berliner Philharmoniker.

Her two other boys were struggling to untangle their grief and all that had occurred. They accompanied their mother to victim support counselling to try and make sense of it all – if that would ever be possible.

Although Joseph was attending school more regularly and had given up most of his money-making sidelines, though he refused to relinquish his pitch with the Co-op trolley returns, which was their biggest earner, he was now clingy and in a constant state of fretfulness. Opening up to the counsellor, he unburdened – *Ah worry bout her every day, ah can't stop thinking about her getting hurt, being deid, not being here.*

Stephen had become insular and withdrawn, refusing to share his feelings with the experts. He blamed himself for the death of his father as he had triggered a chain of events which led to Dixie being lifted off the street and meeting his end. No amount of talk and advice from the police or Cal Lynch could alter his thinking. When not at school his days were spent in his room, allegedly studying, when in reality he was just staring at the four walls. The only glimmer of hope, Grace thought, was he still played for his local boys' club – he was their talismanic player and showed real football talent according to his crazy, slabbering coach.

Evenings were the worst as she sat alone in the living room, the tv blaring in the corner her main companion. She would think of Dixie and the constant noise he would bring to the household or the silence when he was morose or worried about something. She'd burn a Capstan cigarette in an ashtray as she attempted to keep his smell present in the house.

Grace would recall Dixie reaching out and touching her, not in any sexual way, just a touch. She would continuously sit close to him at the kitchen table, pretending to read the paper or folding a pile of washing as he attempted to pull his business accounts together. He'd bang away, frustratedly, at the calculator with his paint-stained fingers, his eyes darting between the receipts and the figures accumulating on the screen while reaching out to squeeze her arm – to know she was there. Or watching the tv in silence, engrossed by a film or an enthralling documentary, reaching out, to know she was there. Sitting alone her mood would darken further. He was tortured, the investigating cop had told her. He would have reached out, reached out for her – to know she was there to help him, to reassure him, hold him.

She flipped from quiet grief to an unbridled anger and thoughts of bringing an insane level of violence, which she hoped she would be capable of, to those who brought heartache and loss to her door. How would she do them in? What type of pain, torture, and death would she choose to inflict. She'd get locked up in the same prison where Suzie would be housed once she gets caught, and attack her, finish her. She would need to think that one through. It would need to be serious enough to get the jail – fraud, assault, or arson. Arson, that'll do, arson. That would certainly attract a custodial sentence. She would check some old files in the office, look for the crimes that have led to prison.

Once she cleared the mist and anger in her head, she just wanted them behind bars and their lives ruined, their power extinguished. Some form of normality is what she really craved for her and the boys.

Or she could just go up Toledo Junction at the weekend and get drunk on gin, dancing with her pals. She'd not had a drink in years, not since the oldest was born, too busy looking after the boys as Dixie got steaming every weekend. An unpredictable pain in the arse at times but he worked hard and deserved his regular blow out, she thought.

Grace tidied her desk for the second time that morning. She was obsessed with routine in the office. Everything in its right place and the day planned out. She felt herself becoming clammy and agitated if her schedule was broken or if anything disrupted her plans. She wondered if everyone was like this, stressed about routine and if it wasn't followed. She lined each page in the diary, underlined each date, each desk item in its proper place, stapler, punch, tippex, pen. Lined up neatly where she wanted them.

'Good morning. Mr Sanders for his appointment with Mr Lynch.' She hadn't heard the door open despite an annoying drag along the newly laid tiles that would require remedial action.

'In the name of Christ…Sanders. Sha…Sanders. Ronnie Sanders.'

'All of the above. Yes. How are you, Grace? Not seen you in a long while,' The man responded, straightening his faded tie, and closing the three random coloured buttons on his ill-fitting suit. Accompanied by a small schoolgirl, he stood, straight backed at around six foot tall and towered over Grace's desk, his lips closed tight in a forced smile. His long, thin face seemed hollowed out with his dark eyes sunken behind a pair of thick, unruly eyebrows with wiry strands darting towards his thinning hairline.

'Right, OK, take a seat, Ronnie, I'll check if Mr Lynch is free,' she replied, directing the visitor and the young girl to the soft, sofas adjacent to the large, gleaming window which looked onto the busy vista of the Wellmeadow.

Cal opened the door ajar, the sound of his latest music acquisition blasting behind him and filling the room. 'Mr Sanders?' he asked, returning to his office. Sanders walked briskly across the room, a folder tucked tightly under his arm.

'I'll wait here, Dad,' the young girl announced, to no response. Grace came from behind the desk to greet her, 'Hi, am Grace. Are you Ronnie's girl?'

'Yeah, I'm Monica. Ah'm in class with Stephen. He's in ma physics, history and reg class.' The girl looked younger than her son and seemed to be underdeveloped. Thin, she thought, though her small face also looked aged, strained. Grace imagined her features would look exactly as they were now when the girl eventually reached for her pension book. As she drew closer, she clocked the faded school blouse, the smell of dampness emanating from her clothes catching immediately in her nostrils.

'Are, ye now,' she smiled, taking the seat opposite and tidying the small coffee table leaflets at the same time. 'He tells me nothing Monica, especially bout school.'

Monica looked up and smiled, 'Ah tell ma da nothing either, not that he'd be interested anyway. Not that you wouldn't like any of Stephen's stuff, ah mean. He's good at history, not so good at physics, ah don't think. Ah like it but ah'm weird,' she added, nervously.

'Well, why don't ye come up for yer tea one night, ye can give him some pointers. Say the morra? And no school the day?'

'Naw, ah'm tae stay aff the day, help him with his social security claim. He's a meeting after this. Another crisis loan ah think.'

Ronnie Sanders settled in the chair, patted his shiny, Brylcreemed hair and opened his file, awaiting Cal's attention.

'So, Mr Sanders, how can I help?' Cal asked, lifting the arm from his stereo, and swivelling in his seat back towards his desk.

'Believe it or not but I'm here to assist you, Mr Lynch. To contribute to the ever-increasing reputation you are building for yourself in these parts.'

Cal looked up impatiently, his agitation coming to the surface as he stared at his visitor, almost looking through him, continuously turning the gold cufflinks attached to his tailored shirt.

'Let me explain. I'm a private detective. Fully trained and ready to embark on freelance work,' he continued, removing documents from the file, and placing them on Cal's desk, 'what you have in front of you are a list of individuals and businesses that I have investigated in the last year who I would imagine you are also interested in.' Sanders crossed his legs, straightened his spine, and pushed his shoulders back. 'I have evidence that those documented,' he added, leaning forward, and pointing a long lanky finger towards the paper, 'are involved in a variety of criminal activities, and are part of an intricate web, on many levels, although they are interdependent, are not aware of the identity of others. Your friend Quinn's empire sits at the top of the tree. I would also advise that these elements can function even if Quinn's empire was eradicated. Some are also the catalyst for miscarriages of justice which you may have an interest in.' He clasped his hands, pleased with his opening statement.

'And what are you asking of me, Mr Sanders?' Cal enquired, closing the file and feeling slightly frustrated with his time being wasted. Impatiently spinning his favourite fountain pen between his fingers he decided he would instruct Grace to get some detail from people seeking appointments from now on, ask more questions – filter them.

'Just some freelance work, anything that you need a discreet expert to check out for you. You see this is my dream job, Mr Lynch. When my former workmates from the Chrysler car factory used their redundancy to buy a taxi licence or get into the pub game, I was investing in my future with a course in York to become a registered, bone fide, private detective.' He smiled; his thin lips closed tight.

'You may have struck a credible blow to our local underworld, Mr Lynch, though from my research I can honestly say that's all it is – a blow. They're functioning quite freely in several spheres which remain untouched and still under the radar,' he added, ominously.

'Let me have a think about it, Mr Sanders. If anything arises, I'll ensure you get a call. Thank you.' He directed his visitor with an open palm towards the door.

Sanders stood behind the chair his tall, thin frame screening the glass door behind him. 'One last thing, Mr Lynch. Have a look at this file,' he said, handing Cal another document. 'That's a note of all your movements in the last four weeks, every movement. That's what I can bring to your operation; inconspicuous delivery, relevant detailed information, on time and within budget. Think about it.' He added and leaving the office, buttoning his faded trench coat over his cheap suit.

Cal scanned the document with a gaping mouth, raising his head repeatedly towards the door. Almost immediately Grace and Jack, the wily senior member of the lawyer's team and resident para legal, occupied his office.

'Right. Whit's he wanting, boss?' Grace asked quickly, pulling Jack further into the room.

'Grace, client confidentiality. Please,' he replied, continuing to scan the papers in front of him.

'Aye, ah know that, but no for him, boss. Tell him, Jack.'

'You tell him.'

'He's worth a watching that one. Do ye know who he is? Even the nickname sums him up. Shaa…Jack, tell him.'

Jack sighed loudly and dejectedly shrugged his shoulders. 'Ronnie Sanders grew up beside me in King Street, boss,' he nodded his head towards the wall, 'just up the road there. Comes from a family of chancers. Known as Shagger. Shagger Sanders.'

Cal raised his head and again looked beyond his staff towards the front door. He could see Sanders standing on the street, a small girl at his side.

'Strange, he doesn't look like the type who would, how should I put it, attract the ladies,' he replied, with a smirk.

Grace fired a sharp elbow into Jack's ribs urging him to provide more detail.

'Naw, it wasn't him, boss. It was his dug. Shagged everything in sight. Pumped the back tyre of John

Canavan's coal lorry without fail every Saturday morning. Lampposts, bins, attempted to hump cats, anything really. Ah'm no that clued up on dug types, but it was a big, massive, chestnut brown hing with a huge, square face and big, mad, scary, wide eyes. Kison it was caud, Kison the bastard was what we caud it, scuse the language. Used tae be murder if it clocked ye oan the way hame fae school, ye had tae run like hell up the close in case it tried tae mount ye. Aye, Shagger Sanders, that's him.'

'Aye, but he's a bad yin, boss. It runs in the family. His Granda dodged the Second World War kidding oan his mental health was shot to pieces and hid oot in Dykebar Mental Hospital tae avoid the draft. His brother, he's a mad gambler and would steal the sugar oot yer tea for a bet. And Shagger, he was hated in Chrysler for sticking his workmates into gaffers for any wee bit of skiving they were up tae. Ah don't trust him, not wan bit, worth a watching,' Grace added, looking over her shoulder.

Cal scribbled on a sheet of paper, ripped it from his pad and nudged himself past his concerned colleagues and out of the office his staff turning to follow him. Heading out the front door he shook Sanders' hand, folded the paper, and handed it to him.

'What the hell's gaun on, Jack?'

Sauntering back towards his desk he responded, 'Unfortunately Gracie, I'm sure we'll find out soon enough.'

Chapter Four

'I'VE GOT THE CHINESE. My brain's numb after the day I've had, so I'm not cooking tonight. Looking through all those bloody files is a nightmare.' Nicki sighed as she dumped her bags on the kitchen worktop.

'No worries, darling. I'll heat the plates. Take a seat and there's a nice glass of red,' Cal responded, placing his hand under Nicki's chin, and kissing her softly as he guided her towards the bar stool.

Henshaw tied her long, blonde hair into a tight ponytail and took a large gulp of the wine, letting out a long sigh.

'Right, here goes, Mr Lynch. We have a further four files to go through tonight. These are the last you'll be glad to hear. You really shouldn't be reading them; they're classified. But I just need your insight and opinion. Then, once you've gathered your thoughts, I'll tell you what's coming next.' Henshaw circled her finger round the rim of her glass as her faced brightened in anticipation of what she had planned.

Cal stared, in awe of Nicki. He loved her ruthlessness in the pursuit of criminals and her relentless work rate to see cases to a successful conclusion. Completing his own agenda was always the main goal but it wasn't too far removed from Nicki's objectives either.

'Can't wait, and your secrets are always safe with me. Nicki, do me a favour – lose the gun? It spooks me,' Cal said, the shining metal glistening off the bright white kitchen spotlights.

'Sorry, force of habit,' she replied, removing the short arm from its holster and placed it in her handbag, checking the safety. 'Are you sure about Frank Lawrie? Do you trust him? No nagging doubts?'

'Absolutely. With my life, quite literally,' Cal responded, assertively.

'Right, eat fast.'

'So…' Henshaw walked round the large, ornate dinner table as Cal piled up the dirty dishes on the worktop, his eyes glancing in her direction throughout. 'We have a whole raft of businesses throughout the country, top cops, councillors, and senior figures at councils, all named by Eddie Quinn in his statements to me. Honestly, I loved those interviews. It felt like he was cleansing himself, clearing the decks, setting the scene for what he knew was coming next and…' She paused, pointing her pen at the documents placed neatly across the table, '…and now those he named, have been verified by sources here and cross referenced in intelligence reports abroad. Unbelievable.'

Cal lifted his glass and walked towards the door to answer the buzzing intercom. He pressed the button and caught Henshaw's eye. 'It's Lawrie. It's fine, just leave the files,' he added, sensing her unease.

'Awrite people. Oh, ah smell takeaway. Anything left for starving me?' he laughed. Throwing his weather-worn trench coat over the bar stool he moved through the open-plan kitchen, picking at the scraps left in the tinfoil containers.

'Wine?' offered Henshaw.

'Cheers Ma'am. What's the occasion, why have ah been summoned? Oh, ah've a bit of news too, well two bits really.'

Cal closed the open files and stood passively at the table, his arms folded across his chest, a glass resting on his angled arm.

'Frank, we've been over this last batch of files. That's three full weeks' worth of reading, checking stories, verifying data, liaising with Nicki's colleagues in London, across Europe and further afield, to nail this thing.'

'Ye've done great, the pair of ye. Hats aff.' Lawrie shook his head in appreciation as he stripped a chicken leg quickly with his crooked teeth.

'Have you heard of something called the Russo?' Cal asked, his eyes fixed on his friend to gauge his reaction.

Lawrie coughed and choked, reaching quickly for his glass. Henshaw moved to a seat beside him, passing a napkin, 'So, you're familiar with it?' She asked eyeing him closely.

'Wow, did you get that from those files? Cop files?' Lawrie wheezed, attempting to clear his throat.

'Various sources, Frank. It keeps coming up.' Henshaw replied.

'Ah, Russo. The Russo. He or she or *It*, no one really knows. Who is spoken of in hushed tones down the station. Everyone's shit scared of *the Russo*. The biggest organised crime gang out there apparently. This has only happened recently, ye know. The high-end criminal underworld are well aware of it, but it's only been exposed since you two arrived on the scene and took down Eddie Quinn.'

'Any leads or thoughts, Frank?' Henshaw enquired. 'The files refer on several occasions to this "figure." I've also had contacts in Interpol throw it out this week to their informers, and intelligence suggests this person or organisation really does exist.'

'The way ah see it,' Lawrie replied, moving to the files opening, and flicking through the pages of each, 'and from what I've heard, the Russo, is the figurehead, the main conduit for everything coming and going through Scotland, England, and most of Central Europe. Controls it all – drugs, people trafficking, laundering, large-scale conglomerate businesses, logistic companies across Europe and some say the policies agreed at Westminster…and ah cannae question their thinking that whoever it is dictates the remit of Jimmy Junior and his crime cartel.'

'How the fuck did I miss this?' Henshaw hissed. 'I worked on Quinn for over a year, and this never came up once, anywhere.'

'Whoever it is, they're good, exceptionally good. Protected, wealthy and at least a few steps ahead of us. But ah wouldn't get too pissed off bout it, Ma'am. The Russo was only exposed when you two started yer, separate, fishing trips into the Quinn empire.'

Lawrie straightened his back, placing his hands in his pockets he added in frustration, 'And that's another reason ah want eyes on Cal 24/7, but being the intransigent prick he is, that's not happening. Ma'am.'

Cal raised an open palm. 'We've been through this, Frank.'

'Looks like I'm here for the foreseeable then babe,' Henshaw rubbed her hand over Cal's thick, wavy hair, resting her fingers on the back of his smooth neck. 'At least when he's with me, I'm still a legal carrier. Right, so how do we catch him, her, or them, Frank, what's your thoughts?'

Frank threw the bare chicken bone into the bin, downed his wine, and flung his jacket over his shoulder.

'Ah think ye just keep doing what yer doing?'

'Eh?' Henshaw enquired, glancing at Cal.

'Look, this scumbag has been in operation for years, decades for all we know. Nobody knew hide nor fuckin hair of this until now. They're now exposed, not totally, just a chink, through Quinn. His operations are, more or less, back up and running. We've hardly made a dent on them. There were no any rivals popping up tae move in on their territory, no turf wars. That tells me all is still in place. Keep chipping away at Quinn's empire, that's how ye find out who this is. Expose the Russo and bring down the whole fuckin house of cards. But,' he paused looking directly at Nicki, 'you need tae be careful. There's powerful people at play here they won't give this up easily. And that includes within the police service,' he added, worryingly.

'Guys, you might have forgotten something – I'm a defence solicitor, not a police officer. I need to earn a living and may end up defending such individuals.'

'Mate, *such individuals* wouldnae touch ye now with a fuckin shitty stick. Yer a witness to an attempt murder, yer own.' Lawrie replied as he edged towards the door.

'And that reminds me,' Lawrie looked at Henshaw, raising his eyebrows, 'Ma'am, ye must have missed yer pager thing. Suzie McGrath's in custody.'

'What the hell, Frank.' Cal stood with his arms outstretched.

'Ah was being mannerly. It was you who called me here. So, I assumed ye had something to say – which obviously ye did.'

'What's the detail, Detective?' Henshaw asked, quickly checking her bag for the elusive pager.

'Bit scattered at present, Ma'am. Picked up from on a raid of a swanky house in Woolton, Liverpool. Current thinking is she's been hiding up there since she tried to weigh Cal in. Superintendent Irvine is on his way down there just now to take her back up the road for questioning on Dixie Clark's murder and his attempt murder.'

'Can you drop me at the station? This Russo thing will have to be put on the backburner for now. We need to make sure the drug-racket charges, and all the other shit, is included in the diet. I'll get on the interview team,' Henshaw stated, quickly collecting the files into one pile, and stuffing them in her large handbag.

'Aye, nae bother, Ma'am. Ah'm going tae drop in on Grace, let her know the script. Ye want to join me, Cal?'

Cal's mind was racing again. He slipped into his own wee world, nothing around him registered as he recalled how close he had come to death and how easily he had embraced it, no excruciating pain, a calmness within his mind, accepting what was coming, just wanting to go to sleep. That scared him.

'Cal?'

'Err, sorry. Could we leave Grace tonight, Frank? I'm just conscious of arriving at her door with the police again, after you know, Dixie's murder.'

'Fair point. There's a press blackout til McGrath is safely ensconced in a cell on Scottish territory. Hopefully, there's nae leaks. You can pass on the good news tomorrow at yer office. Ah'll call in later.'

'You said you had two items of news?' Cal enquired, growing increasingly frustrated with Lawrie's laidback attitude.

'Oh, that's right, so ah did. Jimmy Junior Quinn is on an early morning flight the morra, fae Spain. His extradition has been rubber stamped. After questioning both will be housed at Greenock Prison; the final stage in what we called Operation Safer. Glad it's done to be fuckin honest, been a pain in the arse. Bit of a family get together on the cards, me thinks.

'You're full of surprises tonight, Frank.' Cal shook his head, exasperated.

Chapter Five

GRACE SETTLED INTO THE quietness of the living room, the solitude at times was welcome, on other occasions it could suffocate her. She was at least shielded here, away from people their thoughts and sympathy evident in their eyes now that she was a single mum, having to raise three kids on her own.

Occasionally, on her day off, she would escape to a place where no one knew her, where the eyes wouldn't be filled with sadness. Whether it was a bus trip to Largs for an afternoon or even a walk up the Gleniffer Braes, she could be herself and not worry about the looks and the pity which often surrounded her.

Family photographs hung strategically around the brightly papered living room walls with more of Dixie being added on a regular basis. Sitting in her joggers and an old t-shirt, coffee at her side and a cigarette burning in her mouth, she finally switched off from her work.

She realised she had made an impact in the office and ran it like a smooth-running machine. It wasn't hard to organise as guys are always happy to be led. *The male of the species*, she thought. That didn't mean she was entirely settled or proficient; this was out with her comfort zone. She had to work at it, plan her day and that of others. She had used the experience of her previous life, growing up and raising her siblings in Ferguslie Park as well as organising her husband and three errant kids to help shape her approach to each day.

She quickly grabbed Terence's letter from her bag and smiled as she ran her fingers over the address for the second time that day.

Dear Mum,

I hope you are well, and Joe and Stephen are behaving for you. I'm well settled now though this letter *writing carryon still takes me a while and I'm still confused bout commas and that. This is the fourth go at this one.*

I'm learning lots about classical music and the different composers. There's no orange walks here so I need to use one of the big drums at the academy ha-ha. The food's no bad but not the same as yours, I think am losing some weight.

Everyone is nice, well nearly everyone there's a couple of bampots but there's bampots in Paisley as well, isn't there?

The building we practice in is amazing you can see it for ages before you even get beside it. It has golden, shiny, walls outside. It looks like a spaceship. I think if it was up the Paisley West End one of the local junkies would have stripped it by now ha-ha.

We watch the orchestra play here and the sound is awesome. The performance space is surrounded by about 2,000 seats kinda hanging over the musicians. One day it might be me and Mairi-Clare playing in there.

Mairi-Clare loves it here, it's as if she was always meant to be in Berlin playing her violin. We're both trying to learn the lingo, she's better than me. I can order a frankfurter (that's a big sausage) from the street sellers.

Could you write her a letter she doesn't get much from her maw or da.

I bought new pants and socks when I got my allowance so don't be sending any more of the three-pair-for-a-pound white numbers you always buy off the auld guy down the high street, ta anyway.

I'm keeping my room tidy it's only small but at least I don't need to share with anybody.

Are you looking forward to the Live Aid concert? I think we're doing something for it as well.

Berlin is amazing, really big, and busy, with soldiers everywhere. I travel alot on the trains and trams. I was down at Checkpoint Charlie on Tuesday; you can see the Russian soldiers right across the border or they might be East German. I don't know.

I thought you would be happy to hear I go to mass every Sunday, it's in German but I think they follow the same script as St Mary's. I'm really enjoying it. Honest.

I've been to a few art galleries, ye can spend all day in them, the paintings are brilliant and must be worth a fortune.

Have you heard anything about Mikey's dad? I got a letter from Mikey said his dad is drinking like a madman in Ireland, tanning the local moonshine.

Anyway, that's really all I can think about saying. Write soon and I'll phone on Sunday at six, as promised.

Your fave son,
Terence.

Tell Joe and wee Shada to send me Scottish five pence pieces. I can get packets of fags with them out of the vendy machines cause they're the same size as Deutsche Marks. Just in case they were wanting to make a couple of quid selling them on.

Terence's life had changed beyond his wildest dreams. Six months previously, as he looked forward to leaving school, he had been filling out application forms with his best mate Mikey for apprenticeships in Paisley and now there he was sitting at the prestigious Berlin Academy being taught classical music by some of the best tutors and musicians in the world, at the Berlin Philharmonic.

Grace, read the letter again just in case she had missed anything, looking for any hidden messages contained within it. Maybe he wasn't happy or

46

content; perhaps she was secretly hoping that was the case. She clicked her pen and began her response.

'Mum, ah need tae talk to ye,' Joe announced, bursting into the living room, throwing himself onto the cream leather chair.

'Is there never any chance of a bit of peace in this mad house? Yes…Joseph,' Grace responded, putting down the pen and dragging deeply on her cigarette. She noticed his trousers were beginning to creep up by his ankles, another Provi cheque would be required. She sighed internally.

'Can ah swear in front of ye, just this once?' he pleaded, leaning forward while placing a pile of books at his feet, his eyes wide.

'Yer clearly worked up about something, by the looks of it. Ah'm hoping it's because ye got a rubbish mark in a school test and yer totally gutted bout it. But somehow…ah doubt it?'

'Kin ah?'

'Aye, just this once.'

'Maggie Thatcher is a dirty, cold-hearted fuckin bitch. There, ah said it.'

'Is that right? Where exactly have you been hiding for the last six years, Son?'

'Ah was up the Central Library there, got a load ah books; bout the hunger strike, what she's dain tae the miners – did ye hear what she had the polis dae at Orgreave? And the scumbag who runs Chile? Pinochet he's called, he's been killing and disappearing folk for years and he's, her mate. Unbelievable. And don't get me started on whit she hinks bout South Africa,' he shouted, holding up one of the borrowed books.

'All very interesting, so what ye going to do about it?'

'Mind Da always went on bout how "knowledge is power," and how we need tae teach ourselves bout whit's happening around us. Well ah'm going tae read hunners and teach maself politics and that. And when ah'm aulder ah'll become a politician and wipe the floor wae that witch.'

Grace raised her eyes to the high ceiling. 'Try no dogging school, that'll be a good start tae yer knowledge is power thingy.'

'Will do, Mum. Right, ah'm away to read these bad boys,' Joe replied excitedly, rattling his knuckles off the cover of the hardback book, and moving quickly towards the door. Pausing, he bent down and placed his arm around her bony shoulders, 'Just shout me if ye need me, if yer lonely or that, or if it's too quiet or ye want me tae watch the telly with ye…err ye know, anything.'

'Nae worries, ah will, thanks, Son. And keep the music down in there the night. Stephen's wee pal Monica is coming up for tea.'

'Mum.'

'Whit now?'

'Well, jist to say, ah pray for ye all the time. Jist so the big man keeps ye safe and that. Ah pray for ye everyday…ah pray like fuck.'

'Och, that's lovely. Thank you. But don't you worry bout me. We'll be fine…and yer swearing amnesty has expired.'

Knowing someone was thinking about you was comforting, reassuring, she thought. Picking up the pen she started where she had left off.

'In the name ah Christ, no peace whatsoever,' she growled as the doorbell rang. *She's early –, must be keen,* Grace thought to herself.

Stephen entered the living room with the small visitor following.

'Monica's here,' he announced quietly.

He had retreated into a shell after his dad had died. His confidence was lost and his outgoing, infectious personality had receded with it. She hoped, gradually, by introducing new friends, he could recover, return to his former self, and live a full life.

'Hi Monica, come in, take a chair,' Grace responded, smiling widely and guiding the young girl towards the couch so she wouldn't feel isolated in the single seat.

'Thanks,' she responded timidly, sitting with both hands pushed tightly under her thighs, her knees pressed rigidly together.

'Relax, Monica. Ye know, it's good to have some female company around here. Having tae listen tae those two can be hard, believe me. Though tae be fair, they're no the worst.'

'Same here, Mrs Clark. Mind ah'm stuck with ma Da,' she replied.

'Right, Stephen, shift yerself and turn that oven on, the chips are already in it. Chips and crispy pancakes, Monica, that OK?'

She smiled and nodded.

Stephen moved towards the door and nudged his visitor in passing, 'So, ah hear yer going to help me with ma Physics then?'

'If ah can. Ah'm no great but ah know the basics.'

'Cheers. That auld Curran hates ma guts. Ah'm going tae ask him for help, see what he says,' he responded, smiling half-heartedly.

'It comes at a price, nothing's free in this life,' Monica replied, raising her eyebrows; and nodding her head.

'Ah've no got anything tae give ye.'

'Aye ye have. Ye play fitba don't ye? Ah love it but ma miserable da won't give me any money tae go tae see Celtic. No even Love Street tae see St Mirren play.'

'Yer da's quite right Monica,' Grace interjected, 'the amount ah fighting that goes on at the games is scary. And you don't be slagging yer teacher. They work hard for ye,' she added, pointing a finger at her son.

'Dae ye like fitba?' Stephen replied, ignoring his mother's comments.

'Ah love it.'

'So ye want tae come and watch a bunch ah boys doon the Racecourse?' He laughed, holding out his hands in disbelief. 'Nae bother, that's cool. We're in the semi-final of the Paisley & District Cup on Saturday. Ye can witness how much of a moon man our manager is. Maw doesnae believe me.'

'Well, that's a good start. Now get the chips on before we all starve here,' Grace said, pointing Stephen towards the kitchen.

Grace picked up a polythene bag as Stephen left the room. 'Monica, please don't laugh, right,' she whispered, leaning over towards her, placing the burning cigarette into the overflowing ashtray. 'Ah bought these at Christmas fur him going back tae school after the holidays.' She opened the bag and pulled out the garments, still in clear wrapping. 'Turns oot they're bloody blouses,' she leaned back and laughed quietly into her hand, 'thank God ah noticed or he'd ah had a fit getting ready oan the first day back. You take them, I'd jist be putting them out.'

Monica smiled and ran her small hand lightly over the packaging. The blouse she was currently wearing to school was the same one she had since second year. She washed it most nights but frequently there was no washing powder, or it wasn't dry for the next day, so she just stayed off. Sometimes she just went in with it dirty and accepted the bitchy remarks and sniggering behind her back by the other girls. Some just held their nose when walking by. Her face dropped as she thought about wearing the bleach white, new blouse to class.

'What's up missus. As ah say, I'd only be binning them.'

'Naw it's no that. This is really kind of ye tae think of me, and that,' she replied quietly, turning to look at Grace, 'it's jist, it's…' She sighed, her eyes beginning to well with tears.

Grace reached out and placed her hand in hers. 'It's OK, Monica, what is it?'

'Ah've no really got many pals in school – well cause ah what happened wae ma maw and ma da being how he is. No as if ah kin bring them up tae ma house, is it? It's jist there's a wee bunch of cows in school and they'll notice it's brand-new and gee me more slagging cause ah finally got rid of ma auld one.'

Grace gave her a reassuring cuddle. 'You seem like a strong-willed girl. Jist hold yer head high, they'll move on when they see they're no getting a rise out ye. If that disnae work jist phone me. Ah'll sort them.'

Monica straightened her back and confidently stuck out her chin.

'There ye go, girl. Walk tall.' Grace squeezed her tightly. 'Right, ah better check on the chef in there.'

Grace left them to get on with dinner once she served it up and returned to the living room to complete her letter. The noise and the laughter coming from the kitchen signalled that all was going well.

She scribed the latest news for Terence, giving him updates on his brothers and her job and asking many questions which he would respond to in their regular phone calls. She always read her letters repeatedly making sure the sadness in her heart was not coming through to her son.

She played a similar game with his brothers – who never saw her crying or broken. She displayed an air of normality around them despite the challenges they faced and the horrendous loss they had suffered. The brave face would drop, and the crying would come when they were all in bed and she was alone with her thoughts, in the silence.

'That's me away, Mrs Clark. Thanks for dinner and the stuff,' Monica announced, standing at the door, her head motioning towards the plastic bag.

'Och away, it's nothing. Call up anytime or drop into the office if ah'm no here.'

'Ah'll walk Monica up the road, Mum,' Stephen said, turning Monica gently by the shoulders towards the door.

'OK, Son.'

Stephen stuck his head back in the door and whispered, 'The shirts weren't mine, were they? Did you buy them the day?'

Grace raised her hand, signalling for him to go towards the front door.

'Make sure she gets home alright.'

'Thanks, Mum,' he replied, with a rare smile.

Chapter Six

TERENCE TOOK A DEEP breath and filed into
the seats within the impressive bowl of the Berlin
Philharmonic Hall accompanied by Mairi-Clare and
the fourteen other international students. Voices fell
silent as, from the centre of the impressive valley
deep in the heart of the theatre, their eyes scanned
every inch of the architectural masterpiece.

Designed by Hans Scharoun the building was
located within the Tiergarten district of Berlin,
close to the city centre and the Wall as the West
turned its back on Potsdamer Platz as capitalism
faced off against its communist nemesis. The
building was part of a mix known as the
Kultorforum with streets rearranged away from
Potsdamer and the dreary, vacant sites and dead
ends located towards the East.

Scharoun had sought to generate a sense of
anticipation for the people coming to listen to the
beautiful music that would be on offer. He had
created dark, unassuming, corridors and from these

concrete passageway's visitors would emerge into the galleries and balconies finally arriving, awestruck, at the imposing auditorium which hung over and surrounded the musicians, the large, tent like roof rising and capturing the sounds which would be, skilfully, created below.

The group of young people had been assembled from throughout Europe and offered the opportunity to train and develop their musical talents at the prestigious, Orchester-Akademie der Berliner Philharmonic. They had arrived in a city surrounded by Soviet controlled East Berlin and East Germany. A virtual island which was viewed as a beacon of freedom in the western world and one which was heavily occupied by French, American and British military.

Two million Berliners enjoyed the cosmopolitan lifestyle being promoted in the wealthy city where a variety of cultures were openly embraced, and centres of education were part of everyday life. The affluence, heavily subsidised by western Germany, had also created an underground economy where anything could be purchased, with hedonism and drug taking prevalent within the nightclub scene allowing faceless dealers to ply their trade.

Terence was convinced he was well out of his depth attending such a prestigious academy. His only positive thought was that the other individuals, sitting around him in stony silence, might also be in the same boat.

'Hello Tubbs,' a voice whispered to his left.

Startled he turned to see a boy around his own age in a white Tacchini tracksuit his hair arranged into a tidy mullet.

'Do ah know ye?' Terence asked, studying the boy, and racking his brain for a connection.

'Yer name,' the youth interrupted, his broad cockney accent becoming evident, 'is written on yer bag. You twat.' He laughed, banging his fist on the small desk in front of him, his mouth open wide to the world and displaying a mouthful of fillings.

Terence closed his eyes momentarily and heel kicked his old school bag under the chair. Glancing at Mairi-Clare she smiled reassuringly. There's always one dick to deal with, he thought, where was Mickey when you needed him with his sharp tongue and put downs.

'Good morning, students,' a familiar voice boomed. He scanned the balconies to see, towering above them, the man they had met at their Paisley Town Hall concert.

'Let me introduce myself again. My name is John G. Cooper. You can call me Principal, John, or Mr Cooper but never sir. This is not school. Welcome to the Berliner Philharmoniker,' he announced with a wide smile and open arms.

'I know you are all nervous and very sheepish at present but believe me, when you complete this course, you will be confident, inspired individuals who will go on and achieve wonderful things. And hopefully some of you will graduate to our very own Berlin Philharmonic Orchestra.'

The Scottish accent helped Terence feel at home. He recalled that when they had met in Paisley, this guy had said he was from Royston in Glasgow; and that they would all be speaking English here as the first language.

The tall figure made his way from the balcony towards the imposing performance bowl area they were occupying, the sound generating from his heels echoing throughout the room. He walked slowly between the chairs eyeing the students as he went. Assessing their character, their mannerisms, who was avoiding his stare, who was sitting confidently or hunching their shoulders, or already appearing out of their depth in their new surroundings.

'The course that you are about to embark on brings together people from all backgrounds and has done so since nineteen seventy-two.'

He spoke slowly, accentuating his words, taking into consideration the various nationalities sitting with wide eyes and nervous postures. His hands moved constantly with every syllable to emphasise his message.

'Diversity, your cultural background, your social origin, religious affiliation, or none. Your way of life – all of these are important to society as well as to you as individuals. But no one, none of us, can create music or harmony alone or by our ego. Only collectively,' he announced his arm circling above the students' heads, 'we will learn and create beautiful music which you will showcase in this mesmerising arena. Your studies will revolve around performance. Our concert series which you will be part of will include hosting a diverse range of musical ensembles and performing alongside a mixture of chamber, opera, symphony, and wind orchestras. And of course, you will receive individual feedback on each.'

The students remained silent as Cooper now stood motionless.

'So, what great composers will you be studying, learning from and being inspired by?'

Terence quickly grabbed his notepad from his bag. He had managed to find a couple of books on famous composers at the Central Library in Paisley and had read up on all the greats prior to his first-ever flight out of Scotland and his arrival in Berlin.

'In your first semester you will study the sublime sound of Johann Sebastian Bach.'

Ya dancer, ah heard ah him; Terence placed a tick next to the name in his notepad.

'The profoundly beautiful music of Mozart,' Cooper continued, becoming more animated with each announcement.

Excellent, fuckin know him; adding another tick.

'Hildegard von Bingen, Monteverdi, Handel, Vivaldi and the utterly, fantastically brilliant Debussy.' Clasping his hands under his chin he smiled at his audience.

Terence was grinning back, smug with confidence. *Ah know all their names*, he thought, quietly contented. *Pity ah cannae play a note of any of their fuckin tunes.*

Cooper lifted a seat and sat amongst the group. Scanning the room, he smiled again hoping it would help them relax. 'What I want to do now is to hear where you all hail from. We will play a little game where you tell us this by naming a famous composer or artist from your country of origin and we then guess where this could be, OK?'

Ah for fucksake, a composer fae Scotland? Terence was rubbing his forehead, the stress already beginning to cultivate. He looked over again at Mairi-Clare who just smiled in return, completely relaxed in her surroundings.

'Let's start – with you.' Cooper pointed to a blonde-headed girl sitting with her back straight and unperturbed by being put on the spot.

'Hayden,' she replied.

Cooper smiled and held his hands up to the audience.

'Austria.' came the response.

'Next.'

'Giuseppe Verdi,'

'Italy.' An increased volume of responses.

Terence zoned out; his mind was completely blank. He was totally fucked. He had no clue if any composers came from Scotland. *Mibbae ah could say Alex Harvey*, he thought. His da listened to him and used to dance around the living room after a few beers. *Or Sheena fuckin Easton, she wis Scottish, ah think.*

'Next.'

The cockney piped up. 'Edward Elgar.' He grinned, nodding his head around the room as if he had subjugated the place.

'England.' Everyone groaned.

'Next.'

Cooper looked at Terence, the whole room following his lead. He could feel the heat rising from his neck to his chin towards his already flush cheeks as he grew redder with the fear that what may come out of his mouth could ensure his humiliation for weeks to come.

He had always had an awkwardness about him and an ingrained unease sharing thoughts or answering out and speaking in groups. As he continued to feel hotter, with sweat beginning to trickle from his armpits, he hoped he would just combust on the spot, that would be sound, he thought.

'Eh…Robert Tannahill.'

The cockney mullet sniggered in his ear, 'Never 'erd of the geezer.'

Cooper opened it up to the audience. 'Well?' The room remained silent.

'Ah, you need educating, people. This young man here is from the most beautiful country on earth, Scotland. What's your name?'

'Terence, sir, sorry, Cooper, shit, Principal.'

Cooper grinned widely and shook his head. 'Robert Tannahill, ladies, and gentlemen – the Weaver Poet. A composer of great music which is now heard throughout the world. Your homework – learn more about Tannahill.'

Terence felt his body slump in the chair relieved he'd survived this ordeal.

'Another piece of homework. As you will be aware the Live Aid concert is being staged in the United Kingdom and the United States of America with a TV audience of one billion people expected to watch proceedings. There will also be performances in Cologne and Austria and here in the famous Berliner Philharmoniker we will stage a concert of our own which will also be beamed throughout western Germany and hopefully beyond that monstrous Wall. And you,' he paused and with an open palm waved towards the students, 'you will also be playing on that night. So please consider what we should present. Tomorrow you will meet your section leaders, who are some of the finest musicians in the world and certainly the best and most inspirational teachers in their field. For now, get settled in and enjoy the rest of your day.

Mairi-Clare hooked on Terence's arm as they left the arena. 'Smart thinking there, Mr Clark. I forgot all about the famous Robert Tannahill.'

'Pure brass neck, man. Ah only remembered him cause his hoose was next tae oor auld primary school.'

'Looks like Germany will know all about him soon enough. And Live Aid, that's amazing, isn't it?'

Terence pulled Mairi-Clare to the side and leaned against the smooth, polished, concrete wall.

'Mairi, this is a lot of fuckin nonsense, ah shouldnae be here. Ah banged a stolen drum fae the

Orange Lodge and Cooper there hinks he can turn me in tae some sort of orchestral wonderkid. He's been sniffing glue, honestly.'

Mairi-Clare put her hand around his neck and tenderly wrapped her fingers in his long, unkempt hair. 'Enjoy the ride, Mr Clark – that's exactly what I'll be doing.'

Chapter Seven

SANDERS WAS ECSTATIC THAT his pitch to Cal was a success. Ecstatic, but not surprised. His ego has always overridden any potential doubts and reassured him that this day would come due to the superiority of his intelligence compared with that of his peers. He'd demonstrate how good he was by providing a detailed dossier of all movements of the person of interest. What meetings take place, persons that may be of interest, and note any suspicions while remaining in the shadows, aloof within the surroundings.

Only those who had something to hide, who were up to no good, were cautious in their movements, changed their routines on a regular basis and were switched on to who may be within their vicinity. This wouldn't be a strenuous job, most people, like his target; Father Dan, went about their business oblivious to what was being acted out around them.

He was surprised to find that the local priest was of material interest, but he surmised that this was a test, a dummy run for some more challenging assignments.

Why would Cal Lynch want to have details of daily going's-on of the local clergy? There were rumours – street gossip – that the priest was present when Dixie Clark was murdered. Nothing was substantiated and there was no record of any police interviews having taken place.

Sanders occupied one of the polished wooden benches in the back row of St Mary's Church. Attempting to blend in he followed the actions of the large congregation attending Mass. He observed a mixture of young parents with their children and older adults carrying out their weekly ritual.

He wasn't a Catholic and had left the parental duties to his now long-gone wife who had, allegedly, taken the wee one to Mass each week as well as dealing with the school, running the house, and managing the daily grind of life. She had developed serious issues with the drink, and the family allowance book, along with those belonging to her mates, sat in a pub safe in the West end to be cashed in on a weekly basis to pay off her and her pals drinking club tic sheet.

She blamed him of course for paying her no attention, for his moods and for being detached from her and the child, almost resenting their presence. He threw her intoxicated body out onto the street one wet February evening without a second thought, as Monica cowered in her bedroom hiding from another fight.

He was surprised at the stillness of the chapel, the non-judgemental atmosphere allowed him to relax and reflect on his recent life. What had he contributed to his family apart from half his weekly wages from Chrysler? Why was there such a disconnect with his daughter, why couldn't he talk to her with any level of interest or enthusiasm to help shape *her* life, *her* future – *Monica...You done yer homework...Go and get a loaf...Go get me ten fags off the van.* He was constantly, selfishly, consumed in his own future when he should be giving up his for hers. *Ach well, too late for that now, that ships sailed. She'll be auld enough to make her own decisions soon, no longer his concern,* he thought.

He tuned in to Father Dan's sermon – droning on about piety and the need to be humble. He studied the priest's persona and mentally noted his idiosyncrasies, and characteristics. A red faced, rotund, small framed, grey-haired individual who moved slowly, his shoulders hunched, his eyes constantly looking downwards. *I'll not lose him in a hurry*, he thought.

This will be effortless.

* * *

Father Dan walked the aisle of the local Co-op. With his housekeeper away back home on holiday to Gweedore in County Donegal, he had to feed himself for a week. He glanced at the message list she had left for him, scrunched it, and stuffed it in his pocket. Great, he thought, an opportunity to eat rubbish food rather than the wholesome offerings prepared for him each day by his dedicated helper. He threw some Jaffa Cakes and Blue Ribband biscuits in his basket and looked for the sign for ready meals. He stopped, frozen in his tracks as he instantly recognised a voice booming from the cigarette kiosk. He peered from the edge of the high shelving and caught sight of the back of a tall, thin man, his long, jet-black hair tied back in a ponytail.

'I do love this place ye know. Any time I visit 'ere the people are so welcoming and friendly. I was up 'ere for work a few months ago, had a wonderful time, so I did. Such a lovely wee place, reminds me of home.' The grainy voice, the Scouse drone, confirmed his worst fears.

Father Dan caught the man's reflection in the mirror behind the counter. The long protruding nose, which seemed to take up half his bony face, and the chipped front tooth were all too familiar and engrained in his mind – waking him and flashing before him in the night with the slightest noise or creak in the old parochial house.

He slowly placed the shopping basket on the floor and quickly moved towards the exit. Keeping his head down he hoped he wouldn't be recognised as he slipped past the queue which was growing behind the dark-clothed Scouser who was clearly enjoying his chat with the Co-op staff.

Sanders stood motionless at the community notice board adjacent to the exits, feigning an interest in a Raleigh Chopper bike advertised for sale. He observed the priest's interest and reaction to the individual currently purchasing two pouches of loose tobacco and a packet of Rizla papers.

Father Dan brushed past him, the collar from his black coat tucked high around his chin. He crossed the busy Broomlands Street, shuffling between the traffic and boarded a bus heading towards the town centre.

Sanders was in two minds, should he follow him? *This is where you make your money, with these split-second decisions*, he thought to himself. He'd hang about, find out a wee bit more about the tall man who had just wandered past him, rolling a cigarette, and humming a tune to himself. He'd shadow him, see where it leads. The man had clearly spooked the priest; *there must be something in this*, he thought.

Father Dan took the white handkerchief from his pocket and wiped his neck and forehead collecting the beads of sweat which had begun to gather as soon as he had recognised the voice. It was unmistakably the same individual who had held Dixie captive, joyfully tortured, and put the bullet in the back of his head, leaving him lying in a crumpled heap on waste ground like a discarded piece of furniture.

He recalled the strength he felt that night. He was courageous while facing up to the evil that was in front of him. God was with him, his faith was strong, it stemmed from his friend. Dixie had emboldened him, given him strength that evening while he provided solace and prayer as Dixie lived out what were to be his final moments.

That strength had long since evaporated, his life now a paradox of faith and guilt. The guilt of knowing what had happened that evening yet not sharing, bound by his faith, his dedication and, steadfast commitment to the Sacraments. His whole being.

The room was empty as he approached the tall reception desk at Mill Street Police Station. Catching his breath, he leaned against it as an officer approached from the back of the room.

'How can I help you, Sir?' she asked in a low tone, her eyes purposefully scanning his face and taking in his current condition and troubled state.

'I need to speak to Police Officer Frank Lawrie,' Father Dan replied in a hoarse whisper, glancing over his shoulder towards the door and the large windows which looked out onto the busy traffic junction.

'DS Lawrie,' she responded, searching the contact sheet taped to the back of the desk, 'and what can I tell him it's regarding, Sir? He will be busy at present. Would you prefer to leave a number and I can for the officer to call you?'

He placed his blood-stained Stole on the desk. 'The murder of Mr Clark. I'm Father Dan McDonald. I need to speak to him immediately. I'll not need an appointment.'

The young officer picked up the handset. 'I need DS Lawrie at reception right this minute.'

Chapter Eight

LAWRIE STRAIGHTENED HIS TIE and brushed the specks of dandruff from the shoulders of his faded suit. He had developed feelings for Grace. Her personality drew him in, a little bit more, every time their paths crossed. She had a complex charm about her; and he admired her stoic character and approach to life and behind her tough, protective, persona he knew she possessed a soft and kind heart. She was around his age he thought, still hurting from her terrible loss but if he hung in there maybe one day, she would be open to finding another partner. One day he'd take a chance and ask her out for dinner. He just had to be prepared for when that moment may arise.

He hadn't been in a relationship since his wife had kicked him out three years previously due to never being round for her or the boy. He had learned from that period, no longer going to the pub after work, though the long shifts and dedication to the job was still prevalent and one of the ex-wife's main gripes. She had moved on quickly with a new man ensconced in the house he was still paying the mortgage on though he saw his son on a regular basis and would always be his dad.

'Ye know ah'm pig sick ah guys. They could be the ugliest bastard in the world but cause they're male they hink they're good looking enough to pull any wummin, any wummin. Dosnae matter if it's Demi Moore, Olivia Newton-John, or folk like me. Greasy fuckers like him think they're God's gift.' Grace was standing, arms folded, her eyes burning into the back of a middle-aged man who was making a hasty retreat and brushed past Lawrie as he entered the office.

Not the best of days to ask her out, he thought to himself.

'Ah'll have a word?' he replied, nodding over his shoulder.

'Nae need, he got his character. He'll no be back.'

'OK. Is Cal in?'

Grace flicked open the diary. 'Nope, he's out. Oh, that's funny. Never seen that before. He's away to Greenock Prison, got an appointment with a client who's doing a four-year sentence, it says. He must have stuck that in this morning.'

'Does he usually head down there?' Lawrie's mind was racing. Given Cal's previous planning, anticipating what the lawyer was thinking was now a priority. 'When do ye expect him back, Grace?'

She ran her finger over the diary again. 'Ah check the diary every evening for the next day, that wisnae in there. No even ma writing. Wait tae ah see him, mucking up ma routine. He's down to be there all morning then he's got his weekly liquid lunch at the Vatican.'

'He goes up tae the Vatican every Tuesday?' Lawrie laughed, surprised by the high-flying lawyer's choice of pub.

'Aye, he meets an auld guy up there for a Guinness and each week they try to solve crimes or cover-ups, he tells me. They're working on some dodgy killing the now, ah think.'

'Grace, it's you I came to see, though ah thought he'd speak to you first.'

Grace hated these types of conversations with polis, it was always bad news.

'We've now got Suzie and her da. They're both being held in Mill Street for questioning then they'll be remanded before trial. Hopefully, they'll make a plea when they see the evidence stacked against them, to reduce their sentence, and we'll not have a drawn-out court case. Ah doubt that will be what their lawyer advises or what they would want to dae anyway. You should prepare yourself, and the boys, for a couple of stressful months.'

Grace sat down slowly, her eyes fixed on her desk, staring at nothing in particular. She knew that this day would come, eventually, and they would have to face the trial, press intrusion, nosey neighbours and, worst of all, lies from the defence. She'd speak to the boys tonight and leave a message with Mr Cooper to speak to Terence in

Berlin. She looked up at Lawrie, her eyes full of worry.

'So, they're held just down the road from our house, Frank?'

Lawrie felt the urge to walk round the desk and hold her tight, reassure her everything will be fine.

'Just for a few days, Grace. They'll be moved to a remand wing before they go to trial. It will hit the news tomorrow; I'll make sure the press are kept under control and handled by the station. They'll no be near you or the boys, ye have my word on that. Ye know, you'll get a family liaison officer for the trial, just to help you through it.'

'They can stick that; ah don't want an officer. They're just nosey bastards.'

'I'll be here for ye if that helps. Jist call me, anytime.'

'I know, Frank, thanks.'

Frank glanced at his watch, 'Sorry, I need to go. Will you be, awright?'

'Aye, fine. Jack should be in shortly. Him talking his usual shite will take ma mind aff things.'

'OK, I'll catch up with yer boss shortly.'

* * *

Stephen tapped his fingers on the graffitied school desk, awaiting his classmates to vacate after the bell's trill. He went over in his head what he wanted to say to auld Curran. He'd make sure he was assertive and confident with his proposal, to get his point across. Monica would be waiting outside ready to hear the good news. The palms of his hands began to sweat as the last pupil left the room, quickly he rubbed them on his black, nylon, school trousers. He took a deep breath and strode confidently to the front of the class. The teacher, who, as usual, was wearing his white lab coat, was busily wiping the blackboard clear in anticipation of the next batch of learners.

'Can ah have a word please, Sir?'

Curran turned on his heels and lowering his glasses he glanced at his pupil then quickly scanned the open register to remind himself of his name.

'Of course…Stephen.'

'Sir, ah don't get this Physics stuff. Ah don't get the ticker tape thing, the speed measurements bit, that sin cos san thing, or understand the experiments you huv us dae, and that. It's just, could ah get moved to another class, mibbae general science? It's just ah really want a good job when ah leave school and know ah need good grades.'

'Why did you choose to take Physics, Clark?' the teacher interrupted, returning to his blackboard chore.

Stephen shrugged his shoulders. 'Dunno, ah just thought it would be different and that.'

Curran put down the duster. Rubbing his hands to clear the chalk, he dropped his glasses down his nose and faced his pupil.

'Different and that. This is a science, Clark. It helps you understand the world around you. It stimulates your curiosity. Prepares you for future discoveries in that big, interesting, world out there.'

'Well, ah'm no good at it. Ah've been copying big Gerry for months. Ah don't think he's happy bout that either.'

'You should copy someone who gets the answers correct. That would be a start,' Curran replied, glibly,

Stephen shrugged his shoulders. 'Well, can ah?'

'Can you what?' Curran responded, closing the register, and quickly tidying the large wooden island that doubled as a desk in front of the blackboard.

'Move tae another subject.'

'That will not be possible,' he responded, shaking his head.

'But sir…'

'Do you think, do you honestly think I would allow one, even just one, of my peers to think I have failed in my profession, to have people question my ability to inspire my students? To have a pupil leave my class without completion, to show that level of failure?' His thin face and sharp features were animated as he continued to clear his workspace while glancing intermittingly at his pupil. 'Do you know, do you really comprehend what the outcome of attendance at this establishment is, what the purpose of this school actually is? Where the final destination is for the vast majority of its pupils?

'Tae teach us?' Stephen realised his proposal was more or less rejected, even before he could go on to regurgitate the script that he had practised several times in front of Monica. He had planned to praise the teacher and seek his advice on where he thought he would be best suited to carry on his learning. The conversation hadn't started as he had hoped now it was a waste of time.

Curran was continuing his rant as Stephen tuned in and out of what he was hearing, lost in his own thoughts.

'The service industries: cleaners, bricklayers, grass cutters, office workers, secretaries. That's what. Yes, some may excel and move to the professions. But you and many more such as you will be washing windows or emptying bins. Jobs that require labour to keep the wheels turning. No individual wishes to do such tasks, but we still need each to be done. We produce service workers, sonny, we are a service school. Hence why my enthusiasm is used sparingly only for those who show real talent and a passion to learn and apply themselves to their studies.'

'So, yer no letting me move then?'

'Do you read a newspaper, Clark?'

Stephen shrugged, 'Well, aye, the *Daily Record*.'

'There's a surprise,' Curran muttered under his breath. 'Well, bring your *newspaper* on the days you have this class,' dismissively he pointed his pen towards an empty row of worn, green, leather benches, 'you can sit over there on those and read in peace. Do the crossword? Yes, do that, do a crossword for me.'

'Ye cannae dae that. There's still pure ages to go in this year alone.'

'You have indicated that you are beyond learning about the beauty of Physics or grasping the fundamental knowledge it would provide for you,' Curran replied as he began to wave the pupil towards the door.

'That's no right. Ah just want a decent joab, no tae be a daftie. Ma maw will be up tae see ye as soon as ah tell her.'

'Clark, your mother hasn't attended a parents' night in three years. This conversation is over. On you go, out.'

Stephen moved quickly towards the door, Curran at his heels. He stopped suddenly and turned, startling the teacher. Looking him right in the eye he slowly opened up.

'Ye know, ma da would say that some folks want tae get people like us thinking in a certain way – teach us tae know our place and no tae get *above* ourselves. "Get notions above their expectations, Son," he'd say tae me, "they hate that," in ye know, he was right, ah wish ah paid mair attention. Folk like you are jist snobby bastards, gutted yer left in a shitehole school like this tae teach the likes ah me. Ah'll read ma paper but it's you who's the failure. Ya auld dick.'

Curran's face was turning a lighter shade of purple. He couldn't disagree with a word the boy had said – he was a failure.

'Out, get out…now,' he bumbled in reply.

Stephen was utterly dejected a dark mood overwhelming him. The feeling of hopelessness that he had erased just a few weeks ago returned almost immediately with a fierceness that blackened his thoughts. What did that counsellor tell him to do when he felt like this? He couldn't remember. Ach, fuck it, he thought, whit's the point.

Monica was patiently leaning on the wall and hooked on his arm as he joined her, matching his walking pace. 'Well, is he letting ye move?' she asked, looking up towards him as his frustration was turning quickly to anger.

'Is he fuck, cannae believe it. Tae read the *Record* for the next year, fucksake.'

Stephen felt things closing in on him again. He wished Monica wasn't there, he wanted to be alone. To talk to no one. Nothing had been the same since his da's murder. All because of him, he'd ruined everyone's life – Mum's, Joe's, fuck knows what Terence was thinking. He could feel the stress rising in his body, his mind becoming blurred and closing down.

* * *

Cal settled into his regular, worn-leather seat in the Vatican. The day had been another busy one and he was only halfway through it. Today was important as he required certain individuals to have sight of one another, their eyes to meet – to help him with his next move.

Old George meandered back from the bar with two pints of Guinness in his steady hands. The wide, wooden table had been laid out with a variety of props as the pair prepared for their weekly assessment of unsolved or disputed crimes.

The Vatican, or The Buddies as it was known to non-locals, was located at the busy junction of Broomlands and Maxwellton Street. A traditional auld man's shop, it was home to dedicated regulars who were comfortable in their surroundings. Lazy afternoons would be spent debating politics, ranting about their domestic situations and relationship frailties, playing chess, or just staring into space or more than likely into the bottom of their empty pint glasses.

Dixie had never fully explained the nickname given to the pub. "Something tae dae wae a Celtic supporters' bus leaving fae here tae go tae Paradise or wis it cause it was close tae the Chapel? Fuck knows," he'd replied, his eyes full of mischief.

He had introduced George on one of their many get togethers in the pub and Cal had taken to the older man, his humour and free spirit seeping through his stories and the life experiences he loved to share. They became firm friends after Dixie's passing and had committed to meet up on a regular basis to keep their friend's memory alive. Their meetings wouldn't be morbid affairs but would have a purpose – to solve, in their minds, the world's biggest unanswered questions or far-flung conspiracy theories.

'Cal, to your health,' he announced, raising his glass before taking a gulp and letting out a sigh. 'Lovely. So, how's your week been so far, ready for some light-hearted mystery solving?' He laughed, his shoulders rising in unison with his pot belly.

'Busy as usual, George, which is fantastic of course, but always ready for the Vatican on a Tuesday to keep me sane. Tell me, are they ever going to provide food in here? They're missing a trick.'

George began to rearrange the plastic models around the table. 'Never, I hope. You'll have to use your imagination with these figures, young man. My model-making days are long gone.'

Lawrie approached the table, stubbing a cigarette out in the ashtray. 'Thought I'd find ye here.'

Cal looked surprised, it wasn't the visitor he was expecting, and he would now need to get out of the pub before his anticipated target arrived, 'Frank, pull up a chair, we're just about to start,' he said, hiding his frustration.

'How are ye, Mr Sinclair, keeping well?'

'I'm well, Francis, can't complain. We don't see much of you these days now you're a fancy detective. He's a big knob now down at Mill Street, Cal,' George responded, nudging his friend.

'Too much work, no enough fun, Mr Sinclair. Ye know how it is.'

'George is about to provide his latest conspiracy findings. I then need to return next week with a counter argument to debunk his theory,' Cal interjected, attempting to move things on quickly.

'Drink, Francis?'

'No thanks, Mr Sinclair, on duty. Ah just need a word with this man here.'

'Did you know, Cal, Francis stayed below me in Sandholes Street. Right wee skitter he was, smashing windows, running through my veg plot, mentions all over the close. Now look at him.'

'You kept us well under control, Mr Sinclair.'

'So, George, here we are. Tell us your theory – who killed Kennedy?' Cal said, attempting to hide his impatience while dreading the customary cold breeze entering the pub as the double doors opened and his intended target entered.

George began moving the model car along the table. 'OK, here goes – the assassination of John F. Kennedy, the thirty-fifth President of the United States of America. So, the Dallas motorcade made its way along Main & Houston then turned right onto Dealey Plaza travelling west on Elm Street. Eight secret service guys in the follow up car, eight … then the shots began to ring out,' he paused and raised his head, eyeballing Frank, and Cal.

By now the bar man had stopped his glass collecting and ashtray emptying duties and was hovering over the table. He was soon joined by another bunch of lunchtime regulars.

George continued, mindful of the presence of the growing audience. 'The first shot came from the book depository, that's not disputed. It hits Kennedy and ricochets into Governor Connelly, seated in the front of the limo. Now, this Oswald character, he was classed as a *sharpshooter* twice with the Marine Corps but that was when he was firing at stationary targets and many years before this incident. And not at a serving president in a moving vehicle, who you're obviously trying to kill – so the level of stress and pressure would be exacerbated tenfold. Now, folk begin to realise something is wrong, the president has been hit; and the guys in the black suits and sunglasses need to get him out of there, pronto.'

The pub was silent as George held them in the palm of his hand, lowering his voice for effect and moving his homemade figures slowly and purposefully around the table in between the half-drunk pints of Guinness.

'The motorcade accelerates sharply, the motorbike outriders leading the way. Bang. Another shot takes half of Kennedy's skull off as they speed away. Attention then turns to the grassy knoll, people move purposefully to this area – the shot must have come from there, surely?' He looks around the room, all eyes are fixed on the table as a splash of tomato sauce is added to the small dinky toy car. 'Well, no. It didn't. The fatal shot, gentleman, came from here.' He pointed his thick finger towards the support vehicle where a green plastic soldier holding a machine gun was squeezed into the convertible back seat. 'You see, gentlemen, the Abraham Zapruder tape which everyone thought indicated that a shot was fired from the grassy knoll was in fact a red herring. I've found out that the secret service detail were not on their 'A' game that day. They were actually still drunk from a heavy session the night before and inexperienced personnel had to be drafted in to cover for them. Now, they always carried an automatic rifle with them in the president support vehicle, on the back seat,' George spoke slowly, pausing he lifted his Guinness and took a large gulp licking his lips to capture the white froth around them.

'As the vehicles raced away a secret service man fell back with the sudden upturn in speed and fired the fatal round that blew Kennedy's brains out. So, there you have it - he was killed by his own protection detail.'

'Wow, quite a theory, Mr Sinclair, not heard that one before,' Lawrie interjected, breaking the short silence, 'any evidence to back it up?'

'As with all these cases, Francis, the evidence is suppressed or blurred. Hence why bullet casings matching Oswald's Carcano Model 38 rifle were conveniently found in the president's Lincoln limo and on Governor Connelly's gurney at the Parkland Hospital. And why Oswald was portrayed as a crazy, lone wolf, who happened to be a top marksman. Though, now I will ask, and I hope our esteemed lawyer friend here will provide the answer – why has a presidents security detail never carried a high-powered rifle since 1963? Twenty-two years and five presidents later – no similar weapon is present within a motorcade. Why?'

'Over to you, Cal. Ah might join ye every Tuesday, Mr Sinclair, we've a few cases still to solve. Mibbae ye can help.'

'You have, Francis. The biggest one being our good friend Dixie. When are his murderers getting their comeuppances?' The gathered regulars murmured in support.

'Soon, Mr Sinclair, very soon.'

'Glad to hear it – we've a kitty behind the bar to celebrate when they're all jailed or even better... dead.'

'Cal, can I have a word,' Frank whispered signalling toward to the door.

'Thank you, George, you've thrown down the gauntlet again fella. Hopefully, I'll have counter arguments for you next week.' Cal shook his hand as he rose quickly from the chair and followed Frank outside.

'Quite a guy auld George, eh?' Frank asked, quickly lighting a cigarette in the alcove of the entrance.

'Amazing old man. I might employ him if things stay as busy. Anyway, how can I help?' Cal replied, moving away from the smoke. Walking at pace along Broomlands he buttoned his dapper three-piece suit jacket, his brown leather satchel swinging with every movement.

'Why the fuck were you at Greenock Prison today?'

Cal stopped in his tracks. 'Err, to see a client obviously. Another miscarriage of justice. A set-up to protect a number of individuals and to look after their interests and those of the Quinn empire, I believe. Why do you ask?'

'Bit convenient is it no Cal? Ah tell ye...'
Lawrie looked over his shoulder and lowering his
voice, though his tone remained decidedly irritated,
as he moved closer to Cal, 'Ah just telt ye the day
before bout the arrangements for Quinn and Suzie,
where they'll be housed; next minute you're outside
the very same prison fuckin gates.'

Cal stared unflinchingly in return, holding his
glare. Time to think fast.

'Don't be ridiculous, that appointment has been
booked for months. The client had been phoning
the office constantly, seeking a visit. I agreed out of
curiosity more than anything, and the visit was very
much justified. Look, his file is in the office, one of
the historic ones I seem to have inherited from the
previous incumbent, do you want to come and read
over it? There may be grounds for a retrial. Out of
interest, who told you I was in Greenock?'

Frank dejectedly dropped his shoulders and tried
to hide his disappointment. *Ah saved yer life and
still ye canny trust me, that's good to know. If ah
doubted it before, ah now know yer worth a
watching,* he thought.

'Fair enough, mate. Och, a jist phoned yer office
this morning. Grace said ye were out till bout half
one this afternoon and I'd get ye at the Vatican. No
harm done, jist let me know if yer ever in that neck
of the woods again, will ye?'

'Of course. Are we done?' Cal asked, pointing
towards Wellmeadow and his office. 'It's just I've
court shortly.'

'Aye, aye sure, Cal, we're done. I'll call in later in the week.'

Cal moved quickly along the street, dodging past the shoppers and lunchtime traffic from the nearby high school. He knew Frank Lawrie was not stupid, a wily cop whose default was to trust no one and interrogate every detail. He'd covered himself with his responses, calm manner, and underplayed reaction. No damage done. He wouldn't be seen at HMP Greenock again. He captured the information he required. He'd continue as planned.

Frank meandered back to his car, settling into the driver's seat he lifted the radio handset which crackled into life.

'Johnny, it's DS Lawrie. Get on tae Greenock Prison will ye? Ask them tae send through a copy of today's visitor log. Ah want the names of every visitor who were in the day. Plus, the time of entry and exit, and who was visited by a Mr Cal Lynch, cheers.'

He stared down Wellmeadow as Cal's tall figure darted across the busy road at the West End cross, the early afternoon sun bouncing off the brass buckles of his satchel.

He sighed as he moved the car into gear, 'God help ye when ah find out what yer up tae, Cal. God help ye.'

Chapter Nine

TERENCE STRETCHED OUT HIS legs and rolled up the sleeves of his Big Country t-shirt in an attempt to get some colour onto his milk-bottle white skin as he occupied the bench in the small park a short walk from St Matthias's church. The early Sunday morning ensured the area was relatively quiet, with the exception of some squawking blackbirds, a couple of dedicated dog walkers and the hum of the odd Trabant car making its way along the road.

A small teenager was kicking a ball off the graffitied back wall of a café. The surface was scorched, the grass was long gone as the dust lifted with every quick movement of his feet.

Mairi-Clare would meet him here every Sunday after Mass and they would spend their day wandering the banks of the Spree River, its water winding through the city after weaving its way from the Lusatian Mountains above Neugersdorf, and flowing past the hilltop town of Bautzen, its medieval towers dominating the vista, before meandering through Berlin. The river would be busy, and they would wave at the tour boats or the many small tugs and barges that fed off the commercial activity along its banks. Or they would explore the city centre, observing the natives as they went about their daily lives in one of the most militarised areas in the world Or her personal favourite – sitting reading and watching the world go by in the nearby Tiergarten Park, a huge expanse to explore and lots of people to watch. They would chat over each other dreams for the future and gently rip apart their musical tastes while drinking fancy coffee comfortable in each other's company.

Mairi-Clare would continue to try and learn more about her boyfriend, probe his personality and find out details about his life to date. He was holding back, shielding, or harbouring issues which should be discussed, brought to the fore, and aired, she thought. He seldom spoke about his dad or his premature death. It would come to the surface at some point, she would want to be there when it did. Maybe she was displaying similar traits herself, hiding the anxieties she was facing due to very little interaction with her family. Not surprisingly, Terence seemed oblivious to her worries, so their exciting adventure in one of the world's most famous cities continued with little drama.

Terence recognised the boy playing football as the son of one of the worshippers who had welcomed him to the parish several weeks previous. Their conversation had been stilted due to the language barrier, but he got the jist of what was being said, kept smiling, nodding, and repeating with little confidence, 'Danke, Danke.'

He had turned up late that day, sweating and stressed as he attempted to find the chapel following handwritten directions and an illegible map from one of his tutors. Now it took him just twenty minutes to stroll down Herbert-von-Karajan-Strasse, past the large neon signs continually beaming the western news messages towards the wall and the East Berlin residents. Their Communist counterparts responding with a sign promoting the state-run Ho stores. Turning right onto Winterfeldtstrasse he arrived at the impressive neo-gothic, red brick building nestled on Goltzstrasse its towering spire currently winning the battle with the mature maple trees that encircled the building and basked in the early morning sun.

Designed by Engelbert Seibertz, the impressive structure was not shy or timid and certainly did not fit with the backyard churches constructed in the era of post-reformation Catholic persecution in Germany. Seibertz sent out a statement that this small community was here to stay, and Terence now sought some sort of solace, a connection with the unknown congregation.

Mairi-Clare spotted Terence at a distance playing keepy-uppy and facing a boy located at the far side of the park who was bobbing up and down anticipating the balls flight, his ears encased in a Walkman. *Good, he's made a pal*, she thought.

'Well, if it's not Charlie Nicholas is there no end to your talents, Terence?' she asked sarcastically, occupying the vacant bench as she watched him flick the ball four times in the air then sent it high towards his partner.

'Ah used tae be quite good ye know. But being a fat bastard, they always flung me intae goals.'

'That's awful.'

'Naw, that's life, MC. Paisley style,' he replied, laughing and making light of her concern.

'So, who's your wee pal?'

He shrugged his shoulders as he waited for the Mitre 5 to be returned by the boy currently hitting double figures with keeping the ball up with his head.

'Ah don't know yet. He's no bad at fitba though. Ah was waiting til you turned up, then I'd have a chat wae him cause you can speak the lingo better than me. Here goes.'

Terence trapped the ball effortlessly with his left foot and waived the boy to come over and join them. The boy meandered over, dropping his headphones to around his neck. His white trainers now brown with dust and his small frame dwarfed by an oversized West German football shirt.

'Hallo, wie...errr ... geht's dir?' Terence asked slowly, and with very little self-assurance.

'Hallo, mir geht's gut. Wie geht es dir? Mein name ist Friedrich. Was ist dein?' the boy responded, holding out his small hand.

Terence turned quickly to Mairi-Clare, seeking assistance. She shook her head, 'You know this.

Just have some confidence. He's saying his name's Friedrich, he's fine and asking how you are.'

'Aww, danke, danke, wee man. I'm mir geht's gut, mir geht's gut,' Terence responded, smiling and giving his new friend the thumbs up.

The boy lifted the ball and spun it in his hand. 'You, English? Best we speak English.'

'Well, no English. Scottish, wee man. But your English sounds better than mine so why not. I am Terence, by the way, and this is Mairi-Clare.'

'I am pleased to meet with you. Big Country – Fields of Fire,' Friedrich replied pointing at Terence's t-shirt, the sun's rays bursting from the compass above the emblazoned words. He imitated Stuart Adamson playing the electric guitar. 'Very good music.'

'Aye, ye've got no bad taste, Freddy.'

'Archee Gemmell, Archee Gemmell – he is Scottish too.'

'Who?' Terence looked at Mairi-Clare then he remembered, 'Oh aye, plays fitba.'

'My papa. He wrote me about him all. He scored the best goal *ever* seen in world cup.' Friedrich dropped the ball at his feet and dramatically held up his hands, looking his new acquaintances straight in the eye.

'It's Argentina, nineteen and seventy-eight. The Estadio Ciudad de Mendoza stadia. Scotland will win the world cup, so your coach says. Scotland plays Holland. Archee picks up ball at edge of the box.'

Friedrich took off on a mazy run, the dust rising, the ball under close control. Raising his voice, he filled the peaceful park with unexpected noise. 'Past one, past two, and three,' he curled the ball onto the corner of the café wall, 'then chip over the goalkeeper.' He ran away, defiantly, pumping his thin left arm in the air to an imaginary crowd.

'This wee guy seems sound, MC, wired to the moon but sound.'

Friedrich returned, slightly out of breath from his exploits. 'Six touches, all left foot – Tor, tor. Goal, goal.'

'Aye, ah remember watching it with ma da. Ah was a bit young, mind, but they always show it back home on the telly.'

'Do they show the trophy your nation won...ha-ha,' he asked, an impish smile running across his face as he impatiently bounced from one foot to the other while rubbing his palm over his skull, failing to make an impression on his crew cut hair style.

'Eh?'

'Your taktiker, err, err, coach. The man with the big nose, no? Papa told me in his letters, he tells the world you will win the world cup. He was dumbass, but you all believed, Papa says.'

'Och, we don't tend to talk too much bout Ally MacLeod or that wee aspect of the world cup, mate. That's ancient history, if ye know what ah mean.'

'Do you know...' the boy asked, bringing his hands to his chest, and intertwining his fingers constantly, '...that your brain decides which nostril you will take breath through. It changes the

91

sequence at its own will, sometime two, sometime one nostril.'

Putting his hand over his nose Terence investigated the theory. Turning his eyes slowly he clocked Mairi-Clare's stare and open mouth.

'Where do you live, Friedrich?' Mairi-Clare interrupted, beginning to get bored. The boy pointed towards the large, grey, concrete building across the road, 'Second floor, up there. With Mother and Father.'

A slim-built middle-aged man appeared at his side, who Terence recognised from the chapel. They spoke to each other quickly and quietly in German as he nodded to them both.

'I am pleased to meet you,' he said slowly, revealing a mouthful of crooked teeth within a large smile. He turned to Friedrich and spoke again quietly in German. 'I'm sorry we have to go to see my father.'

'We will catch up with ye again, wee man,' Terence replied, throwing the ball to his new pal.

'My Papa is over there at Wilhelmstrasse; we go and see him,' Friedrich replied raising his arm and pointing towards the wasteland beyond the derelict flats.

'Where is he, Friedrich?' Mairi-Clare interjected, slightly confused.

'Past the wall. He is in the East. Father says we will get him out soon.'

Her eyes lit up, intrigued and eager for more detail. 'Wow,' she whispered, 'could we come?'

The father nudged his boy's' shoulders. 'We go now. Sorry, we must go.'

They waved their goodbyes and headed quickly out of the park.

'Interesting, Terence, interesting.'

'Your minds racing again, ah kin feel it. I've clocked that look before. Fucksake.'

Mairi-Clare laughed and grabbing his hand, they exited the park towards the city centre. 'Mmmm, maybe, Let's go for a stroll.'

They walked on, engrossed in their conversation and not aware of two men who emerged quietly from a black van, split up and walked down either side of the wide pavements. The same two who had followed their every step since they had arrived in Berlin.

Chapter Ten

NICKI HENSHAW STUDIED HER complexion closely in the mirror. Topping up her lipstick she looked for lines, and signs of ageing. This was far from her usual routine prior to interviewing a suspect but this one was slightly different. She tucked in the loose blonde wisps of hair that fell around her forehead, straightened her hip length blazer, tidied her white blouse, and headed for the interview room.

The team had met hours earlier and were led by the experienced, no nonsense, Superintendent Irvine an officer meticulous in his planning and setting out of the stages that would be followed during the interview process.

Irvine was a veteran of the prolific murder scene and local turf wars that had been prevalent in Glasgow in recent decades. His approach was very much focused on ensuring that the available evidence would guarantee a conviction in court without dubiety about the guilt of the accused being a possibility. He always aimed to provide the jury with little room to question or debate the facts in front of them.

'Right team,' Irvine raised his voice and the assembled officers immediately fell silent curtailing their conversations, 'DCI Henshaw, here from the Serious Crime Squad, and I will do the first phase of interviews with McGrath and Quinn. I want you tuning in and picking up on any inconsistencies that may emerge, any points that we need to highlight and drill into in the next phases and follow-ups…and don't be scared to tell us what we may have missed.'

His broad frame and protruding pot belly were in proportion with his six-foot-plus height. Rolling his shirt sleeves up to his elbows he looked around the room at the team who all sat eager and delighted to be part of such a complex case.

'We will nail these two. The evidence is there but I want more, let's leave no gaps. I want to sweat them and get as much out of them before they're charged. We know we can apply for an extension but let's focus on this twenty-four-hour window. Keep chasing down any loose strands, just as we have since last October. You're all aware how high profile this is and the type of organised crime outfit we are up against. We may only have one bite at this to build the case to put them away for an exceptionally long time. So. No. Slip. Ups.'

He nodded to a young officer standing on the periphery of the group who stepped forward and began to hand out files to the staff.

'Once we've broken them in, DS Lawrie you'll lead on McGrath and DS Jackson you're in on Quinn. It'll be round the clock with scheduled breaks. Let's get it right, team. Kick-off in ten minutes.' He clapped his hands together to encourage his staff as they all began to split from the meeting, aware of their designated roles.

Irvine pulled Henshaw aside, 'I'll be pushing on the murder of Dixie Clark and the Peter Turner cold case, Nicki. You poke them on the drug trafficking, money laundering and the like. Let's mix it up. Keep the fuckers thinking, overwhelmed, and on the back foot.'

'Good approach, thanks for the opportunity, sir.'

'Anything you should be sharing with me, Nicki? I'm not going in there with my knob hanging out, am I?' he whispered, looking at her directly from behind his unkempt eyebrows while scanning the room for anyone paying undue attention to their conversation.

Henshaw took a small step forward moving her face parallel to her colleague's ear, 'I'm in a relationship with the lawyer she went out with, the one she tried to kill. It started well after the event itself.' She looked Irvine in the eye and confidently added, 'I'll step back, boss, if it compromises the case. Just say the word.' She waited in silence as Irvine seemed to take forever to respond, tapping his nicotine-stained fingers over his thin lips.

'No, stay on it. It'll rattle them, confuse them, especially her. We're setting the scene for the team to run with it for the rest of the day. They better deliver.'

Henshaw had read over the files yet again as soon as word came through that the pair were on their way back to Scotland. She had worked on the Quinn case, hard days, and sleepless nights, to gather enough to get them to this stage. There were casualties along the way with families such as the Clarks left devastated and not yet receiving justice or any sort of closure. Then there was Cal, still vulnerable, still not sharing what was tearing him up inside. Though he tried hard to keep these feelings from her, she saw a man still to deal with facing death, being defenceless and weak at that moment remained with him. He just had to open up and share it.

Irvine led the way walking briskly down the dank, soulless corridor towards interview room number two. He pushed the door open and stood aside allowing Henshaw to enter. Suzie McGrath was already present sitting with a straight back, a perfect posture, on the plastic chair against the wall. She clocked Henshaw as she entered, her large blue eyes going up and down as she studied the detective. Lowering her eyelids, she picked at her manicured nails and shuffled in the seat to straighten her designer dress. An equally well-dressed female lawyer sat adjacent, her file already open with pen in hand she looked up briefly and returned her focus to her notes.

The officers took their seats in silence facing the two-way mirror as Irvine emptied his pockets placing his cigarettes and lighter onto the faded desk, and slowly opened his file. He sat back in the chair crossing his legs and resting his clasped hands against his expanding gut, tucking one of his thumbs inside his shirt resting it on a button.

'Well, Suzie, here we are…eventually, eh?' A dry smile coming over his face. 'I'm Superintendent Irvine and this is my colleague Detective Chief Inspector Henshaw, who I believe you may, kind of know.'

Henshaw tightened her jaw. She understood what Irvine was doing getting it out there early, letting them know it wasn't an issue, but a heads-up would have been appreciated.

Suzie lifted her chin and pouted her lips, her eyes darting between them both before settling on Henshaw.

'Oh, I am honoured that such senior police officers are here to interview little ole me. What do you think, Ms Lawson, are they really taking this nonsense seriously?' The lawyer raised her pen gesturing to quieten her client. She slid papers across the table and lifting her own copy began to read.

'I am reading and entering into the record the following statement on behalf of my client, Susan McGrath.

I, Susan McGrath, would like to provide the following details pertaining to matters Strathclyde Police are investigating. I am estranged from my father, Jimmy Quinn, and have no knowledge of either the alleged drug dealing which is purported to have taken place in the town of Paisley, or the murder of Mr Clark.

With regards to the assault on the solicitor, Cal Lynch, I was not involved in its planning, instigation, or the shocking assault itself. I believe others, unknown to me, were jealous of our developing, deep personal relationship and as such sought to attack Mr Lynch.

I was aware that the police had wished to discuss these issues with me, though after hearing of Cal's terrible and terrifying assault I feared for my own safety and went into hiding to protect myself.

End of statement.'

Irvine pushed the statement dismissively to the back of his file, not even giving it a curious glance.

'My client has nothing further to add…other than she hopes that the perpetrators of these crimes, of which she has no knowledge, are found and convicted,' the lawyer added robotically, clearly something she had repeated and advised on many an occasion during her career.

Henshaw clicked her Parker pen, flattened her notepad, and addressed her rival.

'So, Suzie. Can I call you Suzie?'

Suzie widened her large eyes and smiled revealing her pearl-white teeth. Henshaw tried hard not to feel inferior. Closing her lips tightly she ran the top of her tongue along the unsightly chip on her front tooth, an injury inflicted while making an arrest some years ago.

'Right, so let's go back to October last year and our investigation into a major drug-running business, centred here in Paisley. An international, smoothly run concern where class A drugs were delivered to your father's businesses here and transported via an elaborate network across Scotland and beyond.'

Suzie glanced at her lawyer who shook her head to indicate; do not engage.

'Let's have a look at this, shall we. Here are business accounts showing significant payments entering the consortium of *A* businesses, including security firms, travel agents and builders. All owned by your father, Jimmy Junior Quinn, and the money subsequently being squirreled away.'

Henshaw was getting into her stride. This is where she loved to be, building the tension, watching them rising and taking the bait and revealing the details that tie them to the evidence – putting them firmly in the frame.

'I own a small hairdressing salon, darling. What has this got to do with me?' A long sigh emanated from the lawyer as she realised that the seal was now broken, and her client would be sucked into a debate that wasn't within their control.

'Well, Suzie, let's all have a look, shall we? And you can clear this one up easily, I'm sure,' Henshaw replied, a tight smirk coming across her face, her eyes firmly on her suspect as she placed documentation between Suzie and her lawyer. Lifting her pen, she began to point her way through the details.

'Here is an example of what we've found – four hundred and fifty-five thousand pound is deposited and quickly removed from A's accounts. We have no knowledge of where it ended up.'

Suzie laughed quietly to herself and began checking her bright red nail varnish, presenting her hand to her lawyer she whispered, 'Not even chipped.'

Pointing at the second document, Henshaw continued, 'Though we have a fair idea. Your *small* hairdressers has outgoings on a monthly basis of hundreds of thousands of pounds.'

'How can I explain it, we were remarkably busy. Small, but thriving.' Suzie shrugged nonchalantly.

'Yer either doing perms for half the population of Paisley or the weans are blagging and buzzing all yer hairspray and fancy nail varnish,' Irvine interjected, 'seventy-five thousand a month for that alone, according to your verified accounts. Ye think we're buttoned up the back?'

'I worked my rear-end off to make that place a success, round the clock, providing jobs for people, giving them a career opportunity, working beside top stylists.'

Henshaw slid another document across the table. 'I thought you'd say that, Suzie, so I had your electricity bills for the last two years sent over. Interesting reading. As you can see you've had an average consumption over the same period that these large outlays were going through your books. All this material and expenditure because you were, as you claim, super busy, *such a success*.'

She paused for a reaction, nothing. 'I even had the bean counters analyse your utility bills and compare them with another business that was experiencing a large turnover similar to your *small* hairdressers. Funnily enough, their bills were significantly higher than yours as well as theirs being a much larger business operation than the one you purport to be running.'

Suzie shrugged her shoulders and slowly bit her bottom lip.

'So the question is, *darling,* how you can explain such a high turnover for such a small business while the money trail shows illicit cash moving from your father's business to places unknown? A father that you kept quiet about while perpetuating the myth that you were the estranged daughter of the late Eddie Quinn. You were washing his money, weren't you?'

Suzie pushed back her shoulders ready to open up as her lawyer placed her hand across her arm.

'I've yet to see any evidence of any crime linked to my client. Superintendent Irvine, this is a nonsense.'

'Och, we've just got started. We've twenty-four hours remember, belt yourself in, hen.'

Irvine removed his bulky frame from the seat with a middle-aged groan. Placing his hands in his pockets he began walking slowly round the room. 'So, tell me what you know of Dixie Clark, Suzie.'

'No comment.'

'Who were the two men you ordered to kill him, sanctioned by your father, that's Jimmy Quinn, by the way? One was a scouser, we know that. We have a positive I.D on that one. Funny, that's where you were hiding out in that nice plush pad, eh? We have forensics that place you at the scene of his torture which, as you well know, was also the location of the attempted murder of Mr Cal Lynch. Who, I may add, has provided a signed statement placing you at that scene, coldly sanctioning his execution, he remembers that vividly,' Irvine leaned over Suzie's shoulder, who sat rigid, 'I think you better help yerself here, love. Tell me who the two hired help are. It may go in yer favour when yer in the dock.'

'No. Comment.'

'Right, we're done here.' Irvine looked at his watch and nodded to the lawyer. 'Half hour comfort break then our officers will recommence this interview.'

Henshaw joined her colleague and made her way to the door. Grabbing the rear of Irvine's shirt, she pulled him back into the room. She had forgotten to ask one of her key questions. She fumed with herself, clear in the knowledge that she had allowed her focus to be slightly distracted by the adversary in front of her, concentrating on her appearance had allowed her to drift from her usual intense preparations.

'The Russo?'

Suzie's wide smile left her face as her eyes diverted quickly towards the concrete wall facing her.

'Who is the Russo, Suzie? We're getting close, ...so close.'

'How's Cal doing, Nicki?' Suzie asked in a faint voice, the large smile returning to her face. 'Is he still out running, staying fit? He used to ask me to join him, not my thing, too sweaty. Do you, Nicki…go…running…with him?'

Henshaw followed Irvine as they slowly walked along the corridor and were joined soon after by Lawrie and Jackson.

'Well, thoughts?'

'Don't think it took long for her to be rattled, boss. The Russo question threw her. I'll keep pushing it once we're in there,' Lawrie replied, as he walked behind his gaffer.

'Agreed, Lawrie, make sure you throw in the forensics from the scene,' Irvine replied, stopping in his tracks he turned to face him, 'and take a female officer in with ye, Nicki had her on edge. You set it up, let your partner fire the questions that she'll flap with. That's where we'll get results.'

'Will do, sir,' Lawrie responded, slightly disappointed by his bit-part role.

'Right, now it's Jimmy Quinn. You ready?'

Nicki nodded, her eyes studying the thick file as they moved towards the interview room.

Quinn was leaning nonchalantly against the wall as they entered the room. His deep tan and muscular frame on show from behind a flimsy, white cotton shirt. He belied his age and clearly looked after himself and took pride in his appearance. His skin was smooth, and floppy, light-brown hair hung loosely over his deep blue eyes.

Henshaw could see the attraction, could imagine how this slick, authoritative figure, who no doubt possessed charisma, could operate in the business world and be comfortable, excelling in those surroundings. The warm climate, untold wealth, and the reputation that he carried as one of Europe's most dangerous and violent criminals certainly helped.

'Take a seat, Mr Quinn,' Irvine announced, setting the tone, 'We'll get started, shall we?'

'You could start by switching on the heating. I've forgotten how cold this country is,' Quinn replied, rubbing his thick biceps.

Jimmy Junior Quinn had been in Spain for twenty years moving around the country, on average, three times a year. He had learned valuable lessons by watching the fate of criminal associates in London who couldn't resist playing the celebrity card and flashing their cash and power, exposing themselves to nosey reporters and generating intrigue into their private and business lives. As the spotlight began to shine ever brighter it would eventually bring them down or piss off their rivals enough that they would inevitably play a part in their downfall.

He had taken over the firm from his ageing father and ruled with an even harder and more sadistic fist than his old man had been infamous for. He was smarter than his da who was only a local hood, come gangster, in the Gorbals area of Glasgow. Jimmy Junior's domain was now colossal, on an international scale, and Henshaw's colleagues at Interpol feared it was now too big, too well resourced, too well protected, to consider the extinction of the syndicate anytime soon. On a scale that it was too vast to fail.

Irvine rattled through the introductions in quick fashion and pressed immediately the topics that he hoped would be the ruin of Quinn and his empire.

'The elusive Jimmy Junior Quinn, here at last. We've done our Organised Crime Gang network mapping exercise on your outfit Jimmy, and you'll be pleased to hear yours is at the top of the tree – access to firearms which you're obviously not scared to use, an established distribution network for your produce and businesses to wash the cash through. How does that make you feel to be at the top of the pyramid – the main man running a thriving OGC,' Irvine asked, staring at his guest.

Quinn returned the glare saying nothing.

Irvine continued, flicking the pages of his file. 'So, we have at least four consignments of Class A drugs with a huge street value which has your name, network, businesses, and dirty paws all over it. We also have evidence that you have been shipping produce via the port of Antwerp, that you have a base established in Berlin and that you transport gear throughout Europe. And how do we know that? Your wee lawyer here will be interested to know. Well, we have a number of witnesses willing to testify against you as well as forensic accountants showing where you moved, laundered, and stashed your ill-gotten gains. So, I don't think this will take too long.'

'You were the one who spoke to my brother in Barlinnie weren't you?' Folding his arms across his broad chest, Quinn's focus was on Henshaw.

Irvine would usually pivot back to the initial questioning, but he was experienced enough to let this develop.

'I spoke to Eddie.'

'How was he?'

'In what way?'

'Was he healthy, happy. You know, content?'

'I wasn't there for a therapy session.'

'Did he mention me?'

'Oh yes, he mentioned you. And your father. He was a scumbag as well, I believe.'

'Did he say anything about us growing up, as kids, I mean. We were always together, running about together. Ye know, best mates.'

'No, he never mentioned that. He did mention how you manipulated him, used, and trapped him. Made him the scapegoat. It's all in the evidence bundle that will be going to the Fiscal. That and a whole host of documentation to ensure you're away for a long time. He may have opened up about his childhood if I had had a chance to talk to him again, but someone murdered him, similar to how Peter Turner was killed. Funny that, eh?'

'Shame he never spoke about me, those were good times. Great wee fitba player, real baller he was. Plus, quite brainy, could do they maths algebra things no problem, in his head,' Quinn responded as if he couldn't care less or was dismissive of the charges he was facing. Henshaw couldn't figure out which.

'Your drug distribution, Jimmy. See, folk have a theory that you were part of the, so called, Ice Cream Wars that were happening last year in Glasgow, punting yer gear round the schemes in vans. But I don't wear that one. You're well above that, aren't you? You're the kingpin, you ensure it gets delivered safely, make sure that there's an endless supply and that the distribution network is in place across the country, similar to all the other countries you operate in. After that, you don't give a shit as long as the cash flows back the same way,' Irvine interjected, in an attempt to refocus the interview.

Quinn stared at Irvine, not moving a muscle. Henshaw tried again. 'The evidence is stacked up against you, Jimmy. We have your most trusted colleagues in witness protection. We also tracked down your banker – and managed to have a friendly chat with him, on tape. See, we know that since Ronald Reagan introduced deregulation to the US financial markets, and his sidekick Thatcher did similar here in London, that you boys have been busy laundering money right, left and centre. Do you know a Mr Felipe from the National Bank of Puerto Rico? That's where you cleaned your money. Buying gold and selling the raw material back to legitimate markets. Mr Felipe was found dead last week, you knew that already didn't you, Jimmy? What is it your Mexican friends say? Oh, that's it – accept the silver or take the lead. Looks like he got the latter. Anyway, our officers will cover this in the next few hours. You could help yourself though?'

Quinn smiled; his eyes still fixed on Irvine.

'Who is the Russo, Jimmy, is that the cover given to your OGC? Any information you wish to provide would be taken into consideration against the lengthy sentence you're facing,' Henshaw persisted. The mention of the Russo did not register a reaction from Quinn, his focus was still on Irvine.

'Superintendent, may I declare before the Great Architect of the Universe that I am not guilty of these crimes,' Quinn announced, in a low deliberate voice.

Irvine laughed and nudged Henshaw with his elbow, 'Bit early for that line, a nice try though. Funnily enough, I actually got to this level in my career without rolling up my trouser leg and getting done in by a bunch of wahoos. I've no time for the *craft*, so no joy there, pal.'

'I did wonder, Superintendent. You weren't present just last year when some of your, shall we say, senior colleagues were able to join me as my guests at the opening of our lodge in Marbella. It was so good to have so many of the brethren with us. In fact, the Worshipful Master from Glasgow visited, you'll know him quite well, what's his name? Oh, that's right, can't say.'

'Very good,' Irvine quickly responded, smarting slightly. 'I'd also like to ask you about the murder of Peter Turner in the Gorbals in July 1962. The one your brother stood trial for and walked free from.'

'Good old British justice.'

'Well, good old British justice has allowed us to reopen the case as new evidence has come to light. New witnesses and the testimony of your brother clearly outlining in graphic detail what happened that night and your role in the murder of an innocent man.'

'Oh, I'd be really interested in hearing more on this one. Sounds intriguing,' Jimmy's replied, his eyes darted between the two officers.

'Oh, you will. Eddie also told us where you dumped the knife. You'll be glad to know we recovered it, and our forensics team are using the latest technology to link it directly to the murder and...hopefully to you. So, don't worry, Jimmy, we've plenty of questions for you in the next few hours.'

'The poor guy who died, his missus, what was her name again?' He paused, 'C'mon you must know,' he clicked his fingers as if to trigger his memory, 'Cathy, Cathy Turner, now goes by Lynch. That's the one. She was younger than my loving father. He was misunderstood, you know. A real softy, an emotional, true romantic but very intense,' Jimmy leaned forward, placing his elbows on the desk he pointed both palms towards Henshaw, 'Do you think sometimes people could kill or have someone killed for love, maybe act of passion? What do you think, Nicki?'

Henshaw watched as Irvine tidied his papers, the signal they were done here. 'Nice to meet you, Jimmy, no doubt we'll see you in court very soon.' Henshaw replied stern-faced.

Jackson and Lawrie were waiting in the corridor as they approached. 'He's a right tricky bastard, dictates the flow of the interview too much. We need that changed. Briefing room in ten minutes – I need a fag. Nicki, what the fuck was that love pish all about?' Irvine asked, slightly annoyed with how their initial questioning had gone.

'I'll need to read it back, sir, either he let something slip or was telling us something he wanted us to know. More likely he wants us chasing down a blind alley. I'll try and figure it out. Leave the Peter Turner files with me, I'll go over them tonight.'

'Cheers, Nicki. And, Jackson, tell me you aren't in that fuckin funny handshake brigade,' Irvine growled, screwing up his eyes.

'Is that still a thing, boss?' Jackson responded, shrugging his shoulders.

'Too right it's still a thing – a manipulative, insidious, power-hunger group who will stop at nothing to assist their brethren – of which that tosser in there is clearly one. Check your team as well – any sniff they're part of that mob get them back to normal duties. Ah want no slip up on this, ye hear.'

Chapter Eleven

THE SHOW SHOULD BE as big as is humanly possible. There's no point just five thousand fans turning up at Wembley, we need to have Wembley linked with the United States, and the whole show to be televised worldwide.

Bob Geldof's distinctive Dublin accent boomed from the transistor radio in Grace's kitchen as he announced the ambitious worldwide Live Aid concert to alleviate the famine in Ethiopia.

'What dae ye think, Stephen, ye think it'll be any good?'

Stephen shrugged his shoulders as he piled the jam onto his morning toast. His mind was preoccupied with other things, one thing after another. He'd tried to be rational, to break down each issue as it entered his head but increasingly, he felt overwhelmed.

'They're aw loaded; they should just pay oot themselves. Especially that dick,' he mumbled under his breath, nodding his forehead towards the radio. 'Kin we talk about school the night, Mum?'

'Course, Son. By the way, ah hear the Cellar Bar is holding a full day event, with the concerts on a big screen. Ye fancy going along, ah'll get the tickets?'

'School. Mum,' he responded frustratedly.

His mum's attention span when in conversation about school issues was never fully focused or delivered with any level of genuine interest. As long as the boys were staying out of trouble, she trusted and left the teaching to the experts, her role was to steer them through the various stages of life, keep them safe through the teenage, impressionable, years and watch them move into the world of work which, given the constant closure of the industries around the town, would be the biggest challenge.

'My undivided attention,' she responded, with a hug and multiple kisses to his now blushing cheeks, 'if yer no in any bother I'll even buy ye a Live Aid t-shirt.'

'Ah new pair ah fitba boots would be better.'

* * *

Grace entered Cal's office as he placed his latest musical acquisition onto the Sony turntable. A cacophony of Irish punk music blasted from the speakers releasing a sound which demanded attention. The gravelly voice of the singer had a distinctive aggressiveness as he sang about streams of whiskey, the love of getting pissed, and storming the BBC.

'Boss, what the hell is that?'

'Grace, I've been playing this all of last night. You need to listen to this group, they're from London. I can't believe I've never heard of them. This album has been on sale since last October,' he responded excitedly, passing the album cover.

'The Pogue's, Red Roses for Me? Turn it down, eh,' she asked, screwing up her face the brash sound grating on her ears.

'You know the young girl, Caroline, who drops in the free newspaper? She put me onto them. Anyway, she was in asking me to be her lawyer, to represent her at court or at an employment tribunal. The Renfrewshire World just sacked her from her paper run, and she wishes to pursue an unfair dismissal case. Kids, eh,' he replied, smiling and tapping his fingers on the desk in time with the fast-paced music.

'Aye? Kids, eh. Is that the wee O'Hara lassie? So, she's the wan who dumped aw the hunners ah papers oot the back there? Wait tae ah see her, ah'll red rose her.'

'That doesn't matter, she's got great taste in music.'

'Boss, yer mother.' Grace folded her arms across her chest raising her eyebrows, awaiting a response. 'No so noisy noo are ye? Look am sick ah tellin her yer no in, that's four times this week alone. Ah feel like a pure bough...just talk tae her will ye.'

Cal shook his head trying to eradicate thoughts of his mother and his continual avoidance.

'I know, I know. I'm sorry, just give me another few days. I'll take her calls by the end of the week, agreed?'

A sharp knock came at the office door, turning, Grace was met by the full frame of Superintendent Irvine filling the entrance, Detective Chief Inspector Henshaw standing in his shadow.

'Apologies for interrupting, we did chap.' Irvine nudged into the office as Cal stood to meet him. 'You having a party? I thought I was in Dublin there for a minute.'

Cal shook his hand and directed the visitors to his new lounge seats in the corner of his office. The influence of Grace was evident with the fresh flowers placed in a second-hand crystal vase brightening the small coffee table.

'Ah'll put the kettle on, boss.' Grace advised, heading out the door.

'It would be better if you stayed, Grace,' Irvine interjected glancing at Cal, 'this concerns you too.' Cal directed Grace to the couch beside Henshaw and then, wheeling his leather reclining chair over, joined them, leaning his polished leather shoe on the table, much to Grace's dismay.

'Take it away, Inspector,' Irvine said, as his eyes scanned Cal's office.

Henshaw swivelled in the soft furnished couch to face Grace lifting the large place cushion and resting her forearms on it. She was aware of her involuntary habit of gesticulating while talking, and she realised, on an occasion such as this, that she had to be less pronounced.

'So, Grace, as you know we have Suzie McGrath in custody, and we have questioned her round the clock on various matters with the main focus being on the murder of your husband.'

Grace stared attentively at Henshaw, not moving a muscle. At this point she would usually interrupt or make a snide or sarcastic comment, not today.

'McGrath appeared in court this morning and has been remanded on charges of accessory to murder, attempted murder, various drug dealing offences and money laundering.'

'So, she's charged wae Dixie's murder?' Grace looked at Cal for confirmation.

Cal nodded his head towards Henshaw waiting for her to continue.

'We can't place her directly at the scene of Dixie's murder, not just yet. We know of at least another two men, both from Liverpool who were involved. If we find them, which I'm confident we will, then it will add to the list of charges she's facing already.'

'In the name ah Christ, so she's going tae walk. Ah don't think yer hearing me, Nicki, ah want that bitch tae rot in jail for the rest of her life, never tae see the light of fuckin day.'

Henshaw leaned forward and clasped Grace's shaking hands. 'Grace, I swear, with the case against her she'll be away for a very, very, long time.'

'We're not finished, Grace, there's more to come her way. We'll still have a full team on this for a long while yet, chasing leads, building the evidence to completely pin her to Dixie's murder. In my thirty odd years as a cop, I don't think I've seen a stronger case. Both of them will be gone for good,' Irvine tried to reassure her, sensing Grace's anger and frustration.

Turning to Cal, Irvine added, 'Cal, our lines of enquiry are still open in relation to your father's case. I'll not lie, this will be a challenge given the time period and lack of witnesses. Jimmy has been charged on a variety of drug related offences which the Inspector here has been instrumental in pursuing.'

'We do have Eddie Quinn's statements to guide us on your dad, so it's not over,' Henshaw added, sensing Cal's disappointment.

'Both have been remanded in Greenock away from the general prison population, they won't have contact with each other, and visits will be closely monitored. We even had the prison service handpick the guards, double checked their backgrounds for connections or any opportunity that may lead them to be compromised. I can't stress enough how much of a big deal this is for us and to colleagues across Europe. We think this outfit are the main players in a number of countries, with a variety of well-established rackets on the go. We won't be taking any chances until their locked up, for good.'

'You'll need tae phone yer maw, boss. Ah'll need tae speak tae the boys the night.'

Cal allowed a small smile to emerge, which relaxed the company. Rising from his seat and lifting four whiskey glasses and a bottle of Paddy's from the bookshelf he started pouring, the rich aroma filling the confined but comfortable space.

'Good old British justice, best in the world, eh,' he said, with a heavy hint of sarcasm while passing the large measures around, 'you only ever get part of it never the full nine yards, that's too much to ask.' He raised his glass as the others joined him. 'Don't worry, Grace, we'll get our justice. Guaranteed.'

* * *

Jimmy Quinn glanced up at the grey clouds that filled the sky. Spits of rain began landing on his tanned, smooth skin, as he stepped slowly out of the security van, surrounded by a posse of officers, and into the reception area of Her Majesty's Prison, Greenock. The dank environment made him shiver as he recalled sitting by his pool in his favourite villa in the Costa, with the Sierra Nevada mountains and the Mediterranean as its south-east backdrop. He would be holding court with his lackeys and drinking his fill of cocktails, the sun constantly warming his skin.

His new digs, in the slightly cooler environment of the West of Scotland, was located on the brow of a hill and within a quiet residential council estate which also offered a stunning view, on the odd clear day, across the Firth of Clyde and beyond the rusting, redundant cranes of the derelict shipyards no longer building and fitting out the luxury liners of its famous past or accepting tons of sugar for the refineries established to make huge profits from the slave trade of the colonies.

If he ever managed to get a look over the large high walls of his new digs, he may catch a glimpse of the Trossachs and beyond. He may reminisce of good times from his childhood spent camping and fishing for their supper at Loch Awe and lazing around the small village of Tyndrum with his da and Eddie, observing the locals bedecked in wax jackets and the numerous hikers with backpacks almost the size of their owners, strapped tightly and high on their shoulders.

Those family trips were always scarce, though he did hold on to them, continued to keep them fresh in his mind, providing him with a sense of inner warmth, of togetherness and a love which was now long lost.

Not long after one of their family getaways he was blooded, enrolled into the family firm, and the thirst, the addiction to the look of fear in the eyes of his victims, and then later the overwhelming craving for cash and the power that accompanied it became his all-consuming priority.

Housing around two hundred and seventy inmates, the prison had received its first inhabitants in 1910. Its primary role was hosting remand prisoners with some long-term inmates also spending time within its walls.

After being stripped-searched and getting dressed in his green-dark remand clothing he was escorted to his new abode, a six by four-foot cell with a desk, chair, bed, and plastic chamber pot. The only natural light emanated from the small, translucent-glass panel high on the wall. His eating utensils were placed on the rigid table, plastic plate, cup, bowl, fork, knife and spoon. An indication of the culinary delights he would have to become accustomed to.

The screws remained silent as they stood aside for Jimmy to enter the cell carrying his second-hand mohair blanket, which reeked of stale urine, and a flat, yellow-stained pillow. A small, bespeckled man appeared at the door and introduced himself as the governor. He was accompanied by another four screws who peered over his shoulder to view their highly prized resident.

'Although you are a remand prisoner, you are Category A status. Your visits will be strictly limited and monitored, and you will be accompanied by two of my officers at all times. All officers are also under strict instructions, by me, not to engage with you at any point,' he announced, a smile and the excitement in his eyes indicating that he was clearly loving the fact that his jail had been chosen to house the most high-profile of inmates for a forthcoming trial, 'welcome to Her Majesty's Prison, Greenock.'

Quinn laughed to himself as the cell door slammed shut the noise of the double lock being turned echoing round the sparse cell. The silence would be ever present as this wing on Ailsa Hall, one of four at Greenock, had been cleared of inmates for its new guests. Suzie, who was currently going through the welcoming routine, would be located at the far end of the wing. Never the twain would meet.

Jimmy had little opportunity to scan the prison or identify any possible weak spots. He'd make mental notes during his daily allocated hour of exercise and together with information attained from visits by his lawyer, the only meeting where screws weren't present, he'd build the picture. He dismissed the governors prepared script. He'd manipulate one or two of the screws, befriend some, if possible, allow them to provide info without even sussing they were doing it. A chat on car engines could reveal what they drive – allowing them to be followed. Looking over the *Racing Post* could lead to a friendly debate on horses and betting – a screw who has knowledge on form will have gambling debts – nobody beats the bookie. He would piece all of this together, see how it all falls, use it when the time was right.

The Russo would surely be pulling together plans to break him out. He was too important to the whole operation, to the business. He knew too much, could make all the connections across the syndicate. The charges against him were undoubtedly challenging and would continue to be if that bastard Irvine and his wee sidekick Henshaw carried on unhindered.

He was utterly convinced, totally assured of one thing – neither him nor Suzie would be going to trial. That wouldn't be happening under any circumstances. How this would be circumvented he was still to establish, but it would not be going ahead, of that he knew.

Chapter Twelve

TERENCE TAPPED OUT THE rhythm on the table with his drumsticks replaying the previous lesson. He was hoping he would find himself with a passion, through time, for the orchestra, the group, and the music in general. He was trying hard. He was someone who immersed himself in his studies and was very popular member of the new class with both the Berliner Philharmonic staff and the majority of his fellow students. First impressions projected a teenager who was enthusiastic, keen, and committed, though his mind would wander to something else that was continually niggling in his mind, nipping away at him non-stop, asking a question which he didn't really know how to answer.

'Hey, sweaty. Give it a rest will ya, bleedn' head is thumping as it is from last night.'

Terence continued to beat out the rhythm staring at the one person in the whole of Berlin who was actually doing his nut in.

Professor Cooper joined the class looking dapper in his turtleneck black jumper and light-coloured suit.

'Students, following on from yesterday's lively discussion. Your homework. Who can fill in the blanks regarding this fellow Scotsman's compatriot, Robert Tannahill?'

'Tannahill was a weaver who wrote poetry and formed a society in honour of Robert Burns,' a voice piped up from behind Terence.

'A composer.'

'He wrote beautiful music.'

'His music has been used in popular songs around the world.'

'Well done, people. You've impressed me.'

'Topped himself, didn' he? He was a coward of a man.'

The students turned to face the Londoner, some open-mouthed, others expressing anger in their eyes. 'Excuse me?' Cooper asked, slightly taken aback.

'He killed himself, didn' he, couldn't handle it. Said he didn't want to die like 'is ole man, bleedn' coward he was.' The Londoner was aggressive in his delivery, sitting upright and glaring around the theatre and catching the eyes, where he could, of his fellow students.

Cooper looked directly at the Londoner attempting to decipher what was behind his cold outburst. 'We all have our crosses, young man. Having empathy is a very worthwhile trait, let's work on that, shall we?'

'So, students, your teachers speak highly of your enthusiasm and willingness to learn your chosen instrument. Early impressions are good, they tell me,' holding up a cardboard box he continued, 'and here we have your four suggestions agreed from your cohort for our recital for the Live Aid extravaganza. As you know our concert will take place in this great hall the evening prior to our pop cousins taking to the stage on Saturday the 13th of July. So, why don't we proceed in choosing our anthem. A simple show of hands will suffice.'

'Professor, our group have been discussing this.'

Terence took a deep intake of breath; he had a feeling Mairi-Clare was up to something with this intervention though he was yet to figure out exactly what.

'If we are to participate in this worldwide, worthwhile event, showcasing how music, and classical music in particular, can help those in need and breakdown barriers, surely, we must highlight how our beautiful music can do exactly that here, in Berlin – with the huge wall that is just a short walk from where we are at present.'

'Continue,' Copper responded, waving his hand as he wandered slowly around the hall, his leather heeled shoes echoing throughout the amphitheatre as he went, intrigued by what might come next.

'Well, we think we should invite some prominent classical musicians from East Berlin to join us in the performance.'

Cooper stopped his slow stroll and turned to the group, 'Interesting, anyone in particular?'

'Yes, Helena Stern. The finest violinist in the world, in my opinion, who lives in the East, why not her?' Mairi-Clare looked round the room to murmurs of support from her peers.

'Let's discuss this later. In the meantime, we will quickly run through these suggestions as you have very little time to learn and perform to the accepted standard for this Académie.'

Terence eyeballed Mairi-Clare who simply smiled in return the slyness he had witnessed previously when she was up to no good, evident in her eyes.

Cooper began unwrapping the suggestions from the box. 'Ah, Mazurka in A Minor by Chopin, that may work. Any votes. No? OK. The great Beethoven, Bagatelle Number twenty-five, one of my favourite pieces. Two votes, mmm. Messiah by the amazing George Frideric Handel – this was actually the first music I played in this building to an audience. Though it may be a bit out of season for July.' Looking around the room a small number of hands were raised.

'And finally – Finlandia by Sibelius?' He raised his head to see a flurry of hands stretched out from their young bodies.

'Interesting, you have chosen a composition relating to the Finnish people's struggle for independence and against censorship by Russia. This is hardly likely to break down the walls that Mairi-Clare here has so eloquently highlighted.'

'Professor, we have chosen it as it encapsulates the whole orchestra: woodwind, percussion, brass and strings.' A soft voice came from within the group.

'Professor, we know the Berliner Philharmoniker included his work in 1902 which Sibelius conducted himself.'

'And this piece they included in 1904,' another voice interjected.

'Professor, another reason to include Helena Stern. As you will know, Sibelius wanted to play violin but gave it up unable to master the instrument. It would be fitting to hear his work resound in this fantastic setting again, played by us students and led by a renowned, world class violinist.'

You're laying it on thick, Terence thought to himself as he sat in silence. Something was being played out in her head, no doubt he'd find out soon enough.

Cooper clasped his hands and smiled towards the young musicians, 'The decision is made. The sheet music will be with your section leads this afternoon. I look forward to hearing your performance. Mairi-Clare, join me in my office directly after lessons today. Thank you, class. Now, let's get on with our work.'

* * *

Sitting on the grass embankment overlooking the student digs a short distance away from the other students, Terence waited patiently on Mairi-Clare, the sun warming his body.

He enjoyed his own company, spending time thinking about the future and, more often than not, the past and how life was back in Paisley. There were, however, memories which he blocked and put to the back of his mind not willing to recall and play them out again. What good would that do? They weren't that serious anyway.

He could interact with confidence, notwithstanding the language barrier, when he had to, but periods of solitude were a valuable commodity. The music classes were very intense, and the creativity and talent being shown within his percussion group had him in awe at times. He would be the first to admit that his learning was not progressing well, and he struggled to match the pace, and what seemed like innate confidence, of the others.

He shielded his eyes against the sun as Mairi-Clare walked towards him, arms folded, head down, though a cheeky grin could be spotted across her face revealing her dimples.

'Right, what the hell are you up tae?' Terence wasted no time as she sat closely beside him, his arm reaching round her petite shoulders, drawing her in.

Mairi-Clare fiddled with the handle of her large handbag, trying hard not to grin. 'Professor Cooper thinks it's a great idea to reach out to Ms Stern.'

Terence lowered himself onto his elbows, 'No shit, Sherlock, I know that bit, but what he doesnae know is whit's spinning round in your seditious napper.'

'Shush, keep it down,' she responded quietly, looking around her.

'Mairi-Clare, these folk hardly understaun what ah'm saying when ah talk in slow motion straight tae their confused faces. So, ah think we're perfectly safe with this conversation. Hurry up, spill the beans.'

She played with his fingers as he leant on the grass, attempting not to meet his eye.

'Well, you know this Helena Stern she's been an outspoken critic of the East Berlin set-up for years. She criticises the government, the Stasi, the Russians, the lot, anytime she travels abroad to play her music. But she always returns to the East after being away, never tries to leave or claim asylum or anything.'

'Does she, very good.'

'Professor Cooper said he knows her from years ago and he thinks she would be up for joining us for the concert.'

'Whoop dae doo, that's amazing. But that's not what you've got that look oan yer face fur, missus, is it? Last time ah saw that I was stealing a drum fae the Orange Lodge and carting King Billy's face about the West End of Paisley. They dafties are still trying tae figure out how it ended up in an orchestral performance in the town hall. So, continue, oh devious one.'

Mairi-Clare looked around her while continuing to play with Terence's fingers. 'Well, I was thinking about your new wee pal, Friedrich. Didn't he say his grandfather was still in East Berlin? I reckon Helena Stern could help us get him to this side of the wall.'

Terence sat immediately upright, stared straight ahead, rubbed his hands through his unkempt hair then slowly turned to face her.

'See when you were growing up in that posh hoose in Kilmacolm, were ye a wean that overdosed oan Famous Five books? Was that Enid Blyton wummin yer hero? Or mibbae you jist wanted tae be that lassie George, the bossy wan? Did you make up yer own adventures – spying on the rich neighbour's tae find out that their grand piano was actually bought wae a Provi cheque, or solving the mystery of the stolen ginger bottles? Seriously, ah cannae keep up with you.'

He lay back down and closed his eyes against the sun, hoping the gathering clouds would reach it soon to provide some reprieve from its glare. Mairi-Clare lay down beside him nudging her shoulder closer to his.

'Let's just get to know Friedrich and his dad better. If we can help them somehow, and it's obviously a big if, that would be a good thing to do. Don't you think? Maybe help his grandfather meet his family again? And I did actually, like the Famous Five.'

They remained silent for what seemed like an eternity as the crows bickered away in the large conifers to their rear only being interrupted by the multiple languages emanating from their fellow students as they played on the lawns.

'You better have a plan, MC, a great plan, a tremendous one, and ah cannae wait tae hear it. Ah'll light a candle on Sunday. God fuckin help us.

Chapter Thirteen

CAL SCANNED THE ROOM observing the small band of regulars hugging their half-and-half pints and tuning into the merciless banter that flowed spontaneously between the individuals as they ripped each other apart on a wide variety of topics from imminent divorces to the poor selection of horses at the bookies or their choice of crap football teams. He was looking for a particular individual, someone he had to do business with and someone he had to have noticed by others. All intricately linked with his plan to finish Quinn.

George duly arrived and they could indulge in their favourite pastime of sampling the perfectly poured pints of Guinness that awaited his presence.

'Please excuse my tardiness, Cal. I have no real excuse to present other than falling asleep in the chair.' He seemed to laugh and groan at the same time as he slowly lowered himself into the worn, leather, lounge seat.

'It's allowed, George, though I know you hate being late, that's why I'm always early for our rendezvous.'

George rubbed his fingers together leaning forward in his seat in anticipation of what was coming next. 'So, Mr Lynch, let's have your counter to my presentation last week then.'

The regulars, realising it was game on, began to gather to hear the lawyer's arguments. They obviously wanted their mate to be vindicated but the opportunity to hear a top defence solicitor narrate and present would only ever be available to them if they got huckled and ended up in court.

Cal began to rearrange the small table commandeering George's toy cars and placing them strategically around beer mats and ashtrays. 'Right, George, let's go back to Dealey Plaza, Nineteen Sixty-Three. Your assertation was that Oswald was in the Book Depository and fired off the first shot. I don't believe this to be the case; there is no evidence whatsoever to forensically link Oswald to the shots fired at the President. I also believe…' Cal raised his head to see Ronnie Sanders standing at the bar, awaiting his presence, 'excuse me for one minute, gentleman.'

'Mr Lynch, this seems a strange place to for us to do business, don't you think?' Sanders whispered, his eyes darting around the room at familiar faces who barely nodded to acknowledge his presence.

'Not my usual approach, Ronnie, but I'm so busy at court these days I'm barely in the office. Would you like a drink?'

'No, thanks, I'm working.'

'What do you have for me?' Cal glanced at the brown envelope nestling under his arm.

'Full dossier on your person of interest for the last two weeks. Some interesting engagements and a more remarkable existence than I would be expecting for a man of the cloth,' Sanders handed over the sealed brown envelope, 'it's all there, every detail.'

'Excellent, Ronnie, can you keep on it for another couple of weeks. I need to hear more,' Cal spoke quietly but assertively.

'You've not even looked at what I've given you?'

Cal handed over a small, folded envelope slipping it into the outstretched hand of Sanders which appeared with remarkable speed.

'I'm confident once I do read it that there will be more to come which will be of use. Keep at it.'

'You're the boss. I'll be in touch, back to work I go,' Sanders replied, as he made a swift exit from the bar.

He hadn't provided Cal with all his findings or interactions, holding back some key aspects. He felt content in the knowledge that the lawyer was clearly withholding information as well as his reasoning behind the need to follow a priest carrying out his daily duties. He'd provide the full dossier later, maybe.

'That'll be Sanders then, my friend?' George whispered, as Cal returned to his seat.

Cal nodded in response, 'It is. Do we need to go over again what is needed?'

'That won't be required. Leave it with me I'll sort it.'

'Thanks, George. I'll meet you anytime when you have something to report,' he responded under his breath content that finally the connection had been made.

Cal took a sip of his Guinness and was now on his feet mingling with the captivated audience, using the sticky wooden floor as his unofficial courtroom.

'So, back to your assertion that the fatal shot came from the support vehicle,' he announced, lifting the toy vehicles and slowly moving them into position, the half-empty pint glass now doubling as the Dallas Book Depository.

'I've checked over and over the Zapruder tape and importantly, George, all available images from the incident. The support vehicle is seen throughout the available documentation and no rifle is evidenced, moreover, no witnesses have mentioned in their testimony to the Warren Commission seeing a rifle being brandished in the backup car.'

George clicked his teeth in disdain, 'The Warren Commission is a whitewash, Mr Lynch, and you know it.'

'I couldn't agree more. What I do know is there are too many unanswered questions.'

'Like what, big man?' A voice piped up from the captivated audience.

Cal began to slowly wander again around the room, his hands in his pockets, holding the audience with his silence. 'Well, let's look at Oswald.' He held up a closed fist releasing a finger with each revelation, 'He defects to the USSR in 1959, receiving his visa in less than two days from the Soviets in Sweden. This is unheard of in any circumstances – remember he was an ex-US Marine. The Soviets subsequently want to send him to a high-ranking *retraining* school in Switzerland. He also applies for a visa to travel to Cuba, as we know a big enemy of the paranoid American regime. And yet...he's permitted to return to American soil without so much as an interrogation or a de-brief?'

Cal slowly glanced around the lounge, all eyes were on him, the chess game paused in the corner, a cigarette burned in the side of a gaping mouth and the overweight barman leaned across the bar, ensconced amongst the empty glasses.

'That's all well and good, my friend, but your theory doesn't explain the injuries or how they were administered.' George sat back and crossed his arms, gutted his research had been debunked with not much thrown out in return.

'I can't disagree with that, George, but what I can suggest is where the true evidence may lie. Over seventy thousand documents relating to the assassination are withheld by the United States Government for national security reasons. The government clearly don't trust their own people with the facts. If they are, and it's a big if, ever released, I believe they will reveal the truth as to how this event was initiated, planned, implemented, and sadly, accomplished. What I will say is that Oswald was placed in a position where one day he could be activated by unknown sources and take the fall for killing the President of the United States. It should be noted also that the day Oswald began his employment in the Book Depository, after failing to hold down three previous jobs. The Kennedy Texas visit, which included Dallas, was announced by the Dallas Morning News – the very same day.' He glanced around the pub, all eyes fixed on him. 'The jury of the Vatican. I'll leave you to draw your own conclusions.'

'Ah've said that for years that Oswald just took the Derry.''

Cal glanced over at George.

'He took the blame,' he smiled in response. Cal nodded, 'Yes, exactly, that's correct, my friend.'

George rose from the chair and stretched out a hand, 'We'll call this one inconclusive, Cal.'

'Agreed,' Cal responded, shaking his hand warmly.

'Next on the agenda, Cal, I want to cover unsolved murders – in Paisley,' the audience that had been rooted to the spot a mere minute ago dispersed quickly back to their preferred drinking locations, 'I've done my research, Cal. I know the facts and where to find the evidence. Christ, the dogs in the street could tell you.'

'Let's think about that one, George. You know we should all be careful about what is aired in public.'

'They won't silence me, Cal, not a hope.'

Cal said his goodbyes and headed for the door. George would need to be handled carefully. Cal was clear with George what help he required. He was confident he wouldn't be let down. There was no room for another innocent death on his conscience. There was though plenty of space within him to house the demise of certain others. That wasn't in doubt.

Chapter Fourteen

SANDERS TOOK A STEP back inside the entrance of number twenty-seven Argyle Street as he observed Father Dan enter Grace's tenement close, directly across from his vantage point.

Almost immediately his eyes were drawn to a police car being parked in front of him, a cigarette being flicked from the passenger's window and landing at his feet.

'Sorry, pal,' the suited officer said, as he closed the car door. Sanders laughed nervously and impatiently looked at his watch and then up and down the street to create the impression that he was waiting for someone to arrive. He recognised DS Lawrie and was intrigued as he crossed the road and also headed up Grace's close.

He'd hang around for a few minutes, but Lawrie's presence had spooked him; and he had prearranged appointment at home in thirty minutes with another interesting character who he would once again ply with vodka to help loosen his Liverpudlian tongue.

'Mum, Father Dan's at the door,' Joseph whispered, pointing back over his shoulder. Stephen sat impassive in the living room school jotters in hand waiting to sort out his Physics issues with his Mum, Monica at his side offering support.

Grace began to quickly tidy the living room, hiding the overflowing ashtray behind the chair and placing the papers and magazines into a neat pile on the smoked-glass coffee table in the middle of the floor.

'In the name ah Christ, ah wisnae expecting him. Joseph, put some water in that holy water font at the door before ye let him in.'

Grace had received a further letter from Berlin it wasn't from her son and one that scared her witless. Despite this she wouldn't call the police; she'd had enough of them and their questions which always were double barrelled or loaded. Frank was trustworthy, she thought, and would keep her right. He was late though and that annoyed her.

Father Dan entered the hall, removing his trilby hat and placing his fingers in the font before removing them hastily.

'Awrite Father, ma mums in the living room,' Joseph advised with a smile as he led the priest towards the open door. Father Dan greeted the family warmly as he entered the room.

'Come in, Father, good to see ye. Take a seat,' Grace spoke quickly, sprucing up the sofa cushions, still scanning the room for any untidiness, 'Joseph, put the kettle on, please.'

'Already boiled, Mum.'

Father Dan rubbed his fingers realising why he had nearly received third degree burns from holy water. 'Thank you, Grace. I won't keep you long.'

The priest would wait for his opportunity to speak to Grace privately. Usually when he entered a room the young folk would make a sharp exit, he hoped this would be the case with Stephen and his friend. Grace deserved to know all he had shared with the police and his presence at the scene of Dixie's torture and what they had spoken about in what, sadly, turned out to be his last words.

'Mum, can we talk about school and Physics,' Stephen asked, his irritation evident.

'Two minutes, Stephen,' Grace glared in response.

Joseph kicked open the living room door, slowly entering with a cup of tea in each hand, he concentrated fully as he placed the cups on the coffee table, letting out a sigh of relief. 'Thought I'd spill that there, Father,' he laughed nervously, wiping his brow, 'ah wis gonnae ask ye, Father, ah want tae get intae politics, ye know tae get rid of Thatcher and that, but ah don't know who's best, Labour or even they Scottish Nationalist or whit bout the Communist Party. What ye think?'

Father Dan spluttered into his cup, 'Let the good Lord guide you, sonny.'

'Another visitor, Mum.' He nudged his head back towards the door as DS Lawrie entered the room.

'Afternoon, everyone,' Lawrie said, standing as he usually did with hands in pockets, his worn trench coat tucked behind them, 'no tea for me, Joe, I've tasted your efforts before,' he added, trying to ease the tension which always seemed to transpire when a cop entered a room.

'You're late, Frank,' Grace spoke in gritted frustration, leading Lawrie's eyes towards the priest.

'Sorry, I got caught up with work. Anyway, I'm here now, how can I help?'

Father Dan took the momentary silence to indicate that his presence was not helpful, he would call back again or catch Grace after Sunday mass. Now was not the time.

'I'll get out of your way, Grace, it was just a courtesy call.' He rose from his seat and tucked his jacket and hat under his arm avoiding eye contact with Lawrie, 'I'll see you on Sunday,' he whispered.

'Thanks for calling, Father,' Grace responded, walking him to the front door.

She quickly returned to the living room; Lawrie was still standing, this time dominating the space in front of the coal fire. She picked up a large, brown, bulky, envelope and handed it to the detective.

'This came this morning fae Germany, it's got the same stamps Terence uses but it wisnae sent by him.'

Lawrie peeked inside the envelope before removing its contents. One by one he flicked through the glossy sheets. 'Photos of your boy, lots of photos of your boy,' He said, glancing around the room.

The black and white images, which seemed to have been taken by a wide zoom lens, showed Terence at various locations around Berlin, outside the Philharmoniker, wandering around Potsdamer Platz and relaxing in a park with what looked like fellow students.

Stephen placed his schoolbooks on the floor, intrigued by what was happening in front of him.

'So, someone has sent you pics of Terence, actually, really good pics. Could some of his pals have taken them?' Lawrie enquired.

Grace crossed the living room and took a small package from her handbag. She handed it to Lawrie and stood next to him, almost dwarfed by his stature, awaiting his response. He glanced inside the small envelope. Taking a paper hanky from his pocket he removed the contents and placed them and the hanky onto the coffee table. He gingerly moved both items around with a chewed biro pen.

'Has anyone touched these?' he asked, looking up to Grace. She shook her head beginning to feel uneasy as she clocked the look on the detective's face.

'These are bullets used in handguns,' he spoke slowly, closely studying the casings.

Grace stood behind him, arms folded in nervous anticipation. 'You see what ah seen; ah'm no imagining it ah'm ah?'

Lawrie shook his head and wrapped the bullets in the hanky, placed it back in the envelope and into his pocket.

'Yep, they've etched TC on the casing. Look, it's probably someone at the wind-up, trying to take a rise out of you. I'll check in with Interpol and the German cops, get them tae pay a visit to the music school. I wouldn't worry too much bout it,' Lawrie advised, trying to reassure the room's inhabitants.

'You sure?' Grace asked worryingly, hoping to grasp onto any guarantee being offered.

'Wait,' Stephen stood up, 'so our da was murdered and the folk that done it have just been lifted and now they've sent this – that they're gonnae kill Terence?'

Grace moved beside him, guiding him back to the chair. 'Ah think Frank's right, Son, it's just a wind-up. We'll speak to Terence as usual on Sunday, he'll be fine.'

Stephen felt his body go rigid as his mum placed her arm over his shoulders, pulling him closer to her. He ran his fingers through his dark hair, tightening his grip at the top of his skull. 'It's aw ma fault, first Dad, now Terence.' He began to cry and shake uncontrollably, his breathing becoming erratic. Grace cradled him tightly her eyes looking up towards Lawrie.

'Don't worry, Stephen, we see this all the time. We have things in place to deal with it.' He knelt in front of the boy, unsure whether he could take in what he was saying, 'Tell ye what, I'll go down the station, make some calls and come straight back up to tell you what's been done about it. OK?'

'Thanks, Frank, we're grateful for your help,' Grace whispered.

Frank lifted the brown envelope and made his way to the door. Grace looked up and with a poised voice said, 'And Frank don't think for a minute that he's getting forced to come home because of this mob. They've influenced our lives enough. No more.'

'Noted, Grace. Ah'll be in touch.'

Lawrie made his way to the station. The short drive had him thinking of a way that the trials of Jimmy Quinn and his daughter could be accelerated. The court system was notoriously slow and bureaucratic, by his reckoning the earliest they would be in front of a jury in the High Court would be August possibly September, July would be a better result. He'd need to support Grace and the boys as much as he could over the next while.

He immediately discussed the situation with Irvine and Henshaw, who in turn spoke to her senior contacts in Interpol. They didn't seem overly anxious or panicked, they'd just be professional as usual; no doubt having experienced similar situations in other high-profile cases.

'German Police will watch the boy, twenty-four seven, from a safe distance. They're also raiding the premises of their resident criminal gangs in Berlin to disrupt their operations. They'll throw in comments to get the message across to stay clear or they'll be back, kicking their doors in, day and night. It helps that I'm owed a couple of favours. The Russo has upped the stakes, Frank. I'd be surprised if they'd be foolish enough to hurt a kid in one of the most militarised cities in the world, but they're putting down a marker. This is aimed at Cal, not the Clarks. We better belt up for a rough ride. Once we're at trial, I'll be happy, not before,' Henshaw said, ominously.

Chapter Fifteen

MAIRI-CLARE KEPT PACE with Friedrich's father as they walked quickly from the church hall along Scharrenstrasse. With the exception of the impressive church building, which dominated the landscape, the area had few discernible features with dull, functional, grey buildings intertwined with wasteland, and wide roads which seemed to have just a few cars occupying them. Terence and Friedrich followed on behind passing a ball between them and stopping occasionally to listen to a song on the younger boy's Walkman. By their actions it looked like they were listening, yet again, to Big Country.

Although the streets were empty on the early Sunday morning the man spoke quietly, wary of any nosey neighbours or Stasi spies. 'My name is Dieter, Friedrich's father. It is a pleasure to meet you both again. My son really enjoys your company,' he announced in slow, broken English.

'I'm Mairi-Clare and this is Terence, who I think you've met already,' she replied, looking over her shoulder.

'He is very good, friendly with Friedrich, yeah. Very prayerful at service also, devoted, I notice. You do not attend service?' Dieter asked, glancing down towards Mairi-Clare.

'Not really my thing,' she replied, assertively.

'Mmmm,' Dieter mumbled in response.

'Would you prefer we spoke in German?'

Dieter shook his head and attempted to clear his mouth of a biscuit; he had just stuffed between his teeth, his pencil-thin, mousey moustache quivering quickly beneath his long, pointed nose. 'It is best for us to practice our English, though this young man, he speaks at tornado speed,' he replied, grinning and pointing his bony thumb over his shoulder at his Scottish visitor.

They had met up earlier in the church hall after Mass, a place where the parishioners would gather for hot soup and coffee and to discuss their everyday issues and the loved ones left behind by the wall that had weaved its way through their community for the past two decades. Today the hall had been filled with noise and laughter as a large tape cassette player; was placed on a pasting table and blasted music leading to parents and small children dancing around the polished floor as other parishioners sat comfortably and sang along.

'We walk to Potsdamer and then reach Niederkirchnerstrasse, then I will show you, yes?'

Mairi-Clare nodded her head, smiling with enthusiasm. She would explain her plan to Dieter, but first she had to get close to the wall and hopefully get a glimpse of his father who remained in the East.

Dieter continued, 'In August 1961 when the German Democratic Republic sealed off the city and began erecting the wall I was a teenager. My sister and I went to our aunt's house near to the cordon and wall. My parents were to follow on a few days after, once mother was able to, she was not well. The short journey was physically impossible for her at that point. Father had refused to leave her side and now twenty-odd years later he is now alone with no prospect of being with us. We talk, across the barricades. That is where we celebrate our birthdays and anniversaries,' he pointed back over his shoulder, 'Friedrich has never met his Papa; their only interaction is by shouting at a distance, stolen moments, or through our letters which are censored by the Stasi. That is why my father writes of things that have happened in the past to limit the black lines through his letters.'

'This way,' Dieter pointed to a large building which was one of several in a row that looked abandoned. The large ornate windows were dirty with, the barely visible internal, faded white; shutters closed tightly behind them. Self-seeding plants had taken root in the rooftop growing freely in the grey stone and from the iron guttering the multitude of purple flower heads fluttered in the gentle breeze. Dieter paused allowing the two boys to catch up.

'Now, we are silent,' he whispered, meeting their eyes.

He led them through the narrow entrance and began heading up the marble stairs, clutching the opulent handrailing as he went. Climbing to the final landing they reached a large open window which overlooked the wall and the empty landscape that surrounded it.

A fresh breeze cooled their skin as they took in the scene in front of them, the barren, dead space, a no man's land which was occupied by only the East German military. Dieter picked up a small pair of binoculars which sat in the corner of the landing and immediately focused on a similar building directly opposite in Wilhelmstrasse.

The building was also uninhabited with all the windows removed and the majority boarded up by the East German security to prevent easy access to the west – just in case any desperate individuals were brave enough to attempt this route for an escape. Only the upper floor windows were open, and this was where Dieter focused his attention, scanning slowly each gap, each window, looking for a sign of life.

'He's looking for Papa,' Friedrich whispered to Terence.

'Wow, amazing,' Terence replied, moving towards the window's edge. Dieter immediately pulled him back and shook his head.

'We stay back so we are not seen.'

'Sorry,' Terence responded, 'the tap dancer, as well, what a view.'

'Tap dancer?' Friedrich was confused.

'Aye, tap dancer, tap floor.' Terence waved his arms around the open space trying to emphasise his point.

'Tap dancer?' Friedrich began moving his heels and toes in an attempt to understand his new friend.

'Naw, naw, high up, up here, Fred. Tap floor. Tap dancer. Tap ah the close.'

'Terence. Shut up,' Mairi-Clare intervened; the boyish carry-on of her friend was mis-timed on this occasion.

'Will do,' he responded sheepishly, moving to the rear of the group.

Dieter checked his watch, 'We are slightly early.'

'Could ye no just take a runny and get over the wall?' Terence whispered.

Dieter gave Mairi-Clare a confused glance. 'How easy is it to escape from there is what Terence is asking, Dieter?'

Dieter laughed to himself, revealing his neglected teeth, with a brightness appearing in his eyes as if the naivety of the question eased his mood. 'The wall is approximately three metres high, four in some parts, there are over three hundred watch towers,' he pointed towards a large wooden structure which sat adjacent to the wall with telescopes, cameras, and gun turrets visible throughout, 'there are bunkers, dog runs, spikes, alarmed fences, and regular patrols. Many have tried. There is no way through this wall. You need connections, the trust of likeminded people in the East, and I would say the energy of youth. My father has none of them. Over there is a restricted zone, buildings aren't open to citizens though access can be achieved for short periods,' he signed, his shoulders dropping despondently.

A figure appeared at a window, a telescope held to his eye, waving a small white handkerchief.

'He is here,' Dieter smiled, raising the binoculars quickly. The man moved slowly around the gap, his tall, thin, body visible as the morning sunlight framed him. He was similar in stature to his son, slim, slightly stooped, Mairi-Clare thought.

Dieter began speaking loudly and quickly in German as Friedrich waved and jumped up and down hoping to catch his Papa's eye.

'Hallo Papa, du siehst gut aus. Wir haben Besucher hier, um Sie aus Schottland zu sehen, winken Sie ihnen zu.'

'Ach Schottland. Hallo. Archie Gemmell, Argentinien,' the grey-headed figure called out and pumped his left fist imitating the diminutive Scottish footballer, a broad smile evident across his face. Friedrich laughed while Terence shrugged his shoulders understanding what had been discussed and pumping his fist in return.

Mairi-Clare attempted to follow the ongoing chat between Dieter and his father though only small parts were clear due to the speed with which they conversed.

The meeting ended abruptly as guards stationed in the watchtower began to patrol the inhospitable surroundings beneath the windows. They waved their goodbyes as the lone figure moved quickly away from the space and disappeared into the darkness.

Dieter did not seem unduly disappointed with the shortness of the *visit* as they descended the stairs towards the street and the growing bustle of the morning.

'It happens often. We just have to see and know he is alive, though he is advancing in years, as you see. You have a plan, I hear?' His eyes fixed on Mairi-Clare then switched quickly to Terence.

'We have a plan which we think will work. I need his measurements if you have them, especially his height,' she put her arm around the boy's small shoulders and pulled him closer, 'your Papa will be playing football with you very soon, Friedrich.'

'Fucksake,' Terence whispered to himself.

Chapter Sixteen

DRIVING SLOWLY AS HE attempted to dodge the potholes in the car park, Cal continued with considerable apprehension as he tried to protect his gleaming BMW and its suspension.

'Don't worry, your little baby has been built with Bavarian expertise and precision, I'm sure it'll be fine,' Nicki teased, lovingly giving the dash a wipe.

'It may well be but I'm sure it wasn't tested against surfaces in such a poor condition as this, unbelievable,' Cal responded pointing out of the windscreen, clearly irritated.

'Oh, stop moaning. It's bad enough you drag me out here on a Sunday morning for a bloody run without having to look at your sour puss at the same time. C'mon, park up and let's get going,' Nicki replied, trying to motivate herself as she tucked her blonde hair inside a woolly hat.

The vast park was sparsely populated with small number of vehicles sporadically dotted throughout the car parks covering both sides of the loch, the majority of local residents favouring a long lie on a Sunday morning. A few couples huddled together on benches holding hot drinks close to their chests. A young mum held the hood of her toddler tightly as she threw bread to the squawking mallards and eiders as they hurriedly tried to get their fill before the mute swans would float over and dominate proceedings.

Reaching the tarmac path at the edge of the loch the wind forcing the fresh water to ripple over the man-made edging, Cal reached for his toes stretching his hamstrings. Nicki stood beside him running on the spot trying to keep the blood circulating around her body as the cold morning chilled her to the bone.

'Can we get going, Seb Coe, I'm freezing, as usual. It's meant to be the summer and this country is still baltic.'

'OK, last week we ran east so let's go towards the west this time, up by the water sports centre, we'll touch the woods over there then back down here for a cup of tea. Remember it's about two and half miles so probably twenty-five to thirty minutes would be a good target?'

Nicki had already taken off, impatient with the cold, her partner's attention to detail on everything and anything and her dislike of the activity in general.

'Such a beautiful loch isn't it, Nicki,' Cal said, catching up with his girlfriend, 'this was actually the location of a village that served the local colliery. It's now submerged in the water.'

'Amazing,' Nicki replied dismissively, her focus on the path and the two plus miles ahead.

'Yes, Bothwellhaugh it was called. There's also a Roman fort across the water,' he added, pointing his gloved finger over Strathclyde Park Loch.

'Jeez, you told me that last week and the week before. You know I hate running and you're making it worse. Best for you to zip it and we'll get this done!' Nicki responded, throwing him a quick glare. The running was tolerable as after it she got to spend time with Cal where they could be relaxed and not concerned with looking over their shoulders. It was also a time in the week where she found Cal most at ease so, despite her protests, she was always happy once they got back to the car.

The route was flat and open around the loch with a slight incline through a recent woodland plantation, the only noise to be heard was the sound of the gravel clashing with the soles of their trainers. They re-emerged at the loch and followed the sharp right along the edge of the opposite car park.

Observing two men sitting in a gleaming red Ford Cortina overlooking the path and the loch, Cal slowed his pace slightly, allowing Nicki to take the lead. Both were smartly dressed in collar and tie with, tidy hair styles. The driver's arm hung lazily out of the window, a filtered cigarette burning between his fingers beside two large, shining, sovereign rings. Their eyes followed Nicki as she raced on in front. Couple of pervs, he thought. Spotting the two aerials located on the roof of the car, he shook his head in disbelief. He had insisted to Lawrie that he didn't want to be followed around by his plain-clothed pals. He'd phone him once he got back to the office to ensure they were stood down.

They continued along the remaining tarmac path route in silence, the only sound their laboured breathing, the steam rising from Nicki's shoulders and vanishing as it mixed with the cold air. Eventually she leaned across the shining black bonnet of the BMW, the agreed finishing line.

'Your best time yet, babe, really impressive,' Cal advised, scanning the stopwatch hanging around his neck. Nicki failed to answer, waving her hand towards the door.

'Why don't we do one more lap, push on further?' Cal asked, his breathing now firmly under control.

'Keys,' she retorted, pulling at the door handle,

'Just one?' he pleaded, clasping his hands in mock prayer.

'Keys. How many times do I have to tell you. I don't chase crims anymore. I catch them with my brain and I'm perfectly happy with my fitness levels, thank you very much,' she countered slowly in a faint voice. Cal opened the passenger door and guided his partner to the seat putting her jacket over her shoulders.

'I'll do one more lap, if that's OK. You rest up.' He reached in and kissed her on the forehead.

'Keys,' she held out an open hand removing her hat with the other and shaking out her hair, 'for the radio please, and don't be long, you moron,' she responded, reclining the seat slightly and stretching her legs out in the footwell.

Cal took off at pace following the same route. He realised this wasn't as taxing as the steep incline of West Brae at Oakshaw though the opportunity to chase an improved personal best would push him on and add to his overall confidence that his injuries were behind him, and that strength was steadily returning to his body and resilience to his mind.

Nicki folded her arms and shook her head as she watched him, smirking as she spent too long staring at his muscular calves and tight arse. She leaned across the driver's seat and turned the ignition bringing the radio to life. USA for Africa, the American musician's effort for Live Aid, wailed through the speakers, We are the World, their contribution to the saving of the starving. She sighed and turned the ignition off, rested her head on the leather headrest, closed her eyes and enjoyed the silence.

Cal kept a steady pace and resisted the temptation to check his time, a glance now may dishearten him, of not being quick enough. The park was beginning to get busy as the locals decided to stretch their legs on the mid Sunday morning. Scouring the car park as he emerged from the woods, he clocked that their security detail had made an exit. Failing to notice an unruly, long-haired, Alsatian dog he tumbled onto the path, slightly winded. He sat up slowly and laughed to himself as the female owner ran past him in an attempt to catch her wayward pet. He rubbed small stones from his scraped knee and resumed his run at a slower, controlled, pace.

A cacophony of noise came from across the loch and the mature woodlands; as the geese and the native crows flew off in unison the outline of their dark bodies and flapping wings contrasting with the low, grey, sky.

Cal reached the door of the BMW; out of breath though still smiling to himself about the tumble he had taken and thinking, thank God Nicki hadn't seen it – he'd never live it down. He opened the door and slid himself into the driver's seat, his hands resting on the steering wheel.

'So, just round the other side of the loch as you come out of the woods,' he started, turning to face Nicki, 'I went...No.' He stumbled from the car. Turning slowly he stared through the open door, his feet rooted to the loose gravel surface.

'Help. Help,' he screamed, looking around the car park and the loch. Running around the car, his eyes transfixed, peering through the windows, he moved towards the passenger door. He opened the door quickly, shattered glass from the window dropping onto the car park floor. He leaned in and wrapped his arm around her neck. Nicki, her body warm, did not respond. A small bullet hole was prominent on her left temple. Immediately his hand and arm were saturated with her blood, the headrest covered in brain matter, hair, and small bone fragments.

'Nicki, Nicki, what happened. C'mon, you'll be… fucksake. Help me,' he screamed to no one in particular. Shaking her body; he tried to find a pulse first on her neck, then moving quickly onto her limp, lifeless wrist. Her head turned her eyes cold, frozen in time. The full extent of her injuries were becoming clear to him with a large exit wound eliminating any notion that she could be saved.

Cal collapsed out of the car and lay on the rough ground. He could hear rushed, heavy, footsteps and raised voices. His mind began to shut down as everything became slower, he could see the outline of figures peering in the open door then moving quickly away. Someone attempted to lift him, shake him from his current state.

Death had a pervasive hold over him, clinging to everything he touched or loved, shaping his past, and dictating his future. He closed his eyes tightly, attempting to blank out the chaos that was enveloping around him.

* * *

Superintendent Irvine leaned on the squad car, dressed in a white, forensic suit speaking into his handset, his eyes scanning the crime scene. He had seen his fair share of brutal murders throughout his career, though this one was personal. Not only was a colleague taken out, someone he had grown fond of and respected, but this was an attack on the force itself. A worrying raise in stakes by a ruthless adversary.

Forensic and senior police officers came and went from the dark tarpaulin tent which screened the BMW within the now cordoned off car park, the flimsy blue and white police tape fluttered in the light breeze. Uniformed cops took statements from the park users who remained at the scene while another team crawled on their knees looking for evidence, marking potential clues for colleagues with bags, who came in their wake.

As Cal sat on the back step of the ambulance, his immediate triage examination complete, he observed the shock etched on Irvine's face. Cal's hands and arms were encased in loose plastic bags, and he wore an extraordinarily large paper suit. He knew he was a suspect, being the last person to see Nicki alive, but there was no need to get a story straight, he just had to provide as much information as he could to help her colleagues. As much as he could remember.

He stood up quickly and stared across the loch. An officer was assigned to him and ordered not to leave his side. 'The car park over there,' he attempted to point his finger through the clear plastic covering, 'you have to check over there. They were sitting watching us, over there. I'm sure,' he stuttered, trying hard to control his emotions. The officer spoke quietly into his radio as Irvine left the tent and glanced in Cal's direction. Immediately officers were deployed to secure the opposite car park, soon the whole locality would be locked down.

'DS Lawrie, it's Irvine here, you've been briefed? I'll be pulling together a team once I get back to Paisley. I need you on this, Frank, focused. Select four officers to help you straight away. You fine with that?' Irvine spoke in a hushed tone over the radio while displaying the confidence of a man in total control, who'd been there before.

'Right, OK, I need you to send one of your guys to Greenock, get their two fuckin cells turned over, forensically examined. There's a specialist team attached to the prison service that do this, they're based at Barlinnie, get them down to Greenock, get someone to call them straight away. And, Frank, the names of every person mentioned in Nicki Henshaw's files, get them pulled in for questioning. If they tell us nothing or don't play ball, I'll drip feed their names to the press for future use. And talking of press – a full news blackout, understand?'

'On it, sir.' Lawrie's blood was boiling as he thought of nothing but revenge, he would need to curtail these feeling, remain focused as Irvine demanded.

'And, Frank, I'll be bringing Cal Lynch in for interview. I can tell you trust fuckin no one so I want you to carry this out, agreed?'

'Absolutely fine to lead, sir, no problem.'

* * *

Superintendent Irvine called the hastily convened investigation team together as they sat in near silence around the sparse room, some talking in hushed tones to colleagues, others speaking quietly into phones or staring out of the tinted glass windows as the late afternoon sun began to burst through the thin clouds bringing some warmth to the cold, lifeless space.

'Right, team, listen up,' Irvine stood in the centre of the group pivoting as he spoke. His shirt sleeves were already rolled up, his Paisley-patterned tie hanging loosely around his thick neck, his shirt hanging untidily over his expanded waistline.

'We've lost one of our own. A thoroughly professional, dedicated officer as well as a good friend. It would be easy for each of us to seek revenge, start nailing those within reach, easy targets. What we will do is follow Nicki's lead, find the evidence…the evidence, team. No ambiguity, just the evidence through old-fashioned, honest policing,' he spoke with determination as he locked eyes intermittingly with members of the team scanning their faces, looking for anger, lack of focus or too much emotion on show, 'there is also a news blackout, so discuss this case with no one. We won't give the perpetrators the satisfaction of seeing their actions in print or flashed up on the news.'

The team nodded in agreement and began splitting into previously assigned groups, ready to begin work and busily hoping to make early progress for their gaffer and more importantly their friend, Nicki.

What Irvine had not revealed was that it had already been decided that Nicki Henshaw, a senior officer, would be reported to have tragically died at the scene of an unfortunate car crash while on holiday in Devon. A Metropolitan Police full honours funeral was already being planned in her native London. No inch could be given to the ongoing fight against the illegal, insidious, organised crime gang. No weakness shown. No losses given up.

* * *

Lawrie sat quietly sipping his coffee and watching his forensics colleague complete their examination. He had now been promoted to a senior role in the case and for the next forty-eight hours he would provide hourly updates to Superintendent Irvine on all aspects of the investigation as it progressed, starting with his findings from the impending interview with his friend.

Cal was limp, his face ashen, and he was in another world as a white suited officer slowly swabbed his hands, cut his fingernails, combed out the contents of his hair, and bagged up and labelled his bloodstained clothes.

The officer removed his latex gloves, closed his faded, large, leather briefcase and tidied several evidence bags nodding to Lawrie that his work was done.

Placing a cup of black coffee at Cal's side he sat close to his friend, thinking of how he would begin the conversation.

'She looked so scared, Frank. I let this happen, I should have listened to you. I thought they were your guys. It must have been them, they followed us,' Cal whispered, staring at the floor and running the images over and over again in his mind.

'Cal, I'm so sorry. Nicki was a good friend and a top, top officer. But now ah need as much info as possible. Ah need ye to be open and honest with me. Ah need everything. So, let's begin with that - have you seen this red car or the guys in it before?'

Cal shook his head.

'First time you saw them was at the loch, today, in Strathclyde Park?'

'Yes.'

'I'll need full descriptions, every detail. Just keep talking, what you don't think is important could be the key to catching these bastards. Bullet casings were found at the scene, big mistake. And given this looks like a professional hit – a bit strange,' he nodded over toward his colleague, 'Sutherland here will be checking the records for incidents where similar weaponry was deployed as soon as he gets finished up here.'

Cal nodded.

'Did Nicki seem on edge, apprehensive bout anything?'

Cal shook his head, 'Nicki hated running. I should have paid attention. Listened to her. I was too casual, relaxed about this whole situation with the court case, with everything.'

'Who would have known of your movements, would have been aware you went running around the loch?'

'No one. We kept everything private.'

'Ah need to know your full movements in the last twenty-four hours, where you've been, what you had for dinner last night, who you spoke to, who Nicki spoke to, what you talked about, who she met, who you met. Understand?' Lawrie lit a cigarette, pulled open his notepad and tapped his pen on the table. 'Everything, Cal, ah need the lot. Fuckin everything.'

Cal raised his head; tears filled his eyes as he stared directly at Lawrie. 'You'll get everything I can remember. I know she was convinced the files held the secrets. She said she was confident that she was really close to cracking it. Though she didn't know who to trust up here. Bloody Quinn and this Russo thing.'

'We're going through the files just now and I've also sent a team to your house, so don't be surprised if it's not how you left it this morning. Right, let's get started.'

Chapter Seventeen

FATHER DAN AWOKE DROWSY and disoriented. His vision was blurred; and he blinked repeatedly to try and clear the fog in front of his eyes. It appeared to be night. All was dark, though he wasn't at home in the parish house. He felt rigid, unable to move, he was in a seated position, and could feel a cold breeze brush around his ankles, cooling his legs. He attempted to move but was held firmly in place, with just some limited movement allowing him to move his shoulders slightly. He tried to focus his thoughts as his brain began to clear the confusion he was experiencing. He could feel particles of dust on his tongue as he rubbed it against the roof of his mouth, attempting to generate salvia to ease his dryness. As his predicament became ever clearer his breathing became sharper, quicker. He began to cough uncontrollably. He heard a voice murmur to his left as the material was pulled from his head. His eyes smarted with the immediate exposure to the bright, natural light.

The priest was in an elevated position, and he noticed a figure, walking back and forth beneath him, the sound of his feet heavy on the floor. A large, thin man stood, looking up at him. His arms were folded across a black, leather jacket and a wide grin broke out across his long face. He need no introduction.

The building was empty with large, iron beams running perpendicular down both sides as light was interspersed along its length, breaking through holes in the smashed windows which were high above the grey, breeze block walls.

How had he got here, what had happened? Maybe he was just dreaming, he smiled to himself. He thought back to his day; early morning Mass with the ten regular parishioners, he was then to head to the hospital to visit the sick, provide solace for the dying and reassure their relatives of a better life ahead for them in Heaven. His last recollection was removing his vestments in the sacristy then feeling an arm being put around his neck and something being placed over his mouth and nose, tightly pressed by a large hand as he was pulled against a body which stood firm behind him.

'So, we meet again, Father. So soon, as well. I just couldn't keep away.'

The voice confirmed Father Dan's worst fears. He knew who was in front of him and the dangerous situation he was now in. He could sense the presence of another individual, picking up the sound of feet shuffling to his rear. He was tied tightly to a chair which seemed to be on some sort of wooden platform with rusted scaffolding poles framing the structure. He could feel a cloth or material around his neck, but he was unsure what its purpose was. His arms were behind his back, stretching his chest, the wood of the chair digging into his forearms.

The building was a derelict industrial unit which looked as if it had been abandoned for several years. Concrete floors were covered in dust, and at various points, wires and metal uprights emerged from the large, grey surface as if they had taken root.

'An amazing building, Father, eh? A thing of great beauty and industrial heritage. Where honest graft was rewarded; and dignity racked up in abundance. My wee Scottish friend behind you there tells me that this place was called Chrysler, where the natives built great cars to sell across the UK, but that friend of the people, Thatcher, closed it down. He also said that the troops were fond of a strike or two. *Time to hit the cobbles,* was the cry as they all downed tools for the most insignificant of reasons and headed outside, most went off to the boozers, he says.'

Father Dan stared directly at the individual as he attempted to figure out how he could extract himself from his predicament. He considered engaging with him in conversation, in an attempt to normalise the situation, which could lead to a route out. That hadn't worked with Dixie. This maniac had put a bullet in the back of his skull. He wanted something, Father Dan realised that, and he was unsure if he had anything to give him that could, potentially, save his life.

'Father. Let's call you Dan, since we're mates,' he sneered in that familiar nasally accent, the word *mates* extending for far too long, he thought. 'My employers aren't too happy. "Clean up loose ends or you're next they said." And a wee Scottish birdy tells me you visited the bizzies recently, just after not saying hello to me in the Co-op, which I have to say, I thought was quite rude. Now, I hope you never broke the seal of confession. The old Pope wouldn't take too kindly to that, would he?' He walked slowly to the edge of the frame and tapped the platform with one, gloved, finger. 'I, my friend, have the power of life and death. So, you have to tell me, Dan, what did you tell the bizzies about the last time me met. Then I might not kill you. Just anoint you with a plenary indulgence.' He laughed again, tilting his head to the side, engaging with the individual to the rear. A muted response was heard in return.

'Dan you're probably wondering, what is this piece of work you find yourself on, no? Well, I know it's not exactly Golgotha where your hero was crucified but a bit of effort went into this, my friend. See, my old man was an engineer and after Thatcher closed *his* factory, he tried to keep his dignity by teaching me how to make things, how to work out and solve problems. Mostly though he sat in his shed drinking homebrew with his mates.

Killed him that did, or was it her? Who knows. It was sad, Dan, sad.'

He bent under the platform, tapped underneath the priest's feet, and continued to speak. 'He taught me how to make the fitting that's preventing you from falling through here, Dan. You see, I need to know what was said or you will die a very undignified death.'

Father Dan ran through some excuses in his head to explain his visit to the police station. What could he say that was believable; a visit to one of his parishioners being held who had asked for his help, attending a community police meeting, reporting a break-in? His mind was still hazy from whatever he had drugged him with, though he realised no concocted story would be sufficient to prevent his impending demise. The scouser had not hidden his face which was a sure sign that he planned for no witnesses to his latest work would be left to tell the tale. He would have to accept his fate.

The stiffness around his wrist ensured any movement was impossible and he had no idea whether his rosaries were in his pocket. He would sing to himself, he thought, it would give him strength to face the demon in front of him. The Creed in Latin which he had loved since learning it as a young boy at Mass in Gourock and it continued to inspire him. He began quietly, noticing the scouser tilting his head to hear what was emanating from his captive.

'Credo in unum Deum, Patrem omnipotentem, factorem cœli et terræ, visibilium omnium et

invisibilium. Et in unum Dominum, Jesum Christum.'

'Ah, the Credo. Sing up, Dan, I love that one,' the scouser responded, laughing to himself. He would get this back on track, witnessing victims trying to zone out, attempting to deflect from the inevitable, was something he had experienced on many an occasion.

'So, Dan, let me explain what's going to happen. I'm not going to *stiff* a priest with a bullet, that would be sacrilege, even in my trade. What we have here is a bastardised, sorry for the language, cam-lock which will withstand thirteen stone of pressure. Remember that number, Dan, that's important. What you also have behind you is a barrel with a tap attached which will fill very slowly with water,' he walked behind the platform as the priest attempted to turn his head to follow his movements, 'now, once it reaches capacity it will add another stone in weight to the platform. You, my holy friend, weigh twelve stones, so guess what happens next, eh?' He sneered again which surprisingly, with all he was facing, was the one thing getting under the priest's skin.

'You will commit suicide. The rope round your neck will tighten as you go hurtling towards the floor. I'll then, with great care, love, and attention,' he laughed to himself again, 'will remove your restraints and you'll be found to have topped yourself. The pressure of leading the flock in such depressing, challenging times was too much for you and led you to succumb, to give it all up here in such a derelict location. Summing up how you feel about society in general. Good, eh, what do you think?'

'Fillum Dei unigentum, et ex Patre natum, ante omnia saecula.'

The scouser looked behind the platform, waving to his accomplice to come forward. 'Turn on the tap…slowly, slowly. We don't want to scare the man.'

The man shook his head not wanting to reveal himself, the self-loathing he felt at being present to witness this would be nothing if he had to lock eyes with Father Dan.

'Don't be shy, my good friend. Come here. Let Dan see you in all your glory, showcase the power you have at your fingertips. I've given you what you always wanted, my friend,' the scouser ordered, beckoning him to the front of the platform.

Ronnie Sanders moved forward, his eyes fixed on the dust-covered concrete floor, kicking small pieces of rubble around like an errant schoolkid embarrassed to have been caught doing wrong.

The scouser leaned towards him and menacingly whispered, slowly, in his ear, 'did you get the impression that I would leave you as another loose end? I get caught you go down with me, and you won't last a minute inside, believe me.'

Sanders took a deep breath, raised his head, and stared directly at Father Dan. 'You don't have to worry about me: I'm enjoying this.'

'You know what to do, lad.'

Sanders moved to the rear stopping momentarily as Father Dan's singing caught his ear.

'Deum de Deo, Lumen de Lumine, Deum verum de Deo vero.'

Immediately a soft splashing sound was audible from behind him, filling the silent void, the water hitting the bottom of a plastic barrel.

Drip…drip…drip.

The sound would change as the volume began to steadily increase; the echo being replaced with the water splashing on contact.

'You'll have a short time before the weight gives way, Dan. Exactly…' he glanced at his Casio, digital watch, 'no, let's keep you in suspense,' the scouser added. 'Told ye, me old man was an engineer. So, start talking priest or you commit suicide.'

'Qui propter nos homines et propter nostrum salutem descendit de caelis.'

'All you have to do is tell me what you said to that copper, Lawrie. You were in there for over two hours, and you handed over your Stole, didn't you. C'mon Daniel, we don't want to be here, do we? Watching you die, do we?'

Drip…drip…drip.

Father Dan flinched slightly, the first sign of fear on display, exposing a weakness, for his torturers to witness and exploit.

The scouser raised his eyebrows and moved closer to the platform, his stale, tobacco; breath reaching the priest's nostrils. 'Ah, Daniel…Daniel. It's only your loving mother who calls you that isn't it. How will she feel when she hears her son, the boy she was so proud of to have joined the clergy, has topped himself, eh? No final confession, no last rites. All that pride wiped out, Daniel.'

Drip…drip…drip.

'People will comfort her, but she will know when they give her a sympathetic look there at the back of their eyes, in their hugs, in their shallow Mass cards, their true feelings will shine through. A failure. A let down.'

Father Dan closed his eyes and shook his head quickly to refocus, to return to prayer. His mother was a devout follower though a realist to the everyday pressure that was being felt by all sections of society across the country. She knew he found his vocation challenging, the loneliness and the harbouring of everyone's problems when he had no solutions to offer, only prayer. If he were to be found, which seemed highly likely, in the condition the scouser described she would hold her head up high and walk behind his coffin as it was carried into the church for his requiem mass.

He felt and heard the wooden boards creak beneath his feet as the pressure on the latch began to increase. He wouldn't have much longer, the sound emanating from the barrel seemed to be closer to his ear, more perceptible.

Drip…drip…drip.

'Can ah turn this off now. He's no going tae tell us anything,' Sanders pleaded, the enormity of what was unfolding filling him with dread. This had gone too far. The scouser had told him he just wanted to scare him, shut him up. Now he witnessed that he revelled in torture and death. He seemed determined on getting a hit, feeding his evil endorphins.

Sanders had pocketed a sizeable sum by working both camps. Cal Lynch wanted information, so did the scouser. That suited him, kept him busy, helped his nosiness while feeding his wallet.

The scouser had clocked him as he followed the priest around town and began feeding him small, but regular sums of cash. He had also spent a few evenings in his house in Ferguslie, drinking and loosening his tongue, much to Sanders' delight. He had asked him to find a building to facilitate a private chat with the priest. No better place than his former workplace – the derelict factory in Linwood.

Drip…drip…drip.

The boards creaked louder, the surface beginning to move slightly, and the vibration was being felt through the soles of the priest's shoes. He braced himself expecting to crash through at any second. He raised his eyes to the sky following the line of the thick rope as it rose to the rusted iron girder above him. He anticipated it tightening quickly, praying it would break his neck instantly and prevent a slow death, choking and grasping for air. He hoped the scouser wouldn't see that, obtain the satisfaction of his fight for air, to look as if he was begging for help.

He was ready to meet his God, his peace made, and Satan hadn't won. He wasn't afraid of dying, his faith was strong, though he did challenge the churches theologians view of Heaven and Hell and the big fire. In his mind, Hell was your worst fears, what occupied your innermost thoughts, what sins you had failed to give up – if you feared death by drowning you would be constantly gasping for breath under water, floundering. If your body shook with the fear of enclosed spaces, being constantly in the dark and being trapped would be your fate. Heaven was everything that gladdened you, made you feel warm and safe, held your most treasured memories and people. He smiled at the scouser who growled in response.

'Et in Spiritum Sanctum, Dominum et vivificantem, qui ex Patre Filioque procedit.'

'Speed it up,' the scouser barked at Sanders, contemptuously staring at the priest.

Sanders moved slowly towards the tap, glancing furtively at the dark figures who were darting stealthy along the edge of the building. They were spread out strategically on both sides of the brick wall, haunching below the broken window frames. slowly making ground, towards the rusted double doors lying open to the elements.

Drip.

'Police. On the fuckin floor. On the fuckin floor!' The shouting came from all sides as individuals, some dressed in black uniforms, their faces masked, others in civilian clothing rushed in creating a scene of total confusion. The scouser immediately placed his hands on top of his ponytailed head and calmly, slowly, dropped to his knees. An officer raced towards him and cracked his boot into his back smashing his skull onto the scaffold pole. He let out a slow groan as he landed face first on the concrete floor the officer's size ten pressed firmly on his back, the muzzle of his rifle stuck rigidly to the back of his neck.

Sanders was lying flat on his chest as the handcuffs were placed tightly on his wrists and he was lifted by the arms and raced towards a waiting police car.

'Sir, you're safe now,' an officer announced to Father Dan as another switched off the water and cut the rope which hung from the rusted iron girder above his head. The priest lowered his chin to his chest and cried uncontrollably. Two officers helped him from the platform as another placed blankets around his back and waist to provide some dignity, hiding his soiled trousers.

Sanders, sitting uncomfortably with the cuffs digging into his lower back stared out of the passenger window as the car left the scene and sped towards Mill Street Police Station.

George Sinclair sat, resting himself, on a road sign opposite the junction; leaning his hands on his chestnut walking stick the grooves of the ivory handle a perfect fit for his wrist. He nodded to Sanders and raised a thumb. Sanders responded with a nod and a smile. Their work was done.

Cal's plan had worked with great precision, though a bit too close for comfort for Sanders' liking. Cal had expected that they would come for the priest, the one loose link and connection to some of their charges. It had to be closed. With the bosses now on remand they needed to spread doubt with what was being presented to a jury while also reinforcing their grip on the community. He also knew they would view Sanders as being of little moral fibre, someone who could be manipulated and exploited. He just had to have everything in place while he awaited the Russo to take the bait. George and the remarkable Sanders learned their roles and played their parts to the letter.

The scouser would now be sent down for an exceptionally long time. He would be housed at Peterhead High Security Prison away from his power base and footholds around the north of England. He knew the drill and would keep his mouth shut during questioning. That would ensure he would be looked after; say one word and he would be dead within weeks.

He would also be questioned on the murder of Nicki Henshaw, but he had, genuinely, no knowledge of that operation. The many layers of the organised crime gang ensured that only those who planned, and brutally delivered that message on the leaders' behalf were in the know.

Sanders, it would be leaked, would be questioned and *officially* charged. His previous life was now over, and he would have to go into hiding shortly, begin again elsewhere. He was happy with that. Paisley held no economic and even less of an emotional pull on him. Young Monica would stay with his sister until she could join him, when she was old enough, if she so wished. He wasn't fussed either way.

In good time George would spread the word in the Vatican that Shagger Sanders was actually a hero and had saved Father Dan's life while catching their dear friend's killer. But that would take place later, he would give it time and wait until he was well away with a fresh identity and a new life established, elsewhere.

Chapter Eighteen

PROFESSOR COOPER CLOSED THE door as he ushered Mairi-Clare and Terence into his office. It was a large space with the walls donned with images of previous Philharmonic leaders as well as prestigious concerts that had been performed in the historic arena. Although spacious, clutter dominated the room, with musical instruments placed on every spare surface or piled on top of filing cabinets.

'Excuse the disarray. Coming from nothing I hate to see good equipment going to waste. I fix it up for students or donate it to local schools.' He leaned on the edge of his dark oak desk with its green, worn, leather surface, which had been installed in that very room by Herbert Von Karajan, the renowned conductor of the Berliner Philharmoniker.

'This keeps me out of trouble. And talking of trouble, tell me, what in God's name is this scheme have you two have got planned?'

Terence shrugged his shoulders and glanced at Mairi-Clare. Although he was attempting to show little interest with her subversive plans, he was secretly enjoying the thrill of the whole situation having lost his enthusiasm for an orchestral career, realising his obvious limitations. He would still show commitment in respect and gratitude for the opportunity he had been presented with, but he was slowly coming to recognise where his future lay, and it was something he couldn't continue to ignore.

'Professor,' Mairi-Clare sat straight back, legs crossed, hands clasped on her knee, 'this man has been away from his children since the wall went up. His family aren't too confident that he will survive another winter on his own, so this may be their only chance to get him out, to have him with them. To look after him in his senior years.'

'Do you honestly expect me to believe, to even consider allowing two of our international students, who have been in this City for a mere five minutes, to be thinking that they can spring someone from the East?'

'We will have a very, very, small part, Professor, it will be the experts who are planning and carrying it out. We just see this as an opportunity to help.'

'There's a thousand and one people who need help, what is so different about this individual, so special?' Professor Cooper challenged the teenager.

'Well, nothing, Professor, nothing special at all. What is special is that…' She looked at Terence for support.

'What Mairi-Clare is saying, boss, is what's special is that, well, we can get him over here. Reunited with his family, wee Friedrich, his grandson, who's never met him. His son, who is worried sick about him. Maybe give them a chance. Like, you did it for us. But we need your help.'

The professor sighed and used his conductor's baton to scratch the top of his head. He eyeballed the youngsters in front of him, their ambition defying their age.

'My old friend Helena Stern is intrigued. What do you need, what's her involvement in this cunning plan?'

'So, you'll help, Professor?' He nodded. Mairi-Clare smiled and leaned forward, enthused by his approval. 'Someone will contact her on the other side. You need to make a request for a donation of some music equipment from Helena, a donation from eastern Germany? The Stasi will have Helena's phone bugged, so they will hear your plea and hopefully take the bait. They'll see it as a good public relations opportunity – Orchestral Academy in the West seeks help...'

'When will this go ahead?' he asked.

'Our concert's on the Friday before the main Live Aid gig?' Mairi-Clare asked.

He nodded.

'We can say Helena is coming early to teach the students and practice before the event, do things such as interviews. They'll use the opportunity to get her to speak positively about eastern Germany. So, the Tuesday afternoon is what we were told to ask for. Everything is ready to go ahead. They are just waiting for your approval. The Girrmann Group are assisting.'

Cooper raised his eyebrows in surprise knowing the Girrmann project ended a long time ago.

'Well, it's people who are following what the Girrmann Group have done previously and want to keep the name and the escape network alive. We just need Ms Stern's confirmation; can you get that?' Mairi-Clare responded quickly, sensing his concern.

'Take it as being confirmed. Helena is an exquisite violinist and a world class performer. How good she is at lying and fooling the Stasi? For your friend's sake, I hope equally as good.'

Chapter Nineteen

JIMMY QUINN WRAPPED THE worn prison issue towel around his thick neck. The dank, barren yard where he attempted to exercise was also not in keeping with the luxurious surroundings of his many villas and numerous hideouts spread out strategically around the Costas.

As he entered the visitors room, Jimmy found Angie Fields, his lawyer, waiting patiently, pen in hand, head lowered, studying papers and underlining paragraphs which she wanted to go over in the next hour. This was the only visit where no guards listening in to every word were permitted to attend. The one time where he could talk freely, though his inherent suspicion ensured that the conversation was controlled and cautious at all times, unless he wanted to share information with any of the cops that, he assumed, were tuning in.

Angie was a seasoned operator who had collated and devised successful defence cases for many high-profile underworld figures in Glasgow and

Edinburgh, setting up and structuring the evidence and allowing the appointed silks to add their touch of magic and the establishments vocabulary which their high court judge friends were comfortable hearing.

She knew Quinn would want to manipulate their meetings, garner news from the outside. While he paid the exorbitant fees she would play the game, give him what he wanted and remain gainfully employed.

Quinn dabbed the little sweat he had managed to generate from his run round the four high walls from his tanned forehead as he took a seat, his eyes scanning the document in front of him.

'Angie, you're going to tell me my bail hearing date is sorted; and that you have enough detail in the files to get these daft charges thrown out of court at the earliest opportunity. And your pal will be doing the same for Suzie.'

The lawyer sighed, rolled her eyes; and lowered her pen, clasping her manicured hands together. 'Mr Quinn, you really need to answer my questions today to help me gather all the relevant information to present a picture, and build the substantial, credible case required to counter what the fiscal will be pulling together against you. Look how confident the officers were at your questioning. This will be no mean task, let me assure you.'

Quinn lowered his chin, glowered up at her and leaned forward across the table, tapping his fingers impatiently. The lawyer lifted the pen, turned her leather file to face her client and stared directly at the reinforced glass window within the door behind him. With the nib of her engraved fountain pen she led his eyes to a sentence on the lined paper. Quinn glanced at the words in front of him a broad grin beginning to stretch across his face, his eyes coming alive.

The lawyer turned the file quickly and ran the pen several times over the paper, the dark ink staining instantly, leaving a large smudge on the page. Quinn leaned back in the chair lifting his arms above his head, the smile still present, his mind content with what he now knew lay ahead.

'Right Angie, let's get started then, just tell me what you need, ask away. I don't want the Scottish justice system to incarcerate an innocent man and have me spend the rest of my days in here. Do I.'

He hadn't seen Suzie since their remand hearing; and he longed to spend quality time with her after all their years apart as they built the business on two fronts as well as living a lie. He knew he would have to control her; she had a vindictive streak and was purposefully evil at times. He was concerned by her addiction to inflicting pain and by the sadistic enjoyment that she derived from witnessing people suffer at her own hands or from her orders. He preferred to do that type of work himself, not receiving reports of his lovely daughter carrying it out. That though was for another day, once they were out and back running the show; he'd rein her in, allow her to reveal her softer side.

They would then disappear as planned and live out their days on the ranch he owned in Bolivia, just one of a number of boltholes had had yet to set foot in. He would get to know her better and make up for all those years they were apart. He knew they had a lot to catch up on; to be together as a family. Before their retreat to South America, they had issues that were still outstanding in Scotland which continued to eat away at him. Questions would be getting asked about his grip on activities if he didn't show his authority. His partners would soon be aware of his ruthlessness.

Chapter Twenty

GRACE HELD HER ARMS wide as she paraded around the office imitating the stick-thin models from the catwalks, pictured in the glossy magazines that she flicked through occasionally.

'What ye think?' She laughed as her two colleagues glanced at each other, Jack expressing bewilderment. It wasn't what usually greeted them first thing on a Monday morning.

'Very you. Grace, very you,' Cal responded, with little enthusiasm.

'Well, it'll be very all of us on Saturday down The Cellar Bar for the Live Aid concert,' she replied as she threw a white, Live Aid emblazoned, t-shirt to each of them. Jack immediately lowered his eyebrows in distaste, scanning the guitar emblem which allegedly symbolised the only hope left for the African country. 'No excuses, Jack,' she prodded her finger into his arm, 'ye can stay out the bookies and yer local for one day, help feed these poor starving weans.'

'Grace, I don't know,' Cal interjected morosely, 'I've so much to catch up on with client files to go over. I was planning on working. Look at the diary, I've court dates all this and next week.'

He had returned to work after his sabbatical, dried out from his binge drinking following Nicki's murder, his body cleansed, and the apartment cleared of all temptation - even his much-loved Malt Whiskey's had been poured down the toilet. He would attempt to reset his mind and focus on his mental health. He was back too soon, he knew that, he had not healed or recovered from Nicki's execution. But time was against him, and plans were in motion and moving quickly and if all went as expected, he had to be around the office as the world tuned in to the music extravaganza.

Nicki had always encouraged him to consider speaking to an expert about the historical issues which continued to plague him, had him crying in his sleep by night and seeking his retribution by day. Now her murder had been added to the list he carried on his mind and deep in his soul. One day; he would speak to someone, just not now. What he didn't want was to spend Saturday sipping iced water in the Cellar as the locals grew steadily more inebriated – all in the name of charity.

'You'll be there, boss, even if ah have tae drag ye kicking and screaming. It'll dae ye good tae be in company,' Grace responded assertively, eyeballing her two colleagues, 'Ah've a busy week maself. Stephen has his cup final on Wednesday and Terence is playing a concert oan Friday in

Berlin. Ah wish ah was there tae see him, but hey-ho, hopefully there'll be other times.'

Cal held up his hands, 'OK, you win. I'm setting up a TV in here to watch it while I work. I'll come and join you later in the day.'

Grace sat down at her desk as a track-suited man appeared at the door, made his way towards her, leaned across, and spoke in a hushed voice.

'Yes, yes, OK...of course...Ah will, sorry about that,' she replied, holding her hand up and shaking her head in frustration as the man left as quickly as he had come in.

'That bloody boy.'

'Problems?' Jack whispered.

'Just the usual. That wis Stephen's coach, he's not been at fitba training in two weeks. He says he's thinking ah dropping him for the final even though he's the captain and their best player. And ye know what else – ah've ah feeling he dogged half his exams in school. Ah better have calmed doon before ah get up the road or the boss will be defending me in court on a murder charge.'

* * *

Lawrie entered the office, full of business with a police radio in his hand and tidily presented, for a change. Usually, he would hang over Grace's desk, ask about the boys, how her weekend went, her hobbies, hint at how lonely he was, which seemed to go right over her head. Today he moved quickly past her with a nod.

'He in?'

'He is, Frank, but he's a client due in five minutes.'

'No probs, I'll be gone in two.'

Cal was tidying his record collection trying to select an artist to help keep his mood upbeat and prevent him from falling into a sullen stupor. He held a couple of vinyls in his hand – Closer by Joy Division, with the Appiani family tomb of Staglieno adorning much of the sleeve and a playlist including uplifting tunes such as Isolation. There's not a chance that's going on, and certainly not his new favourites, The Pogues, they'd have him have wanting a drink before the needle reached the second song.

Frank threw himself down on the soft leather chair, releasing a long, heavy, sigh. The pressure of multiple open, unsolved, cases and the expectation from Superintendent Irvine that he step up and lead them to their conclusion was beginning to take its toll on him. It was gradually dawning how shallow his existence actually was, that he had no life outside the force, no hobbies to allow him to switch off, or, tellingly, very few friends that he would consider to be genuine, that he could confide in, be himself with. Whatever the fuck was in store when he retired was not worth thinking about. Probably back on the drink and dead at fifty-six or maybe even worse, working as a poxy security guard in the Paisley shopping centre chasing shoplifters and not giving a shit whether he caught them or not.

'Come in, Frank, make yourself at home, tea, coffee, cake?' Cal said sarcastically, leaving the vinyls and swinging his chair round to greet him.

'Coupla secrets for ye, Cal. First one,' he whispered, looking over his shoulder, 'word is young Terence in Berlin is getting followed more intensely than first thought. Interpol think the Russo are going to try and snatch him shortly. And...the shit has well and truly hit the fan with the raids Nicki instigated in Paisley and Glasgow. There's senior officers running for cover, here, there; and fuckin everywhere.' He leaned forward rubbing his hands across his cheeks and lined forehead in frustration. 'I've been *warned* by a Superintendent, one of the handshaking brethren, to tread carefully or they'll turn on me, dig up dirt and instigate a suspension. The usual junk that they get up tae when their weird world gets threatened or exposed.'

Cal moved to the seat opposite his friend recognising the stress that was clearly affecting him. 'You're not overly worried, are you? They'll not have anything on you, will they? I know you've cut a few corners from time to time but that's not reflected in any complaints or previous investigations or notes on your record, I would assume...is it? Plus, you just got a commendation last year for saving my life, remember?'

'Doesn't matter does it, Cal. They manky bastards can stitch you up should they decide to turn on the switch. Ah told ye before, you and Nicki have shone a big, massive, fuck off searchlight on this whole corrupt, shithole. The bent folk with the power? The ones working for Quinn and this fuckin Russo thing? They won't give that up or get jailed, not a chance. Irvine's got ma back so that's one thing at least,' he replied with a hint of frustration. He stood up quickly and fiddled with the buttons on his radio, banged it against his thigh and moved towards the door.

'Fuckin thing only works when it wants tae. Sorry, ah just wanted a sounding board.'

'We need Quinn and Suzie on trial as soon as possible, Frank. That'll shape how this all unfolds. I think it will draw the Russo out even further.'

'Aye, well, that was the other big secret. Ah'll mibbae call you later in the week. Ah think there'll be movement soon. Top secret, mind, but folk are getting nervous after Nicki was taken out. Irvine pushed for prompt action and ah think he got it. They're going tae be moved, covertly, tae the court's holding cells for the trial, which is being scheduled as we speak. There's been a block on any leave for the cops based at the High Court, a kitchen to feed them has been put in to avoid any mixing in the canteen and a hush-hush schedule for them to be moved is getting put together…so this week it'll all start, ah think.'

Cal pretended to show little interest, flicking through a file that Grace had left on his desk for a waiting client. 'Oh, well that sounds positive. Keep me posted, Frank, and if I hear anything I'll call you, obviously.'

Frank shook his hand and made his way out onto the busy street. Picking up the phone Cal's eyes followed him as he completed each step until his swagger was gone from his view.

'It's on. Make sure everything is prepared and you are ready to go, nothing left to chance. Understood?' He replaced the receiver and tapped his pen on his smooth, chiselled chin. *By the weekend this may all be over*, he thought, *finally. Over.*

* * *

Stephen tidied his room for the third time that morning. Moving his possessions around he placed the small number of books and albums he kept onto the wooden shelves his old man had put up for him when he was a small boy.

He smiled to himself as he recalled his dad telling him he had to help. He had pierced an extra hole in his joiner's belt so it could hang from Stephen's wee waist, the pockets full of nails, screws, and pencils with the hammer swinging at the side, almost scraping along the carpet. He'd pass the materials when asked, studying closely the way his dad went about his work. The marking, the levelling, tapping of screws, the noise of the drill screeching forcing him to put his fingers in his little ears.

'Yer ma apprentice, wee man. Ye can come and work for me soon as ye get finished wae school. Just don't tell yer maw ah said that,' he whispered, rubbing his callused fingers playfully over Stephen's head and grinning widely as the smoke from the cigarette burning in the side of his mouth caused his eyes to blink repeatedly.

Stephen had not long started school, but he knew then, at that very moment, he would work with his dad, smoke fags like him, wolf down his dinner as quick as he did every night and make folk laugh just as he did. He wouldn't stagger about like him as he did on some nights, he knew that, he wouldn't scare his weans like him when he was drunk and being crabbit.

He looked in the mirror and ran his fingers through his long, unruly, dark, hair. It was to be styled by one of Monica's cousins at a fancy salon once it got to the required length. Ah well, he thought, that won't be happening now.

What about Monica, how would she feel? They'd become close, she had helped him, took him out of the depressing hole he'd fallen into on several occasions, made him laugh again, and for lengthy periods forget the guilt that eclipsed him. The feelings that followed him everywhere; had eradicated any self-worth, taking with it any sense of the possibility of seeing a positive future or even the ability to look forward to the day ahead or the day after that.

He scanned the labels of all the medication he had lifted from the bathroom cabinet – dothiepin, amitriptyline. He laughed quietly to himself – not only was he shite at physics, but chemistry wasn't a strong point either. Some of the tablets were his own that the counsellor had gotten prescribed, and he had refused to take, though most of the bottles

195

were his mum's, just to help her sleep the odd night, she told him. He emptied the contents onto his single bed and the capsules spread across his smoothed-out eiderdown.

He was dressed in his best clothes – Levi jeans, still to be cleared from the Provi cheque, and his short-sleeved black and white checked shirt. He placed the two letters he had written onto the dresser, leaning them against his player of the year trophy. He'd hoped he'd said enough in them, covered everything, said sorry. Sorry for Dad and now, sorry for what might happen to his big brother. He opened the bottle of Irn Bru he had laced with vodka.

He began.

* * *

For the first time in a long while Grace had a feeling of foreboding about going home. She didn't have the energy to argue and fight with Stephen again. She was tired of the confrontation which had been a prerequisite of their interactions for the past few months, if not years. The continual visits to the high school about his non-attendance, and recently the resurfacing of his stresses and anxieties around his feeling of guilt, which she had the inability or expertise to counter.

She would play it calm, comfort him, suggest he go back to counselling, if he was depressed or that or if he wanted to that is. His non-appearance at football had surprised her, she knew how much he loved being on the pitch. He was never boastful though she knew he loved having his pals look up to him, follow his lead as they beat all around them to reach their first cup final.

He had seemed so calm over the past few days, contented even, after a lengthy period of being withdrawn from the family and snapping at any question or comment which was directed his way. He even tidied his room to a level not seen in years and was ever generous with his hugs for his mother, though he still grunted at his younger brother.

She crossed the Wellmeadow, darting between the orange buses, the hue of blue fumes from the diesel engines catching in her throat. She immediately bumped into her neighbour, Sadie McIntosh, who, as always, looked her up and down and pulled a small smirk over her lips. She was the last person she wanted to see, being the resident stuck-up boot who thought she was above everyone else. Her boy was pals with Stephen so Grace would always bite her lip and avoid telling her what she really thought of her, though this was long, long, overdue.

When Dixie had been drunk up the west end of Paisley, she could tell her the full script the next time they met, everything that was said, by who, and any arguments that had transpired. All Dixie's fault, she would say, well, so she heard, she was just saying, as her friend, obviously.

Their eyes connected and Grace gave her a broad smile, 'Sadie, how are ye?'

'Lucky, I seen you Grace, still working away; I see,' she looked her up and down again. Grace bit the inside of her lip praying this one wouldn't keep her too long.

'Whit it was. Is. Your Stephen gave my John a pile of football programmes and cassette tapes. And ye know how ah like a tidy house, Grace. It's just more clutter in his room.'

'Och, Stephen's always kind that way with others less fortunate than himself, Sadie. Maybe he thought young John was missing out on things. Anyway, I'll say you said thanks. Need tae go, Sadie,' she replied with a smile and brushed past her heading towards home.

'But…' Sadie stood open-mouthed, raging at not having dispensed with all the snide comments she had planned to unload.

Now he's giving his stuff away, what is it with that boy, she thought. Nobody in the house was allowed to touch any of his things, football programmes all placed in running order by date, music stacked by year then changed to favourite tunes. *He's just maturing, wanting to experience different things; and not wanting to have stuff around that reminds him of being a kid.*

She bumped into Monica as she turned into Argyle Street. She had missed the wee girl calling up, having moved away to live with her aunt as her dad had been remanded or disappeared somewhere after being lifted for stealing all the metal from the old Chrysler factory, so the sweetie wives had said, anyway.

Monica seemed well-settled, was smiling, and smartly dressed in a knee-length summer dress and white cardigan. Being away from Shagger looked to be doing her good. She waved as their paths crossed on the pavement.

'Hi, Mrs Clark, good tae see you. Ah was going up to see Stephen. If that's OK?'

'Course it is, love. And less of the Mrs Clark. Ah told ye, it's Grace,' she nipped her rosy cheek, 'yer looking well, Monica.'

'Aye, well one of the joys of no staying wae ma da is that there's always food in the fridge.'

Grace screwed up her eyes and tightened her lips, 'It's a godsend you're here, actually. You'll stop me from creating a bloodbath once ah get tae the hoose.'

'Oh-oh, Stephen's in trouble again,' the young girl responded warily, as they climbed the close stairs.

* * *

The flat was quiet as they entered and made their way to the kitchen, Grace flicked the kettle switch on as she dumped her bags on the worktop. She'd make stew tonight but keep the potatoes separate, might just roast them. Maybe Monica would stay for tea. The kitchen was how she had left it this morning at nine o'clock. Joseph walked out with her following up on his latest obsession, politics, and a talk he was eager to attend about *Trotskyism and like-minded radical voices in Scotland* which was being held in the Mitchell Library in Glasgow. Stephen persisted in leaving his cereal bowl and cup on the table each morning, so she realised he hadn't been out of his bed all day.

'He's turning night intae day since he stopped school for the holidays, Monica. That's awright for a coupla days but it's no oan aw summer.'

'I'll make ye a tea if ye want tae go and check oan sleeping beauty and get him up,' Monica replied.

'Thanks,' Grace raised herself slowly from the chair, her palms flat on the kitchen table gearing herself up for the impending confrontation, 'Och, ah'll have a fag first, might calm me doon a bit,' she slumped back in the chair pulling her cigarettes from her jacket pocket, 'ye can tell me all bout yer auntie, who looks to be looking after ye well.'

Monica placed the two mugs on the table and sat fiddling with a teaspoon. 'Ma da; just phoned the house and said he had tae go away for a bit cause of work and he'd arranged things with Aunt Margaret. Didnae even say look after yersel or fingers crossed for yer exam results, nothing,' she sat up and smiled across the table, 'Aunt Mags is different, so kind, she took me shopping for new clothes. I've even got my uniform for next term already, though ah don't need blouses cause ah've got yours. When ah told her what ye done, she said you had a very kind heart and she'd love tae meet ye one day.'

'Och, that would be nice,' Grace took a long final draw of the cigarette and stubbed it out into the glass ashtray, 'well ah think that kind heart ye speak of is just about tae go into hiding once ah pull this lazy lump from his bed,' she replied, sighing as she made her way to the door. Monica sat in silence anticipating Grace's booming, authoritative, voice and Stephen's sleepy, groans in response.

A piercing scream startled her; forcing her to inadvertently push over her cup across the table. It sounded as if it came from the pit of the person's stomach and met the very hollow of their mind as it bellowed from their mouth. She rushed to the bedroom, unsure of what awaited her.

Grace was crouched over the bed cradling her son, her feet surrounded by empty medicine bottles. She stared at Stephen his eyes vacant, his body limp, unresponsive to his mother's shaking, shouting, and smothering kisses.

'Stephen, wake up, Son, wake up,' she pleaded. Vomit covered his favourite shirt and cotton pillowcase. Grace placed her fingers in his mouth trying to make him sick again. She put her ear tightly to his chest, she shook him frantically, she put her ear to his mouth, stretched his eyelids, his long black, beautiful; eyelashes almost touching his forehead.

'Whit will ah dae, whit will ah dae,' she screamed.

Monica called an ambulance and left the front door open. She ran back to the bedroom with a wet cloth and began rubbing his face and neck. 'Grace, we'll get him on his feet, get him walking, it might help.'

'Aye,' Grace replied in shock.

Lifting his body, he felt heavier than the thin frame that was under their forearms, unresponsive his legs dragged behind him as they made their way to the hall and back to the bedroom.

'If we put him oan his side he won't choke when he's sick again,' Monica said quickly as they placed him back on his bed as Grace tucked his vomit covered, congealed hair behind his ear.

A Paramedic appeared and placed his hand firmly on her shoulders and moved her gently to the side. 'What's his name, dear?' he asked, as he began to look for signs of life. His eyes scanned across the well-worn bedroom carpet. 'I need all those bottles into this bag,' he said assertively, his eyes fixed on Monica who was standing in a corner, the world turning very slowly for her, 'now, pal, now,' he said, sharply.

His colleague slipped his arms under Stephen's body and gently lifted him, placing him on the stretcher, wrapping a thick blanket around him and strapping him in. They were on the close landing as Grace and Monica ran after them, down the stairs to the ambulance. Neighbours, who had clocked the ambulance, stood in silence on the pavement while others peered from behind their curtains.

Grace sat at his side holding his hand and rubbing his pale face as the medic worked around her. Within minutes they were at the hospital.

She attempted to provide details to the nurse standing at the emergency entrance though she thinks Monica answered for her. As her boy was rushed through the double doors, she caught sight of the medical team lining the corridor awaiting the trolley and its unconscious inhabitant. His life was now entirely in their hands.

She reached and held Monica's hand tightly. Staring ahead she whispered, 'this is our secret, anyone asks, he took a funny turn, had a fall. We'll figure it out. We don't want folk talking about him when he's better and back home.'

Chapter Twenty-One

MAIRI-CLARE CLOSED the room door quietly and sat opposite Terence as he leaned over his small desk studying yesterday's music notes, hoping he would initiate the conversation.

The room was untidy despite its lack of comforts or reminders of home that she had filled her own space with. The exception being a family picture of Terence and his brothers narrowing their eyes against the sun as their parents stood behind them beaming with pride, held in place by drawing pins above his single bed.

'Where did you go after that, you know,' she nudged her head towards the door.

'Ah went down to the chapel. Father was there, talked tae me for a while. Ah don't know if he actually understood what ah was saying but we had a good chat. He heard my confession, suppose that's meant to make me feel better, cleanse the soul, and aw that. He's a good guy, inspiring. Ah seen wee Friedrich and had some craic with him, took ma mind aff things,' he replied in a low voice.

'Terence, the guy's an idiot. He's clearly got issues. I'm surprised he got to you over your hair. It's not like you to get annoyed…or violent.'

Terence raised his head quickly to meet her eyes, sensing her fear. 'Ye know ah'm not like that, don't ye? Ah usually just come back with a wisecrack, ye know just slagging tae shut them up. He just pushed the wrong buttons the day, that's aw. The professor says the talk of Robert Tannahill triggered him. His old man died, suicide, left him and the mother to fend for themselves. He then went aff the rails and was constantly getting intae trouble in London. This is his only hope cause he's got real talent with music, and that. Ah really shouldnae have done it.'

'I know you're not like that. It was a fine headbutt though. Don't worry, you didn't ruin his good looks,' she responded with a smile, attempting to lighten his mood.

He turned to look out of the small window, moving the faded lace netting to view the green expanse of lawn which, as usual, was occupied by students and staff enjoying their surroundings.

Terence and his cockney colleague's paths had crossed in the corridor earlier in the day as they moved between strings and percussion lessons. He had listened, for days now, with no response, as the Londoner cracked jokes at his expense. One word too many, the final snide remark, which pushed a button that he was unaware was present in his makeup, left the cockney lying on the polished floor of the corridor holding his nose as the blood poured between his fingers. He opened his eyes occasionally glancing up worryingly at Terence, awaiting further retribution as fellow students stood around their mouths agape.

Professor Cooper had strolled past, stepping over the prostrate youth, crying in agony.

'I would have done that in the first week, young man. We'll talk later,' he whispered to Terence, the noise of his leather heels mixing with the boy's moans as he continued on his way.

'This place, being away from home, it makes ye think bout things, and that.'

Mairi-Clare leaned forward as he continued to stare beyond the window. 'We could find a hairdresser in town if you want to tidy it up. Though, I don't think it's your hair that's got you annoyed, is it?'

Terence took a deep breath and dropping his shoulders he began to talk in a hushed voice, as if he was afraid of what he would say, of who would hear his innermost thoughts. 'Coupla years ago, ah was growing ma hair long. Ah was dying to get a mullet, just like ma pals and aw the fitba players. Then one Saturday ma maw sent me up to Wee Frankie's the barbers, up the West End to get it cut. "Jist a trim?" ah said, "nae bother, son." It was Easter, so she wanted it tidied up a bit for going tae mass the next day.'

The room fell silent for what seemed like an eternity as he replayed the scene out in his head wondering whether to continue, to attempt to put into words the memories that constantly swirled round his

and squeezing his limp hand tightly with no reaction forthcoming.

'Ah dae love him and miss him. Ah just think maybe if he hadn't been, killed, if I'd went out working with him, ye know, got tae know him a bit in his world, we would've got oan. Stephen would have worked with him, nae doubt. I'd have done the odd shift if there was a coupla quid going. And he did work like fuck for us. But, it's always the same when somebody dies isn't it, some memories are missed or wiped oot. Only their best bits talked aboot.'

Terence could hear his voice beginning to falter, he knew if he turned round now, lost his stare out the window, he would break the pretence and lose his masculine shield. He tasted the tears as they ran down his cheeks the warm saltlike particles running over his lips and distracting him for a split second.

'Ye know,' he paused, a deep intake of breath filling the silence, 'I had a routine when he was oot on the booze, learnt it the hard way. If he went oot early on a Saturday; and wisnae in for bout six it meant he'd be pure buckled when he landed back. So, ah would go tae ma bed early, kid oan ah was sleeping when he'd eventually stagger in the door. Ye see, one time ah was sitting watching Match of the Day on Saturday night. He came in, pished, aggressive, shouting shite to no one in particular. Ye could tell his pals had been feeding him cheap, shitey whisky, probably arguing with somebody in the boozer. He made sure the mood always came hame wae him. Ah always sat on the floor watching the telly across fae *his* seat. That night ah could feel, actually feel, his eyes staring intae the back ah ma head, fixed oan me. He was desperate tae start oan me, ah'm sure of it, for breathing, ah think. Ah kept saying tae maself, don't turn, don't turn round, no even a glance. Ah coudnae even see the telly, the tears were blinding me. Ah felt fuckin trapped. Ma maw saw it, never did a thing, said fuck all. Ah just kept thinking this guy fuckin hates me. Ah just stared at the telly for ages till ah heard him snoring in the chair then got up as quiet as ah could; walked by ma maw, who threw me a sad look, and went tae ma room. That's who ah remember and that cockney fucker got it cause it jist became a bit clearer now.'

Terence could hear Mairi-Clare quietly sobbing as she placed a small white hanky in his hand.

'It's done and forgotten bout. I can live with it. None of us are perfect and he had his troubles when he wis young so that didnae help him, ah don't think. Ah've learned a lot since ah've been here with you. The wee priest at St Matthias is a great help as well, puts things into perspective and hands out good advice on forgiveness, and that.'

Shaking his head to try and snap out of the thoughts that were surrounding his mind he quickly ran his sleeve across his face to soak up his tears. 'Ah'll say sorry tae that guy the morra if ah'm no kicked out ah here before then. Anyway, let's go, we need tae join Dieter and wee Friedrich down at Checkpoint Charlie. Today's the big day when you help him tae meet his granda.'

Chapter Twenty-Two

HELENA STERN SAT POISED in her, much loved, Barkas 1000 dark blue box van as the queue of vehicles edged forward, slowly zigzagging through the red and white barriers towards Checkpoint Charlie. The Barkas two-stroke engine purred amongst the noisy lengthy line of Trabants attempting to cross the border into the West at Friedrichstrasse-Zimmerstrasse.

Her line of sight toward the security cordon was clear owing to the elevated seat, which also helped her view the activity ahead of her and the frustratingly long, detailed checks that were being carried out on each and every vehicle which reached the East German guards.

Opening the window to try and generate some fresh air she considered lighting her third cigarette within the last ten minutes, though she was aware that this may reveal her nervousness as she would no doubt quickly finish it in a few puffs and then be looking for something else to do with her hands.

She realised that eyes were everywhere at the border, on every street corner, watching, scanning for any unnatural movement or indiscretion which would then lead to more intense questioning and the stripping bare of her vehicle once her time arrived at the front of the queue. She tried to zone out, think of the music she would be teaching and playing with the orchestra at the Philharmonic over the next few days in preparation for the live concert on Friday.

* * *

Helena was born, raised, and continued to live in the small East German town of Bautzen. Its medieval, scenic location on the banks of the River Spree guaranteed that it was hard to consider relocating anywhere else despite the all-encompassing oppressive regime ruling the country. Known for its churches and compact and well-preserved surroundings it was also home to the feared Ministry of Security where prisoners and dissenters were held captive within the imposing fortified prison.

She travelled the world playing her music to large audiences; enthralled by the self-taught, accomplished, violinist who portrayed the other side of Germany. A country which she was proud to highlight still possessed a vibrant culture and a creative vibe that the communist state could not curtail. Although her travels were extensive, she was always happiest at home despite the hardships placed on citizens. Her frequent trips allowed her to get an insight into how others lived, their luxuries, and at times obsessions, and intense levels of consumerism.

Some saw her as a poster girl for the regime with her youthful looks and piercing blue eyes, drawing in those who met her gaze, framed by her high cheekbones and blonde hair, which was permanently pristine.

Behind the beautiful veneer was a strong willed, highly motivated woman who knew how to manipulate the system for her own ends. She contributed to several escapes of those desperate enough to take the chance of achieving their freedom.

The regime was predictably proud to call her one of their own having financed and nurtured her natural talent at the Staatskepelle Dresden Orchestra. Since the late seventies she had emerged as the star performer, composing several arrangements which would lead to her eventually outgrowing the orchestra and playing her music elsewhere.

Today the rear of her prized van was packed to the roof with donated orchestral equipment for, as the regime put it, *a contribution to those struggling to achieve musical parity with the standards of their counterparts in Dresden. We seek to assist you by providing these gifts.*

* * *

Terence, Mairi-Clare, and their German friends stood behind a large dark window on the first floor of a tobacconist shop surrounded by boxes of biscuits, tinned fruit and cigarettes which were stacked high around the grey walls. The windows overlooked the check point and a large sign advising, *You are now leaving the American Sector.* The building, taking in the length of Friedrichstrasse, was the ideal position for watching the cars being processed by the Eastern Block security.

The shop was shrouded by tall, smog-stained buildings on each side, while some regeneration and modern architecture was beginning to emerge on the western edge of the border. It was constantly busy with military and locals buying their fill of western cigarettes, newspapers, and bootleg produce sold from under the counter. The presence of a few additional individuals coming and going would not draw any suspicion at the busiest location in the city.

The volunteers had endlessly studied the shift patterns of the guards noting who were the laziest, who seemed dispirited, who was trying to make a name for themselves and climb up the ranks, what day and time was best to attempt an escape, when to avoid the border – preferably when diplomats were crossing from the West which seemed to trigger intense activity on the ground.

A member of the new Girrmann Group talked quietly into a two-way radio as others sat around drinking tea and awaiting instructions.

The original Girrmann Group had been active since the sixties and had led many escapes over and under the wall, through sewers, using hot air balloons and packing shelled out cars with desperate people.

Now, beating the regime was proving ever more difficult with the only perceived weak spot being the opportunity to play on human error at the border crossings.

After an initial rush of adrenaline when they first arrived in the early afternoon the day was becoming tedious for Terence and Friedrich, their similar short attention spans meant the boredom was now beginning to set in as they moved into the early evening.

Dieter stood against the wall hugging Friedrich tightly. The boy released himself and came and stood beside a bored but equally nervous, Terence.

'How long do you think, Terence?'

'Fuck knows, wee man.'

'Her van is in the line,' one of the Girrmann Group announced, passing the binoculars to Dieter who in turn passed them to Mairi-Clare. The large bug like headlights were switched on as prearranged to signal that all was going to plan, so far. 'It won't be long now, maybe one hour at most.'

'There's yer answer, wee man. Whit's the first thing you'll do when ye meet yer granda, Friedrich?'

'Father told me often Papa gives really strong, bear like, hugs. I'm going to do the same, squeeze him really tight. I think that will surprise him.'

'Ah'm sure he'll love that, wee man.'

'My friend,' Friedrich whispered, 'you like Big Country, yes? Agree?'

'Aye.'

'I listen to your Scottish group, Altered Images, on our radio. *Happy birthday, happy birthday.* Do you like them also?'

'Aye, they're no bad, aye.'

'Do you know of Clare, the singer?'

'Aw, aye, Friedrich, of course ah know Clare. Look this has got a wee bit tense now to be talking about music. Don't ye think?'

'You know of Clare? You have met her?'

'Of course, ah used tae see her up the Co-op getting the messages for her maw quite a lot. She seems tae like crispy pancakes gaun by her trolly. Always singing away to herself so she is.'

Friedrich produced a neatly folded, glossy; poster from his denim jacket pocket wiping his hand over the image of the singer, her spiky, two-tone hair framed by large earrings and her bright red lipstick highlighting a captivating smile.

'Really? I love Miss Clare Grogan. Do you think one day I could come with you and meet her at her messages. She may like me; we then fall in love and marry and live in a castle in Scotland or Bavaria, I think it would be warmer there.'

'In the name ah fu...aye, wee man, I'll take ye one day to the messages. In the meantime, keep praying ye get to meet yer granda,' Terence responded, pointing towards the window, smiling, and wrapping his arm around Friedrich's neck pulling him closer to give him a reassuring hug.

Mairi-Clare had taken up position at the window, her eyes fixated on the blue and white van with the large headlights and shiny front grill, which a single white female driver occupied, trudging along to the awaiting security detail.

'Err, I think we have a problem,' Mairi-Clare whispered, 'a man has just got into Helena's van.'

The volunteer grabbed the binoculars as another spoke quickly into the radio handset.

* * *

'Ah, Ms Stern, leaving us at our famous Grenzübergangsstelle, are we?'

Helena smiled at the tall figure who made himself comfortable in the passenger seat. Her stomach was turning while she tried to hide her nervousness and frustration at the intrusion.

'You know I am, Herr Wolf; you signed the application. Remember?' She flashed her teeth as she let out a laugh, attempting to appear composed.

'I did, Helena, of course. You are appearing at a charity concert for…erm Live Aid, to feed the poor people of the West, yes?'

'The poor people of Ethiopia, I believe.'

Colonel Markus Wolf sat, relaxed, as the car came to the border running his hand through his swept-back dark hair the edges above his ears beginning to turn white. He looked younger than his years, his perma-tan projecting a look of healthiness with the made-to-measure, dapper suit, and small tie, which matched a beige coloured trench coat.

Wolf was raised in Moscow and climbed to the heady rank of Head of the East German Foreign Intelligence Service. He knew of all defections, the failed attempts, relocation applications and, worryingly for Helena, he had taken a keen interest in her movements throughout the West, attempting on at least two occasions to have her spy and report back on activity in Dresden.

'Tell me, why have you never applied for relocation permission? We have approved hundreds to transfer to the West last year, though I note that you haven't applied, no?

'My home is Bautzen, and it will remain so,' she turned and met his eye, 'Michael Bittner applied for relocation, do you recall? You refused and then he was murdered. I'll take my chances where I am. Thank you, Markus.'

'That was an unfortunate incident, yes. Which, as you know, you will not speak about. We must protect the state, Helena,' he waved his hand towards the window, 'keep it psychologically and physically intact while we show the world that we are open, all embracing. Hence allowing you to travel freely.'

'Ha-ha, having my husband and children under practical house arrest each time I leave to play my music, until I return, does not, to me, seem to be a state confident in having support for the policies it implements.'

Markus raised his eyebrows from behind his large, tinted glasses and held his hands up, feigning responsibility, 'Erich Meikle is the boss, I follow orders as you know. Anyway, this monstrosity of a wall will be removed, I predict, within ten years. The country will be unified. Then, my friend, you can come and go as you please,' he replied, smiling and accepting one of her cigarettes. He lit them both with his gold zippo lighter and took a deep draw blowing the smoke through his large nostrils.

'And what will happen to your eighty thousand Stasi then, just disappear?'

Markus laughed heartily, 'what will happen to us all.'

The outside of the van was now being given the once over by four Stasi guards carrying out their customary checks, their level of enthusiasm rising when they recognised Colonel Wolf sitting in the vehicle. They immediately saluted and he waved in return.

He glanced over his shoulder scanning the large black boxes stacked in the rear of the van. 'For now, tell me what you have behind you here.' He pointed to one of the guards to examine the rear as his colleagues looked over Helena's paperwork.

Helena switched off the headlights.

* * *

They stood in silence as they watched the scene play out from the window, everything seemed to move in slow motion as the guards raised the rear door of the van and began removing the containers of musical equipment and lining them up on the tarmac for inspection.

'I think we are busted,' the Girrmann volunteer sighed dejectedly.

Other activity was also taking place directly below their viewing point, outside the tobacconist's front door. A black van was being surrounded by soldiers in full combat uniform and gas masks.

The door of the room immediately burst open; and all the occupants turned, startled. Two men rushed into the room, flashing their identification cards. 'Do not worry, we are Interpol. Mr Clark, for your safety, with us, now.' They grabbed Terence under both arms and quickly dragged him through the door.

Dull explosions were heard from around the van below as smoke billowed towards their window blocking their view. They could hear voices being raised and see figures through the smog being pulled from the vehicle and dragged to an awaiting military lorry.

* * *

'You are well aware what is in the van, Markus. Was it not yourself who authorised the donation, remember, for the poor western students?' Helena attempted to keep her cool as one by one the black cases containing instruments were placed on the street, easily carried by one guard. Within minutes they would reach the bottom of the pile, the double bass case containing the old man, and the bass drum which held a five-year-old boy who was destined to live with his godparents in France, if all went to plan.

Both had been given a strong tranquilizer to relax them and knock them out thirty minutes before they commenced their journey to prevent them from moving in their uncomfortable hiding spots and to reduce the risk of any such movement being overheard.

Helena was convinced she was being set up by the colonel, exposed at the border for the world to see which would lead her straight back to her hometown of Bautzen, though it would be a damp cell where she would find herself, not with her loving family.

'Wouldn't it be hilarious, Colonel, if your Stasi officers found escapees within the gifts which you have provided,' she threw her head back and laughed out loud, 'and you, you Markus Wolf, sitting in the same vehicle. I think it would be the Gulag for you, no? Ha-ha.'

The colonel looked in the rear-view mirror as the guards opened the first of the black cases, revealing various musical instruments, throwing them back in the red velvet casing. He summoned the guard standing to attention at the front of the vehicle and spoke to him quietly. The guard immediately moved to the back of the van and assisted his colleagues in reloading the items carefully back into Helena's B 1000.

'We will see you in a few days, Helena, back home, yes?' He looked over the border as four men all dressed in black were being dragged across the road as smoke billowed from a parked van. Grinning he added, 'looks as if you have a welcoming committee.'

She nodded and smiled as he left the vehicle, tapped its side, and ordered the guard to lift the barrier.

* * *

Entering the first floor flat her presence was met with quiet elation. 'Well, this wasn't the welcome I was expecting.'

Mairi-Clare stepped forward with an outstretched hand, 'Ms Stern, it's an absolute pleasure to meet you,' she announced nervously, 'I've followed your career. The way you play the violin … I love your music. I'm really looking forward to learning from you.'

Helena smiled at the young girl in front of her who was looking back at her, starry-eyed. 'You were the young lady who set all of this up, yes?'

She nodded in response and looking around added. 'With lots of help.'

'Let's hope your imagination stretches to your instrument, we shall see,' looking around the room she added, 'for now we have equipment to unload, yes?'

The lead Girrmann volunteer stepped forward, 'Johan will drive with you to the rendezvous point. We have a doctor waiting to assist with your cargo. We will follow shortly after.'

Dieter hugged Helena's tightly, unable to speak with sheer emotion. She smiled and rubbed his shoulders then quickly followed her guide from the building.

* * *

Beaming widely, Principal Cooper came from behind his desk and embraced Helena. Laughing quietly in her ear he said, 'Helena, you always make a grand entrance. Thank you for joining us, our students are super excited to hear you play.'

'I was almost playing from within a Stasi prison. My heart was pounding,' she laughed, returning his warm embrace.

A sharp tap came to the door and the two Interpol officers entered, Terence and Mairi-Clare following behind them. 'Sorry, Professor, but it wasn't…'

The professor held up his hand and guided everyone into the room. 'Terence, I've known about these guys here for the last three weeks. They have been keeping an eye on you, protecting you. That is why I was not overly worried when you approached me with your cunning plan. I'm sure they have told you that today the organised crime gang who murdered your father were planning to kidnap you and use you as leverage before their big bosses go on trial back home?'

Terence lowered his head, 'Yeah, they did. Thanks, officer,' the officer nodded and smiled. 'How's Friedrich's granda, has he met him yet?'

Helena was first to respond, 'you have done a very brave thing today, you and your young friend here. You should be very proud, a small but important part of history,' she lifted her violin case and held out her hand, 'now we play beautiful music, yes?'

'Professor, I've called ma mum, she doesnae want me tae go home, she's adamant ah stay here, but ma brother is in hospital now as well. Sorry, it's a bit of a shambles so, ah'm sorry but ah need to go.'

'Of course, Terence, I'll have flights organised at the earliest opportunity. At least you will have some time playing with our guest. The officer and our staff will escort you onto the flight.'

The officer nodded his head in confirmation, 'we'll be around here until you go home, Mr Clark. They won't get anywhere near you, trust me.' he said assertively, as he walked his colleague from the room.

'Wish he'd stop calling me that it makes me feel like an auld git,' Terence whispered to Mairi-Clare, attempting to lighten the mood.

'Well Mr Terence and friend, lead me to your great auditorium. Shout on your friends. We make music.'

Mairi-Clare sat with Terence as Helena chatted to the tutors, awaiting the arrival of their classmates. There was no euphoria or excitement at their plan going well and Friedrich finally getting to meet his Granda. Their thoughts were of home and the additional troubles arriving at his mum's door. She held his hand loosely, running her fingers over the small blisters he had developed from excessive use of his drumsticks.

'They'll soon disappear once you're home,' she said quietly, her eyes fixed on his broad hands, 'you're not coming back, are you?'

He couldn't imagine playing here as part of a full orchestra, being good enough to be part of an ensemble that held an audience captivated, sitting thrilled to hear more, their eyes darting from the strings to the percussion to the woodwind. He knew Mairi-Clare would thrive and feed off any performance she participated in. This was her world, her dream and she was made for it, ready for it.

'Once Stephen is fit Mairi-Clare ah'm not hanging about, but yer right, ah won't be coming back. For the first time in my short, fat life ah know what ah want tae do,' he said softly. Squeezing her hand, he rose from the chair and looked down at her flawless features, her blonde locks still bobbing on her shoulders just as they were when they first met, her large blue eyes filled with sadness met his.

'Ah need to go and speak tae someone. Is ma hair awrite?'

She broke into a smile, 'One day I'll have that styled, believe me. On you go, I'll help you pack when you get back.'

Chapter Twenty-Three

'YOU LEAD ON THIS this one, Frank. This will be hard, so best go in sensitively, I'll dip in and out.'

Irvine removed his tie and occupied the worn leather sofa in the office he had commandeered at Mill Street Station, as Cal was guided in by a uniformed officer.

'Cal, welcome, join us. I've just made a pot of fresh coffee, the beans come from Guatemala, best of stuff, allegedly. Here, take a seat.'

Cal looked uncharacteristically flustered as he had rushed from the court to make the meeting and his mind was also on heading back there shortly for another case.

He was most comfortable in the courtroom where the intensity of the criminal cases and the daily drama allowed him to lose himself and concentrate fully on defending his client. Added to that, the rush he experienced when interacting with witnesses who took the stand, anticipating their responses; and reading their mannerisms, continually filled him with a childlike enthusiasm and curiosity each day he presented in the courts of the West of Scotland. The tedium of repetitive cases, which not all his peer group enjoyed, were equally appealing at times as it allowed him to switch to auto pilot and let his mind drift to other matters and his plans for ensuring that Jimmy Quinn and Suzie were put away for a long time and their syndicate left in pieces. This was never far from his thoughts.

He hoped this meeting with the police, if it brought more unwelcome news, did not send him spiralling out of control again.

'Thanks, Superintendent, it certainly has the climate for it and a strong coffee is what I need right now.'

Irvine eyed Lawrie as he began to pour, the rich aroma filling the room.

'Cal, we'd just like to update you on where we are with Nicki's case and ask you a couple of things.'

'Fire away, Frank,' Cal responded, laying his court robes on his lap and reaching for the mug in front of him.

'Ye remember Sutherland, our senior forensic officer? The wee baldy guy?'

'Should I?'

'Probably not. He swabbed ye last week. Anyway, he's really detailed in his work, very meticulous – a top officer our Stuart,' Lawrie attempted to lighten the mood, 'he talks like fuck right enough. Sometimes we need tae give him a body swerve or ye widnae get a thing done wae his incessant ramblings,' lifting two sheets of paper from the small table he added, 'he's come back with the ballistic reports on the bullets used. They're from a point 357 Magnum, nine-mil rimmed casing. Fired at close range. She didn't stand a chance, Cal.'

'Can you find the gun then? Your team must have carried out the searches nearby, did they uncover anything?'

'Nothing of interest was recovered. Sutherland has checked the database against the pattern on the casings and it's matched exactly with bullets that were found at two separate incidents in London, just last year. So, we think a hired assassin, or a team, more likely, were sent up to carry out the hit. They're certainly confident they won't get caught given that they don't feel the need to clean up after themselves,' Lawrie leaned forward sipping his coffee and pausing for a second, 'last year when you had dealings with Eddie Quinn and that maniac McGurn did they let slip anything about connections they may have in London?'

'Not a thing, I'll check my notes once I get back to the office, but nothing comes to mind. That sounds quite positive then. Who were the other victims?'

Irvine opened his paper file, 'First one was a rich businessman who brokered insurance for large companies from his Covent Garden office. The other was a property developer linked to the sale of wasteland at the London Docklands, a married father of three. The MO was the same for all three incidents, two bullets to the head while sitting in their car with evidence left at the scene.'

Cal lifted the mug to his mouth and took a long, slow sip of the coffee, attempting to ensure the thoughts running through his mind weren't evident in his eyes.

'You're right about the coffee, very nice. I don't think they mentioned any links; but as I say I will check my notes. To be clear though, it's not the type of thing we would have talked about,' he moved to leave.

Lawrie noticing a slight change in his demeanour, similar to when he questioned him on his visit to Greenock Prison.

'That's great, Cal, I'll call in. No rush.'

'I'd love to stay, gents, but justice beckons for those in need. Thanks for the coffee, Superintendent.'

'Just one last thing, Cal, before you go. You may wish to sit down.' Irvine's eyes were on Lawrie yet again as he then diverted himself to tidying his files. He was never good with the softer side required in policing and always struggled as people's emotions came to the fore when unwelcome news was being communicated.

'There's no easy way to say this, Cal. The postmortem confirmed Nicki was pregnant, around eight weeks. I'm so sorry.'

Cal sat in silence for what seemed to the officers like an eternity, adding to Irvine's unease. He was going over all the conversations and intimate moments he had shared with Nicki, their discussions on starting a family, how many kids they would have, pondering names and laughing at the most ridiculous ones, which they would never dare use. Would their own childhoods shape the next generation? He thought of how Nicki would have been feeling, how she would have been desperate to share the news but remained consumed in her work, waiting for *that* day when she would smile, hug him, and whisper in his ear that they would be having a child. Was that her last thought as she died? Did she reach towards her stomach? Why didn't he see any signs, notice anything, ask her how she was feeling. Maybe that would have led her to opening up. He prided himself in being able to read people, gauge them by their reactions and body movements yet he couldn't pick up on anything from the person he loved.

'Wow, she never said. Why wouldn't she have said?' he asked out loud to no one in particular.

Lawrie moved beside Cal placing his hand on his forearm, 'Cal, we checked Nicki's medical records, she had a couple of miscarriages a few years ago, both at twelve weeks. If she hadn't told you ah think she was worried the same would happen again, mibbae waiting to get over that hurdle, and not to tempt fate.'

'We'll never know will we…I think…I think. The thought of becoming a dad and all that would bring, our baby being present in the world. Being a good dad, doing everything with them.' He was beginning to babble, 'Do they know... did the doctors say, was it... a girl or boy?'

Lawrie shook his head.

His mind was swirling, he wanted out of the room, to be alone with his thoughts, to get back to his flat close the curtains to block out the world and try to fully absorb what he had heard and importantly – to comprehend why, yet again, he had failed a person he cared deeply about. Why Nicki didn't think she could be totally open with him, to share her thoughts and fears. Maybe it was his mannerisms or how he presented himself. Whatever it was he continued to let people down.

'You had a right to know, Cal. It'll also form part of the charges when we catch the folk who did this, Lawrie responded assuredly.

Cal stood up slowly, his eyes staring at the floor, 'Good luck, gentleman. I must return to court.'

* * *

The chatty female police officer led him along the narrow corridor towards the exit. Her friendly persona and conversation was lost on Cal as he nodded and smiled not wanting to appear rude. As he reached the reception he asked if he could use the phone. He couldn't return to court; he was in no fit state. They would need to reschedule the case.

He made his way home, closed the curtains, and removed the phone from the hook. He searched the cupboards frustrated with himself that he had cleared the flat of all forms of alcohol just a week previous.

Climbing into the king size bed he felt tiny, vulnerable, and weak. He loosened his tie and the buttons on his silk waistcoat as he stared at the ceiling and the darkness. A darkness which completely suited his mood.

Tears rolled down both sides of his face running across his ears as he lay, his body shaking.

He realised that he had no-one, absolutely no-one, who he was particularly close to, who he could turn to or confide in – to share how he really felt. All his life friends and romantic relationships were either at arm's length or turned out to be a disaster.

His mother was of no help due to her harsh exterior and suspicious attitude to any everything in life.

He had finally found the person he could share his innermost thoughts and who he would share the rest of his life with. He had ruined it, put everything on hold, again. Allowed Nicki and his baby to be murdered as he pursued his ultimate revenge.

He committed himself to finding peace, an inner contentment where hatred, vengeance and hurt played no part.

One day, he thought one day.

Chapter Twenty-Four

GRACE RESTED HER HEAD on the edge of the bed in the room she had occupied for almost two days as the doctors continued to monitor Stephen's condition. The consistent beeping in the corner of the machine rigged up to her son was her reassuring companion.

The specialists had advised that his statistics and vital organs were good, and it was just a waiting game for his body to decide to wake up and begin the next stage in the recovery process. He was young and his body resilient to trauma and, thankfully, he had been caught just in time to prevent any lasting damage, they asserted with confidence.

She had allowed herself to slip away for a quick wash and change of clothes, with Joseph and Monica convincing her that they would phone immediately should anything change in her absence.

She had also taken the opportunity to return to Stephen's room and scour for any indications which may allow her to understand why he had taken a concoction of tablets. Was it a cry for help or a genuine attempt to leave them all behind?

She opened the envelope he had left addressed to her, absorbing the contents as he said goodbye, and sorry.

Once he had recovered, once he was home smiling again, annoying his brothers; and complaining about his football manager the letter would be ripped up and put in the bin, the thoughts contained within it remaining unsaid.

His demeanour over the past few months had been erratic, at times he appeared contented and happy with life. This switched when chats centred around school or his brothers time in Berlin, he would retreat into himself for prolonged periods, closing down conversations and not sharing his feelings or thoughts. Discussing his dad's death or even happy family memories was not an area anyone ventured into in his company. That was still too raw for him, though one she hoped, through time, he would learn to accept and live with.

The only items which were out of place in his; obsessively; tidy room was a stack of newspapers, all dated for Tuesdays and Thursdays, folded open at the crossword page with varying degrees of success in completion evidenced by his distinctive, cramped handwriting.

Other than Joseph and Monica the only person to visit Stephen was Father Dan, praying at the bedside with Grace and leaving a set of rosary beads and a small bottle of holy water from Lourdes on his pillow.

'Ah admire yer faith, Father, and thanks. Mine's a bit thin jist now. Ah think the Big Man is ripping the pish out of the Clark clan, testing ma patience, tae be truthful,' she said with a sorrowful honesty.

'Grace, I, at times, question this also but let me have enough faith for both of us just now. This isn't Stephen's time to leave us, I'm convinced of that.'

The repetitive sound of football studs scraping along the linoleum floor of the ward failed to stir her as she slept soundly gratified that by Stephen's breathing; long, deep breaths and the repetitive beeping of the machine it meant that he was still with her.

She felt a soft tap on her head, slow but continuous. Stirring sluggishly, she reached out towards the source and felt Stephen's, long, bony fingers, trying to rouse her. Opening her eyes quickly she smiled as Stephen looked at her and indicated with his eyes that she should look towards the bottom of the bed.

A group of teenage boys stood dressed in soaking wet football strips, stained with mud with a trail of soil leading directly from the ward door indicating their path. As if returning from battle without any spoils to present.

'In the name ah Christ.'

Monica stood amongst them, a huge grin across her face as she saw the improvement in Stephen.

'The cup final, Grace, it was the night. The team wanted to come and see their mate.'

'Sorry, boys, ah don't think you should be in here, the ward sister will do her nut when she sees the mess you've made of her floor,' her eyes darted towards the door clocking the nurse standing with her arms folded across her large chest.

'This sister is not in the slightest bit fussed with the dirty floor, Grace. The place is too sterile anyway and these lovely fellas asked permission to come in,' she said and left, her singing being faintly heard as she moved between the rooms.

A small boy wearing a goalkeeper's outfit, mud caked to his face and congealed to his ginger hair, stepped forward from among the crowd.

'Are you the goalie?' Grace asked, tilting her head and failing to hide her disbelief.

'Aye, ah ah'm,' he shrugged.

Stephen tapped her hand and in a low, croaky voice said, 'He might be wee, but he can spring like Tigger. Can't ye, Tigger?' he laughed quietly.

'Mate, we won the cup. It went tae penalty kicks, they bottled it. Ah think ah psyched them oot, ah managed tae save the first two.'

'Well done, boys, that's brilliant,' Grace said, clapping loudly.

'Mate, we won, but we aw feel,' he looked quickly to his left and right, 'well, we aw agree, that the cup's no won til the captain lifts it above their heid. We were just going tae leave it here with yer maw but since yer awake...here it is. Paisley and District Cup Champions, 1985. Us.' He stepped to the side of the bed and handed Stephen the large silver trophy with the team colours of green and black tied to the large lugs of the impressive, silver jug.

A single tear rolled down Stephen's cheek, leaving a thin track line on his pale skin in its wake. He ran his hand over the engraving. He lifted his chin and caught the eye of each and every one of his teammates, his pals, who he now realised should be a consistent presence in his world. He saw their happiness, their togetherness, the bond that would stay with them forever. They waited in anticipation. All eyes on him. A genuine, wholesome grin came across his face, for what seemed like the first time in years. Stretching, he raised the cup proudly as high as he could manage, the bright fluorescent light bouncing of its polished, silver surface.

The room erupted in shouts and cheers as the boys crowded around the bed, each attempting to get closer to their pal, some giving him hugs, the majority shaking his hand or just punching his arm. Pushing herself backwards Grace squeezed herself out of the teenage scrum and pulled Monica close to her.

Stephen knew at that moment, his moment, that life was good, people, mates, family, even his mad manager were worth being around. He had a lot to give and even more to live for.

Chapter Twenty-Five

JIMMY JUNIOR STOOD HIS back straight, arms folded across his puffed-out chest waiting for the governor to visit. He had refused to leave for his daily exercise and was threatening to smash up his cell unless he had a meeting. Right now.

The governor duly arrived flanked by two heavily built wardens, all three men displaying a visible disdain for the inmate, as if he was something they had collectively stood in.

Quinn had become more demanding in the past week, asking for meetings, having to be physically returned to his cell from his exercise period, demanding free association with other inmates, and challenging his lack of access to his daughter who was being held only a few hundred yards away.

'What can I do for you, Quinn? My staff advise me that you have become, how should I put it…decidedly awkward or, in their words, "a pain in the fuckin arse." So, tell me what the hell is going on?'

Jimmy moved to the rear of the cell, his back placed against the whitewashed, rough wall, the sole of his right foot leaning against it emphasising the large quadriceps bursting out of his green prison issue trousers.

'There's a list, Governor, a long list. If I'm; going to be stuck in this hole for the foreseeable future, which let's face it looks to be the case, according to my brief. As an innocent man, I want some home comforts...'

The governor let the speech wash over him, twenty-five years in the job had taught him not listen to a word inmates uttered – he had no control over any trials and no interest on how his inmates viewed the rules he set within his prison.

He was aware though that the man standing smugly in front of him; knew everything about his life and his foibles. This was highlighted by the delivery to his home of a bouquet of lilies, his wife's favourite flower, which he had managed to intercept before they reached their intended recipient. They had, allegedly, been sent on behalf of the Prison Officers Association offering sympathy, for the sad loss of her husband. There was also the medical course their daughter was attending at Edinburgh University; mentioned by Jimmy while in earshot as he passed one morning. He knew Jimmy's reach and power were widespread. He was retiring in eight months; he wouldn't be taking any chances for anyone.

'What do you want?' he replied, his jaw tightening.

'For a start, I want more shelves for all my books and case notes, in fact I want more books. I want new towels and more time in the yard, and I want to see my daughter, please.'

The governor placed his hands in his pockets and slanted his head to his left keeping his eyes firmly on the man in front of him who he had grown to both hate and fear in equal measure, 'Give him more access to the library, once a week for two hours. An extra fifteen-minute recreation time and change his towels. You can see your daughter in the dock when your trial starts. Move him to the bigger cell at the end of the wing,' he turned on his worn heels and sauntered down the empty wing, 'that'll do you, Jimmy.'

'We need to build a positive relationship, sir, if I'm going to be staying with you for a while.'

The heavy iron door slammed shut and the keys turned quickly in the lock. Jimmy Junior sternly faced the spy hole as it went from dark to bright, artificial, light. He allowed himself a small smirk. The governor can stick his towels, he'd be back in luxury soon; all was in place. It was just a matter of time until the plan would be activated.

* * *

Cal shook his head in frustration and glared into the reception area for a second time as, yet again, the phone rang unanswered at Grace's desk. Jack was on phone duty in her absence, *just take a message or transfer through to me* he was told. That proved to be too difficult with calls being constantly missed.

'Send that through, Jack,' he hissed. *The sooner Grace is back in here the better* he thought to himself. He lifted the receiver and immediately raised his hand towards Jack to signal his annoyance. Jack responded with a glaicket look, having no idea what he had done wrong.

'Mum, how are you?' Cal smiled rising from his seat and closing the office door.

'Ah've no heard fae ye for a while, how are ye?' Cathy was always straight to the point, no going around the margins. She had asserted previously that small talk was, "a waste of fuckin time."

'I've been really busy, flat out with cases, Mum. I was hoping to call you at lunchtime today to catch up.'

'Aye, ah'm sure ye were. Ye never came down to the wee lassie's funeral, ah thought she was yer girlfriend?'

Cal tapped his gold fountain pen on his desk as he thought of an appropriate response, one that wouldn't generate more questions. His mother would never open up or drop the harsh veneer she consistently displayed so showing his emotions could be met with ridicule or a curt dismissiveness.

'I thought it would be best if I stayed away, made myself scarce, to be honest, Mum. I was to blame for her death, remember? Seeing her family devastated would have sent me over the edge.' He waited for her brusque response.

'Son, did you really like her...like...love her?' Her tone was softer, slightly concerned, even motherly. 'Ye've never said.'

'I did, Mum.' He wanted to tell her about the loss of their child, but he couldn't find the words. It would be real if he said it our loud and he wasn't ready for that, not yet. The line fell silent for what seemed like an eternity as he awaited her reaction.

'Ah'll pray for her,' she eventually blurted, her voice breaking.

He changed the subject quickly, feeling uncomfortable with her showing any emotions, 'While I've got you. Years ago, you worked in Covent Garden and at the Docklands, didn't you, who was that with?'

'Och, ah had jobs all over, Son. Covent Garden, Convent Garden...,' the line went silent, 'err, ah cannae remember. Ah ran an office there at wan time, ah think. Why ye asking, has someone been asking about me, nosing aboot?' she responded defensively, adopting her usual persona.

'Well, it was about...oh it's nothing, just an old school friend contacted me out of the blue mentioned something about Covent Garden that jogged a memory, that's all.'

'Ye sure?'

'Positive. Look, I'm sorry, I really need to go; my office manager is off just now, so this place is in organised chaos. I'll call you tonight, to discuss what we spoke about before, do you remember?'

'Aye. that's fine.' The line went dead instantly.

He tapped the handset on his smooth forehead, eyes closed as he attempted to stimulate his memory of her varied work history. She was hiding something; he sensed the tension in her voice.

It was undisputed that she had worked every day, tirelessly, since they had landed in London, but how had she managed to pay his private school fees and put him through law school with office and admin jobs? He had a weekend job at the local Safeway store stacking shelves and filling bags, which covered very little of his expenses – a couple of cheap, shiny suits for his placements and some second-hand clothes in the latest fashion trends from Camden Market was as far as that stretched.

Her intrinsic sense of secrecy and an elusive facade was something he was comfortable with and understood to a certain degree, but this felt different. His experience of, continually, being around criminals listening to their lies, their subtle quirks when being questioned during interview or even holding back on him, their lawyer, despite client confidentiality, had allowed him, to instinctively sniff out when someone was hiding the full facts with their vagueness.

How had his mum's work life covered all their needs and the expensive fees which had set him on the path towards establishing himself within the law fraternity? What were the details she was hiding? He didn't know the answers, but he knew he would have to find them out. Once other matters had been dealt with.

Chapter Twenty-Six

TERENCE ROLLED UP HIS clothes and stuffed them into his tattered leather case. Mairi-Clare removed them and folded them properly. They worked slowly attempting to delay the goodbyes and inevitable tears.

She broke the imposing silence with a little laugh, 'You packed plenty of gear anyway, mister.'

'Yeah, plus ma maw kept sending me over scants and socks, ah better make sure they're in or ah'll be dead. Oh, and can you check ah've put in the Union Berlin strips for ma brothers? Ah think they'll like them.'

Mairi-Clare sat on the edge of the bed continuing to organise his luggage in an orderly fashion. 'Will you come back and visit me?' She looked up, her deep blue eyes filled with sadness.

Terence moved closer and lowering his body he wrapped his arm round her slender neck becoming intertwined with her blonde curls and resting his chin on her slim shoulder. 'Ah'll be travelling the world listening to you, pal. This is your scene, not mine, you're just so at home here it's where ye belong. But thanks for all ye've done for me, it helped me no end tae decide where ah want tae be. God bless ye.' Mairi-Clare lowered her chin and snuggled her face into his neck pulling his body to her for comfort, smiling at his choice of phrase.

A chap at the door pulled them apart as the professor entered the room dressed, as ever, in an impressive three-piece suit and starched white shirt accompanied by a green tartan tie, 'Time to go, young man?' He nodded to Mairi-Clare. Standing slowly, she attempted to smile as she left the room.

'It's been a pleasure to have you here, Terence. You know, you may never play in an orchestra and experience the all-encompassing thrill of being part of an ensemble, to hold an audience in the palm of your hand. But what you have...' he leaned forward to meet his eye fixing his stare on him a wide smile opening up across his stubbled face, '...is an ability to put everyone at ease. You don't view them as competition, you treat everyone for who they are. A humbleness. And a vicious headbutt. Your soul is clean, young man, it shows every day, in your eyes. Thank you,' he said, giving Terence a gentle slap on the head. 'It is a pity you'll miss the performance of Finlandia, I'm expecting a mesmerising rendition. Now, come with me. It's time for you to go home and help your mother.' He stood at the door awaiting him. Terence closed his case and followed the luggage bouncing off his lower leg as he struggled with the weight.

The professor led him from the dormitory, turning left down the dark corridor towards the auditorium, whistling to himself as he went, 'Ye know, Gabriel Faure has always been my inspiration, such a great composer,' he paused, losing himself yet again as he talked about music, 'The way he draws you in and doesn't let you go until you're exhausted and have left everything at his feet.'

'That's magic, Professor, but we're away the wrong way. Is the janny no picking me up out there?' He nodded his head towards the door behind them.

'That's correct. But first, young man,' he opened the oak door leading to the impressive grand hall, the instantaneous bright light shining directly onto Terence's confused face, 'your friends and teachers here at the Philharmoniker wish to say; thank you and of course, goodbye.' He held the door open encouraging Terence to enter first. The students who were assembled within their orchestral groups, stood in unison to greet him.

Timidly he entered the imposing tentlike structure with its seating surrounding the polished honeycomb floor and rising in irregular lines towards the roof, it's bright white lighting strategically placed to focus solely on the performers; adding to the suspense and the anticipated drama of an audience watching the recitals unfold.

The professor guided a startled Terence to a front row seat as he moved towards the podium lifting his white baton as the ensemble reoccupied their seats.

Mairi-Clare sat beside Helena Stern both with their violins placed in readiness under their chins, eyes on the professor, bows held in anticipation close to the bridge of the well-used instruments.

The professor tapped the large music stand with his baton leading to the cockney teenager to make his way to a mic placed to his left and close to Mairi-Clare.

Sporting the evidence of his run-in with Terence he smiled and nodded towards him, grinning as he ran his finger over the white plaster covering the bridge of his nose.

Terence had apologised profusely for his actions and the cockney had softened his outward brash exterior and opened up about his father's suicide and his own spiral into disorder. A teacher at his comprehensive had him play his favourite tune on his prized saxophone in front of an old friend, who happened to be the touring professor. Terence sensed his continued pain on the abrupt passing of his dad, they had that in common, he was not experienced or worldly wise enough to offer solace or words of real comfort or substance. That would have to come if he wished to follow the path; he had set for himself. He asked, strangely, for advice on how he should speak to his brother on the issues that led to him attempting to take his own life.

'I wouldn't say fuck all, if I were you, mate,' the cockney responded confidently, 'he'll have enough geezers nipping at his skull, he'll just need folk like you to treat him the same, ye know have a laugh, rip the pish if that's your thing. Just be his brother.'

They would never be the best of friends but a mutual respect and understanding of each other's loss and imperfections was evident. 'Cheers, pal, I'll do that,' Terence replied shaking his hand tightly, 'ah'm sorry bout the nose and that.'

The professor raised his baton and slowly waved it towards the orchestra. The cockney raised his head and began to sing, his precise tone and harmonious vocals filling the empty Grand Hall and emphasising the uniqueness of its design.

O the summer time is coming
And the trees are sweetly bloomin'
And the wild mountain thyme
Grows around the blooming heather
Will ye go, lassie go?

The string section came to life with the flick of the professor's baton; led in perfect unison by Mairi-Clare and Helena the harmony, gracefully leading the cockney into the chorus.

And we'll all go together
To pull wild mountain thyme
All around the blooming heather
Will ye go, lassie go?
I will build my love a bower
By yon pure crystal fountain
And round it I will pile
All the flowers of the mountain ...

Terence could feel the temperature of his skin rise by the second, he'd imagined his face would be fully red by the third verse. He was humbled that the group felt his leaving should be marked but being the centre of everyone's attention was not something with which he was ever comfortable. He'd concentrate on the music and the great voice of his cockney companion.

Robert Tannahill's poetry had never sounded so good, certainly better than his auld man's version that he used to have to listen to from his bedroom when he came home honking and in a singing mood.

Helena lowered her bow and turned her sheet music whispering in Mairi-Clare's ear. She then signalled to the professor to stop the performance. The music came to an abrupt, undignified; end as Helena walked towards the cockney apologising for her intervention. She turned to face the ensemble leaning to speak into the microphone.

'We are celebrating your friend's time with you here. While Robert Tannahill continues to inspire generations of poets, composers, and musicians we should allow this young man to leave with a large smile on his face, yes? You have learned another one. Sheet two?' The group nodded in agreement turning the sheet music and preparing for the professor's instruction.

'Mairi-Clare, join with me here,' Helena instructed, reaching out her hand.

The professor raised his baton, 'Your best performance, ladies, and gentlemen. Young at Heart by the Bluebells.' The baton swirled in the air as Mairi-Clare and Helena led the violins, their bodies moving in perfect unison. Helena had called it right thought the cockney, this would be uplifting and a great tune to see his wee, fat Scottish friend away home.

He approached the mic smiling towards Terence. His timing was impeccable as he patiently waited for the violins to peak and then move to their lower harmonies.

Young at heart
Yet what a start
Old before their time…

Terence sang along shuffling his body in the seat. His eyes were diverted to movement in the area located above the orchestra as three figures appeared in the front row. Friedrich waved down to his friend his other hand grasping his grandfather's. The three generations, together now for the first time, lifted their left arms and smiling broadly pumped their fists, Archie Gemmell style. Terence laughed, and beaming with pride returned the salute.

The caretaker duly arrived and lifting Terence's case nodded to him that it was time to go. The ensemble played on as he headed for the door. Mairi-Clare began her solo piece, the precise playing reverberating through the building. A building built for her talents and one in which he was sure she would become an accomplished performer. He turned to face her, the open door at his back. Her eyes were closed tight, her body moving with each stroke as her blonde curls bounced around her shoulders. Tears landed on her prized violin; she knew he'd be gone by the time the piece was finished.

Chapter Twenty-Seven

JIMMY JUNIOR LAY ON the thin mattress skimming through the pages of his latest library book, a novel by Robert Ludlum about a man with an unbelievable survival ability as well as being a professional assassin. The Bourne Identity was close to his own personality, he thought, having to survive and fight for everything was part of his own make up. He wasn't slow either to murder anyone that got in his way.

From the corner of the large cell Radio One blasted from the small transistor radio that the governor had kindly presented him with. Gary Davies was excitedly telling his listeners of the entertainment which lay ahead – full coverage of all the performers at today's Live Aid concert from Wembley, 'But please make a donation,' he pleaded.

Quinn smirked to himself.

The lock turned quickly; and the door swung open with a creak that irritated him each morning.

He turned his head slightly to see a screw throw him a bin bag, 'Get packed, Quinn, yer moving.'

He sat up on the bed swinging his legs to the ground, 'You can piss off, yer no ghosting me. Ye think yer sending me to Peterhead or some other shithole, yer not on. Get ma solicitor on the phone.'

The screw ignored his ranting and dismissively turned to exit as quickly as he had come in, 'Calm yer jets. You's are moving tae Glesga, yer trial starts next week. Start filling that bag, the van leaves after breakfast. And take that swanky suit as well, ye might need all the help ye can get when yer standing in the dock of the High Court on Monday.' The screws grained laughter could be heard from the other side of the thick door, the key rattling as he moved along the empty wing.

Quinn rolled up his designer shorts and t-shirts and placed them neatly in the bin bag, he stacked his case files on the bed and lifted his library book. I'll not be needing you, he thought, throwing it back on the bed.

He took a deep breath, holding it for a second; he closed his eyes, thinking everything through. He was meticulous in his planning; he was also particularly scrupulous in deciding who he employed and trained to the standard he expected across his various activities. And who he selected for particular tasks. He would now rely on them to deliver; God help them if they failed.

* * *

The large wooden gates of Her Majesty's Prison, Greenock, opened allowing the four motorcycle cops, on gleaming white BMW bikes, to ride in and park up. The yard overlooked the damp grey walls and the rusted iron bars of four floors of cell windows which were equally depressing as they reached towards the dark clouds overhead with just a glimmer of July sunshine beginning to sneak through.

Dismounting, one of the cops walked past the white prison van and raising the visor of his helmet introduced himself to the armed officers relaxing in a battered Land Rover their feet hanging over the open doors.

One had his eyes closed a cigarette burning between a pair of thick lips while his colleague, lovingly, ran an oily rag over a Heckler & Koch assault rifle.

'Jesus, the full armoury is out today, eh?' the cop said, nodding his head towards the gun, 'I'm Sergeant McWilliams, we've been dispatched to take ye up the road.'

The armed officer placed his ten high Doc boot on the dashboard, wrapping his hands around the rifle, 'I'm Sergeant Ritchie, that hungover fucker is Sergeant Waddell. It's a beauty, isn't it? I'm actually wanting tae fire it in anger, but Scotland is too quiet these days.'

'Careful whit ye wish for.'

'Ah know, ah know. How was the road on the way down?' Ritchie asked, his eyes still on the rifle.

'Saturday morning, nothing out there at all.'

'That's good tae hear. Anyway, are all your guys radioed up and briefed?'

'Aye, of course, that's all sorted.'

'Good, gaun tell that prison officer over there tae bring ye out some tea and biscuits. Very obliging lot doon here, so they are.'

'Cheers. We on schedule to leave at twelve hundred hours as planned?'

'We are. The sooner we get these two bastards up tae the High Court cells the quicker we can all go home and enjoy whit's left of the weekend. We'll check radio signals at eleven thirty hours and be facing that gate at eleven fifty. They'll be loaded by then,' Ritchie advised as individuals began to emerge from a back entrance of the admissions block.

Suzie's eyes smarted as she entered the courtyard looking up at the patchy grey clouds above her. An outbreak of noise from the male inmates gawping from their cell windows rose to a crescendo with wolf whistles, shouts and plastic cups being cracked against the iron bars. She stopped and flicked her long, glossy black hair over her right shoulder and flashed her pearl-white teeth towards the cells, the yelled responses merged in an inaudible clamour.

Handcuffed, she moved at the slow pace of the female warden she was attached to. The cops stared at her as she strolled towards the rear open door of the prison van, her posture perfect. Her time on remand had not had a negative impact on her looks or her ability to draw admiring glances from the opposite sex. The warden guided her forward and placed her into the small, claustrophobic cubicle for the journey ahead. The cuffs were removed; and Suzie rubbed her wrists as the cubicle door was closed and locked by the van driver.

Throwing the bin bag containing her clothes into a vacant cubicle the warden turned and smiled to the driver, 'She's all yours now. One more on the way down then yer good to go.'

Jimmy Junior stood at the reception area of the prison he turned his eyes to the governor standing at the back of the room. 'If this is a shift to some other dump, Governor, where I'll have limited access to legal representation; my lawyer will rip you and the Prison Service a new one,' he declared loudly so all the wardens congregated didn't miss a word as he attempted to show his authority.

The governor moved towards the large reception desk, leaning his elbows on the worn surface he eyeballed the vacating inmate, 'You're going to the High Court, as I've told you. Once you receive your full life sentence, there will be no better place for you than Peterhead, Quinn. Enjoy your trip.' He turned and walked towards his office, leaving the glass door open he read paperwork on his desk. 'Get that fucker processed and out of my prison.'

Chapter Twenty-Eight

CAL FIDDLED WITH THE thin metal aerial at the rear of the small television he had set up at the reception area of the office. Stepping back, he checked the quality of the picture which was blurred at best and not something he could live with for the full day of music that lay ahead.

He had been at this for far too long and now regretted that he hadn't accepted Jack's offer to have it up and running yesterday evening. He had downplayed his interest in Live Aid as, potentially, having Jack join him in the office on his day off was not something he had added to the list of scenarios for what may unfold in the hours ahead. 'I may come in, Jack. Though my current plans are to stay at home. Just leave it, it's fine.'

Like the rest of the nation, he was fascinated by the concept of the world's best musicians, performing in an all-day concert to save a starving nation, their actions being the catalyst to encourage others across the globe to donate money to alleviate hunger. His social conscience nagged him that surely people don't need to be entertained to save others from dying needlessly.

His mind wandered back to his teenage and early adult years recalling how he had toured the music venues around London to hear the emerging sounds of the day. His studies were always paramount with his future mapped out on the assumption that he achieved what was required to practice law. Nonetheless the night he heard the Damned at the Marquee Club up the West End had been mesmerising and, laughing to himself, he recalled another drunken night closer to home, in the cold winter of seventy-nine, as he trudged through snow to the Dublin Castle, Camden, to listen to the Camden Invaders. The warmth of the pub, the good company he was keeping, as well as the amount of lager being consumed, certainly meant; that however bad they were; he wasn't leaving early. At least he could boast he had seen the first incarnation of the now famous Nutty Boys, Madness.

As with everything in his life his obsessive personality fed his preoccupation with the latest sounds to emerge and meant that he became engrossed in any genre that caught his attention. He jumped from punk to ska and dabbled in the up-and-coming new romantic scene with great enthusiasm. A fixation with jazz soon developed, brought on by spending far too much time in the Jazz Café in Newington Green. This led him to change his whole wardrobe and to be seen walking around Camden in fedora hats and wing-tipped black and white patent shoes, to match his colourful suits. His mother laughed; others at his work placements just stared.

The small screen came to life with a burst of colour and noise as Status Quo came on stage, shook their long hair, and strummed electric guitars as the audience bounced along to Rocking All Over the World.

He had the full day's programme, from the *Daily Record*, on his desk with certain artists underlined indicating when he would take a break to watch their much-anticipated sets. The afternoon list certainly caught his eye, no doubt a marketing ploy for when people would be more susceptible to parting with their cash.

He glanced at his watch, yet again, as he looked down Wellmeadow, which was unusually quiet for a Saturday. He locked the office door and headed to his desk lifting the freshly made pot of coffee as he went.

Grace had been pushing him to go to The Cellar Bar for the full day's gig though he hoped, now that Terence was home and Stephen recuperating from his time in hospital, that her day would be fully occupied; and she would be too busy to come looking for him.

He sighed as he pushed the stack of folders in front of him, all in chronological order for the week ahead. He dived straight in hoping to find a challenging case that would get his adrenaline going. He glanced over at the grey metal filing cabinet; one day he would tackle the alleged miscarriage of justice drawer, packed full of inmates professing their innocence. However much it pained him, he had to stick to the here and now and deal with the cases needing his immediate attention.

Continuous chapping at the door interrupted his concentration. He glanced again at his watch. The timing was about right.

He strolled towards the office door singing along as Tony Hadley from Spandau Ballet sweated through his set in the bright sunshine, his fashion statement of a long leather jacket and trousers combination certainly adding to the heat he was experiencing. The huge audience at Wembley swayed back and forth to the hit single, True, as Tony's powerful voice filled the stadium and boomed out of Cal's small television set.

He glanced both ways down the street then, leaving the door ajar, he made his way back to his office, his eyes on the screen.

'Come in, Frank. There's cold coffee in the pot, help yourself.'

'Why are you in here the day?' Lawrie appeared exasperated, certainly more so than usual. He fiddled with the buttons of his handheld radio as his faded trench coat swayed from side to side, 'Fuckin thing is useless,' he muttered to himself as he banged it off the edge of Cal's desk then placed it back to his ear.

'To pay the bills. What other reason would bring me in here on such a beautiful day. Why are you in here today? I thought you were joining Grace in

The Cellar?' He placed the fountain pen in the edge of his mouth exposing his perfectly formed, teeth. His manner was relaxed, almost nonchalant, and he would aim to maintain this in the hours ahead as the day unfolded. Given that Frank was in a heightened state of anxiety he would have to maintain this pretence.

'Is there a problem, Frank?'

'Too right there's a problem. A huge fuckin problem.'

Chapter Twenty-Nine

THE PRISON VAN TURNED slowly out of the large gates onto the Old Inverkip Road and began to pick up speed as it headed towards the dual carriageway. The blue lights sitting on metal rods to the rear of the police bikes flashed intermittently through, the small, darkened windows, of the cramped cubicles as the first outrider sped ahead to stop the traffic at the forthcoming junction.

The twenty-five-mile journey would be carried out at high speed once they had navigated their way out of the winding roads of the Greenock housing estate. With the dual carriageway ahead, the route would be straightforward, aside from the odd drop in momentum as they approached several, unavoidable, roundabouts prior to reaching the motorway and then onto Glasgow's High Court.

The radio crackled into life, '*Kilo one to base. We have dispatched, arriving in approximately twenty-eight minutes, over,*' the officer announced as the clear expanse of the River Clyde came into view.

The water appeared still, almost inviting, with a crystal haze that stretched towards the banks of Ardmore and the tip of Ben Lomond in the distance as the sun slowly made an appearance in the early afternoon.

'Received, over.'

'Kilo two to Kilo one, first junction secured, over.'

Today was the culmination of weeks of planning at the highest level, with security clearance and full knowledge of the operation given to only a chosen few. The plan was straightforward, deliver the country's two most wanted criminals to the holding cells of the High Court in the Saltmarket – with the minimum of fuss. The road network, having been checked the previous four Saturdays at various hours, was deemed to be quiet at this time with the only pressure points located on exiting Greenock and the entry to Glasgow's Saltmarket; the busy city centre and High Street being areas of most concern.

The day was chosen specifically to coincide with the nation being glued to their tv screens and the musical events in London and Philadelphia.

It was calculated that the sight of a prison van, with motorcycle cops and an unmarked, beaten-up Land Rover travelling through the streets, would not register much interest.

The holding cells would be vacant with their trial the only show in town for the coming weeks. A full array of services, replicating those of a traditional prison facility, accompanied by armed officers, would be deployed from Saturday morning. Only when their guests arrived would those present be fully briefed and realise who they were hosting.

Quinn knocked the thin fibreglass frame wall of the cubicle, 'Suzie, are you in there?' He shouted over the constant drone of the engine as the driver shifted through the gears. He turned his ear hoping to hear a response.

'Dad, where are we going?'

'They're taking us up to Glasgow, to the courthouse, Suzie. Don't worry, we'll be fine.'

To avoid a panic attack due to her fear of enclosed spaces Suzie removed a small emery file from the lining of her trousers and tried to concentrate on shaping her manicured nails. Her thoughts turned to facing Cal across the courtroom and she hoped he would return her gaze and, genuine, loving smile. She would have, if time had permitted, had him killed, though that didn't diminish the emotional attachment she felt. She had thought about giving everything up, throwing in her lot with him completely. He was the only man who had come close, really close, to having her undivided attention.

She smirked to herself, the thought dissipated very quickly as she banged her fist on the side of the van recalling how Cal had managed to survive his execution and would now testify to put her away for a very long time. She had trust in her dad and the organisation, its contacts, power, and unbridled access to those it had corrupted. Maybe the trial wasn't the forgone conclusion that everyone was predicting.

The convoy continued on at a steady pace barely slowing as it manoeuvred the large roundabout on Greenock Road overlooked by the imposing Ferguson-Ailsa shipyard, its tall cranes defiantly reaching towards the blue sky signifying that the area's expertise and future in shipbuilding was alive and well.

'Kilo two to Kilo one A8 Woodland roundabout secured, over.'

'Noted, Kilo two.'

The officer placed his rifle on the back seat of the Land Rover, lovingly patting its trigger as he carefully laid it down, 'We'll be home in no time. Might even get to see some of that concert everyone's going on about.'

'Fuck that,' his partner responded, 'I'm going for a curer. You're welcome to join me but you'll need to keep up, I'm choking for a drink.'

'That sounds like a really enticing offer, Bobby. And you know how much ah value yer drunken company, but ah'll pass,' he said sarcastically.

The radio crackled into life again, *'Kilo two to Kilo one. We have a problem, there's a lorry overturned blocking the A8 roundabout exit at Langbank. Local officers in attendance. Permission to divert, right, right, onto the B789-Old Greenock Road, rejoining the A8 in approximately 10 minutes.'*

The officer took a deep breath and glanced at his partner for comment who shrugged his shoulders, *'Permission granted, kilo two. Send another dispatch ahead on the B789 and provide a status report asap, over. Kilo one to base, did you get that?'*

'Affirmative.'

The prison van slowed as it swayed right, then left, leaving the dual carriageway following the signs for Langbank as the driver lowered his gears to climb the steep hill of the leafy suburb's main road.

The road was lined with a mixture of mature trees with multiple shades of green prominent in the canopy as it stretched across the road directing the sun's rays through the gaps in the branches. Accompanied by pruned hedgerows and bordering large, lush agricultural grasslands the area had a distinct countryside feel to it despite being minutes away from the harsh industrial face of neighbouring Port Glasgow and its big brother, Greenock. The busy road, with oncoming traffic passing freely and farmers spotted working their machinery in nearby fields allowed the officers to relax slightly as the convoy pressed on.

As they reached the top of the brae and proceeded down a large dip in the road the brake lights followed by the hazard lights of the white prison van sparked into life. The Land Rover slowed behind it as the driver peered out of the side window.

'What you seeing, Bobby?' Sergeant Ritchie looked over each shoulder as he reached and lifted his rifle off the back seat, his eyes scanning the hedgerows for any threats.

'Looks like one of the outriders slipped on some oil. He's pulling his bike up now, he's waving, he's all right. Here's their sarge coming,' Bobby added, sensing the tension emanating from his partner.'

The motorbike came to a halt as it reached the passenger door of the vehicle. Simultaneously a fellow officer had caught up with the convoy, slowing his bike to the front of the Land Rover.

'Sorry about this, guv,' the helmeted officer announced.

'Is your man, OK?' Ritchie enquired while rolling down the window which screeched as if in pain.

The officer slipped his hand inside his fluorescent jacket and, producing a Glock pistol, quickly fired two bullets into Ritchie's face. His accomplice fired directly through the windscreen at the driver ploughing four bullets into his chest, then, casually, walked to the driver's door and emptied another two into the back of his victim's head as he lay slumped over the large steering wheel.

'Base to Kilo one, sit rep, over.'

Lifting the radio, the assassin launched it over the hedge into the overgrown field as a large red tractor exited the gate. The driver attached a thick chain to the rear doors of the prison van and reversing the powerful vehicle ripped them from its hinges.

The driver of the van, dazed as blood poured from a head wound, was marched to the rear of his vehicle as a pistol was placed at the back of his ear. He stood rigid, his partner equally disorientated at his side, as one of the team entered and released the prisoners from their small cubicles.

Quinn rubbed his hands together and greeted his team with congratulatory hugs. 'Like clockwork, boys,' he said, laughing energetically.

Suzie stepped down onto the road taking in the scene around her with a wry smile. 'We were never going to go on trial, were we?' She asked, not expecting a response. 'What happens with these two?' She eyed the two prison guards standing in fear for their lives, the bloodied remains of the two policemen in their eyeline.

A uniformed gang member stepped forward and placed an envelope into the top pocket of their bloodstained shirts saying, 'What you will read in there will be familiar to you. Your address, family names, age of your kids, what's in your bank accounts and where you do your drinking,' edging closer to one guard, who was shaking uncontrollably, 'and for you some nice photos of you at the public bogs where you get your cheap thrills. You're both being spared. One word, just one word, anything you share in a statement which ends up in court – I'll be back to kill you…slowly. Now get fuckin in there,' he growled.

The guards were shoved into the cubicles previously occupied by Suzie and Quinn. their piercing screams being heard as they were pistol-whipped into unconsciousness. Their mouths and eyes were crudely sealed with gaffer tape and the cubicle doors locked. A small package was left strategically at the entrance to the van with wires attached to suction pads placed onto the van's frame. Just enough for anyone to think twice about entering the vehicle in a hurry.

A black transit van with smoke-glass windows screeched to a halt, its side door opening immediately.

'Let's go,' Quinn announced, grabbing Suzie under the arm. She stopped, resisting his momentum.

'Wait, my clothes.'

'Jesus, I'll buy you gear.'

She glared at him, displaying a distinct level of disdain, as she lifted the coat from the ground brushing the dirt off the garment. 'That's my favourite red coat, Dad. I'm not leaving that, not a chance.'

The van took off at great speed as the motorbike drivers retraced their previous route and disappeared from sight.

It had been a long couple of days for the gang as they put in motion months of planning to free their leader. Each, *official*, police outriders house was visited at midnight by Russo members and their families bound and gagged and removed from their homes. After reporting for duty and leaving on their route to Greenock the officers were instructed to drive to an industrial estate and hand over their bikes, uniforms, radios, and details of their duties that day. They were interrogated on how many armed support officers would be attending, the route that was planned, the number of times they were expected to call in. Over and over the same questions, by several gang members at separate times, asked slightly differently, followed by warning of unbridled violence on their loved ones if the smallest detail could not be corroborated with previous answers. Instilling unadulterated fear and intimidation was the gang's method of operation, every aspect controlled, with the understanding that at any minute you or a family member would be shot. No one would stand in their way.

Once the boss was out and in the safe house the officers would be released, dumped naked into an empty industrial estate, a key and address placed into a shaking hand informing them of where their families could be found.

Quinn and Suzie stretched out on the plush leather seats as one of the team handed them soft, hot, towels and a glass of champagne. 'From your welcome box, boss,' he grinned. Quinn buried his face in the cloth appreciating the small touch of luxury.

He reached over into the box sitting at his employee's feet, 'Everything else in here I asked for?'

'Of course, boss, everything.'

He lifted the Glock 17 handgun and ran his fingers slowly over the black, pebble finish and groove-less frame. Slowly placing the magazine stack into position, he caressed the weapon like a long-lost friend, 'Nice, how many rounds does it hold?'

'Ten, boss.'

'That'll be plenty,' he replied, smiling at his daughter his eyes diverted to the box, 'there's a wee gift in here for you, Suzie,' he handed her a small silver Browning, pocket pistol.

She placed it in her coat pocket not bothering to give it a glance. Wrapping the red woollen garment around her thin body she said disdainfully, 'I would've preferred a new handbag.'

The driver glanced in his rear-view mirror as the police radio could be heard in the background – encouragingly there was still no acknowledgement, as yet, of their breakout. 'The chopper's fuelled and ready to go, boss. You'll be outta the country in no time.'

'Once we deal with our unfinished business, stick to the plan, Fergie. You know where to take us.'

Chapter Thirty

'THE TWO HIGHEST PROFILE fuckin crims in the whole of the country and they daft bastards let them escape.' Frank Lawrie was pacing the floor in Cal's office, perspiration gathered on his forehead and rolled slowly down his pale skin onto the two-day old greying growth gathered around his thick jawline. 'They only had two armed cops on duty, two. This is the Russo, fuckin Jimmy Quinn. Unbelievable.'

Cal removed his white silk handkerchief from his dapper suit pocket and handed it to his visitor.

'What do you mean, escaped? Here, sit down, take off that big jacket, Frank' He guided him to the lounge seats in the corner of his office and poured them both some iced water from the jug on the small coffee table.

'It's a bit sketchy at the minute. We think they've broke out of the van, whit we know is that two officers are dead, the place is cordoned off the now, they're waiting for the bomb squad cause there's a device in the van. We don't know if they're in it or no. There's no chance they're still in it, they're fuckin long gone. Some fucker is at it, ah'm tellin ye. Ah saw the roster for this op three days ago – two vehicles, each carrying armed support, plus observation teams dotted along the route. All fuckin stood down last night by some top brass – bar the two cops left tae dae it aw by themselves.'

Cal sat directly across from Lawrie, sipping his water, his eyes taking in every movement and expression of his visitor.

Sting could be heard belting out Roxanne from his Live Aid performance, an event which was now paling into insignificance as the minutes progressed.

The day was unfolding just as Cal had been told to expect and prepare for. The notable exception being that a detective was now occupying his office. He would have to come up with a plan to remove him from his personal space, to give him the room to manoeuvre should it be required, and to allow events to progress as he was told they would.

'Frank…why are you here?'

'How?'

'You've just said that Quinn and Suzie have, you think, escaped from custody. Which is not only a huge embarrassment to your force but something you would think that all of you, collectively, would be keen to rectify even recapture them?'

Frank was suspicious of Cal, wary of his smart-arse phrases and eloquent use of words. He knew he did this to project an image of someone who was in complete control and full of confidence in his abilities, in addition to, at times, confusing those with a weaker grasp of his rich vocabulary, resulting in them submitting to his superior knowledge.

He always suspected Cal of knowing more than he was letting on, he knew he had lied about an earlier visit to Greenock Prison. He reminded himself that Cal had previous for setting his enemies up for a fall, something he had chosen to turn a blind eye to. Whatever was going on today, whatever was going to happen, the epicentre was right here in the shape of the smooth, calm and controlled individual sitting in front of him without a care in the world. This is where he would stay.

'Why are you dressed in a fancy suit on a Saturday?'

'Why…Frank. Why are you…I always wear a suit to work.'

'On a Saturday?'

'I'm working. I wear suits to work, the day in question is inconsequential. Why are you here?'

'As soon as ah heard, Cal, ah came over just in case you were in. Ah was worried the Russo might want tae target ye, tae tie up loose ends.'

'That's very thoughtful of you, Frank, really it is, but there's no need. That would be a completely irrational approach from what, as far as I've learned so far, is a very well resourced, calculated; crime group.'

'Ah'll just hang around, Cal. The Serious Crime team will be leading the chase for those two fuckers.'

'Frank, tell me, how will you save me? Your radio isn't even functioning properly,' he asked, flashing his broad smile.

The detective lifted the handset and banged it off his broad palm, 'Aye, yer right bout that. Tell ye wit, ah'll phone the station, they can bring a new battery up to me. Sorted.' He moved towards Cal's desk and lifting the phone he punched in the number, 'Don't worry mate, ah'm here for ye.'

Cal lowered his head attempting to disguise his frustration at this deviation from his plan and interference with the potential events that lay ahead. Picking up on Frank's phone conversation it didn't sound as if a radio fix would be a feasible solution.

'Well, we're fucked, Cal. There's not a single cop spare to drop aff a radio. They're aw oot searching for they two bastards, and armed support is at a bank robbery which has turned into a siege in Johnstone - shithole of a place that. And there's also a full-scale fuckin battle going on in a pub at the other end of the town they're aw steaming already cause ah that concert. The fuckin Africans must be well pleased it's this shower ah shite that's saving them. So, anyway, they cannae help little auld me,' Frank sat on the edge of Cal's desk, folding his arms across his faded shirt, 'anybody would think these incidents were aw linked, even staged, Cal.'

Cal strolled towards the reception area lifting two crystal glasses as he went. 'Well, if we are here for the duration, my friend, we may as well have a drink and enjoy the music.' He arranged two seats and a small table in front of the coloured portable television and poured two shots of Jamesons.

'Just a wee one for me, pal, ah'm no a big drinker these days.'

Chapter Thirty-One

THESE PERSONS ARENT PLAYING for the benefit of their health. They're playing for the benefit of other persons' health. So, get your money out now.

And the address is...

No, fuck the address. Let's read the numbers. Cause that's how we're going to get it.

Bob Geldof sat forward, wide eyed, facing the presenter running his hands through his unkempt hair. His frustration was growing by the minute with the lack of donations that his much-heralded event was yet to generate. He needn't have worried, by the end of the day a huge sum would be raised to stop the hunger and to, hopefully, eradicate the famine in Ethiopia.

'That Geldof guy's a pure knob,' Stephen whispered into Monica's ear.

Grace danced around the living room, glass in hand, as the music blared from the telly in the corner of the room. Her three boys sat open-mouthed. Monica leaned her head on Stephen's shoulder and laughed at their shocked gapes.

'C'mon boys, dance with yer auld maw,' she encouraged them, attempting to pull Terence to his feet, 'Ma three boys all safe and in the one place.'

She was against Terence being forced to leave Berlin and the thought of Suzie McGrath and her gang dictating how they went about their day to day lives added to her complete hate of that woman. In hindsight though she was relieved he was home, and with the trial starting next week they would soon be able to put all this behind them and Terence could go back to Berlin and carry on with his music.

She raised her glass to the ceiling in defiance, its contents running down her thin arm, 'Fuck, Suzie McGrath.'

'Mum,' Joseph tutted.

'Sorry, sorry,' she covered her mouth as Joseph buried his head behind his copy of the Socialist Worker.

'Yer not watching the concert, Son?' she asked, nudging in beside him on the single leather seat.

He lowered the paper and pointed at the television as Paul Young, with a spiked mullet and dressed in an open-neck shirt, slid across the white stage on his knees beneath the large *Feed the World* banner, his raspy vocals serenading the audience and telling them that – every time they went away, they took a piece of him with them.

'These events are just to make people feel better, Mum. They won't end hunger; it might *feed the world* for a wee while but then everyone will go back to their day jobs, and nothing will change.'

'Awrite, Son, lighten up.'

Joseph sat forward in his chair, tidying the collar on his khaki jacket, 'This has a world audience of what, a billion? What if that billion turned on the politicians, the establishment, made them share out the wealth and natural resources they've stolen? Then they would *feed the world*. This is just another distraction, aided and abetted by the powerful,' he sat back in the chair with a sigh, 'It's aw just a sham.'

'The wee man's turned intae Arthur Scargill. Good on ye, Joe. Ah know what yer saying, but the musicians are just trying their best, doin whit they know,' Terence interjected, lending his brother some support.

'That may be right, Terence, but ah bet after this concert their individual record sales will go through the roof, they'll go on country-wide tours, European wide tours, mibbae even world tours on the back ah this. In stadiums as big as Wembley. And ah bet the millions they make fae that wulnae find its way tae feeding the world.'

'Ah get it, brother, but ye can only do what you think is right. Ye don't have control or influence over these folk. As long as you try and help people where ye can and be true to yerself, wee man, then yer fine.'

'Very prophetic, Terence. Berlin has done you well,' Joseph replied, returning to his paper.

Grace placed her glass on the mantel piece and stood, hands on hips. 'God, you lot are depressing. Ah'm going tae The Cellar tae watch the rest of the concert. Any of ye want tae come? Didnae think so. Ah'll be home soon.' She gave them all a hug and kiss, slipped her Live Aid t-shirt on, readjusted her long red hair into a tight bobble in the mirror and headed out the door, singing to herself as she went.

'Ah'll go out after her,' Terence said, sensing the concern of his brothers. He'd also have a word about his future. The timing was about right with her relaxed mood and the trial starting shortly.

Mairi-Clare had called last night after the concert, her voice full of excitement. The choice of Finlandia had went down very well. Friedrich and his family had been the guest of honour, though Mairi-Clare didn't go into much detail due to fears of the phone being bugged by the Stasi.

Helena Stern had headed back to East Berlin taking with her a letter of gratitude from Principal Cooper for the kind donation of the much-needed music equipment. She would deliver it to the Stasi sitting outside her house, awaiting her return. Mairi-Clare was lucky enough to have an afternoon's personal tuition from Helena who reinforced in her that her future lay in Berlin, developing her talents and her love for music.

Terence had to tell his mum about his life-changing choice, he hoped she would support him, be proud of what he would commit to and understand that it was something he couldn't ignore any longer, no matter how much he had tried to block it out.

* * *

Lawrie removed his shoes and stretched out in the soft office chair, his holed socks resting on the smoked-glass table. He sipped the whiskey intermittently. Ensuring he had a clear head for whatever may unfold was his priority.

'Who the fuck's he?'

'Who?' Cal asked, scanning the screen.

Lawrie's eyes never left the screen as he pointed his tar-stained finger, 'That wee dick wae the boots oan wae the heels.'

Cal sat forward in the chair neatly rolling up the sleeves of his; light blue, Dior shirt, revealing his muscular forearms. 'That's Bono, he's the lead with U2. They've a great following already,' the camera took in the packed crowd as banners were waived proudly catching in a light breeze, 'see, look at the flags with their name on them.'

'Fuckin acting like a pure eejit. Look. He's jumped intae the crowd now, he'd be jailed if ah wis there. Even the band are raging wae him, poncing about like that. Left them standing there like spare parts.'

Cal glanced out of the large office window his eyes diverting quickly again to his watch, 'He's a showman, Frank, an entertainer, he's working his audience.'

'Aye, nae bother. Looks like a prick tae me.'

The door swung open with its usual screech as Grace bounded in, smiling at her two friends, throwing her office keys on her desk. Frank immediately straightened himself, replaced his shoes and ran his fingers through his thinning hair.

One day he'd have the courage to ask her out, though his ability to gauge when that should transpire was not one of his strong points. When would he think she would be over or have come to terms with the death of her husband and be ready to share her life again with another? He would just hang in there; it would happen naturally or hopefully she would catch on to his pitiful preening and take the hint.

'Ye better no be stinking oot ma office wae yer sweaty feet, Frank,' she laughed, pulling a chair beside them, 'and why were you two no in the pub? Ah'm sitting doon there maself like a lemon, everybody's pished as farts; already. And auld Jack never bothered tae show up, as per, but ah thought you two would at least stick yer head in for a wee while.'

Cal passed her a crystal glass of golden liquid, the rich aroma catching in her nostrils.

'Have this Gracie, you're going to need it.

* * *

Quinn tugged on the starched collar of his white shirt as Suzie ran a comb through her smooth, silken, black hair placing a small ceramic butterfly clasp to the side of her head to keep her long fringe in place. Cal had given it to her on one of their romantic trips to Edinburgh after he moaned at her for having to constantly tuck her fringe behind her ear. He said, although it was cute, it spoiled his view of her captivating blue eyes.

The van made its way along the quiet Paisley street keeping well within the speed limit so as not to draw any undue attention.

Some early casualties of the day's drinking could be seen staggering on the pavements using the sandstone walls of the tenements as their very own personal pin ball machine and relying on an inbuilt radar to reach the sanctuary of their homes.

'Update Fergie, is all going as planned?'

'All going like clockwork. The main road diversions are in place, there'll be no traffic through the West End until you've exited. The polis are tied down all over the outskirts of town and we've a bit of organised mayhem starting in Glesga tae ensure they're busy up there as well. There's still radio silence on yer breakout, unless they're using another frequency or call sign that's no been shared, we've no picked up anything, we're scanning them aw though. Ah think they're still waiting for the squad tae deal with the booby trap. Fuckin magic.' He laughed, glancing in the rear-view mirror and despite having a malicious look in his eyes he still sought some shred of appreciation from his master.

Quinn lifted the mobile phone pulling out the large antennae, 'You checked that this thing is working?'

'It is, great things them, ah'm thinking of getting one maself.'

'Is he where we expect him to be?'

'He is.'

'What time was the last recce?'

'Fifteen minutes ago. He's got a couple of visitors in, nothing of great concern though.'

Quinn clutched his daughter's hand tightly as he broke into a huge grin, the excitement beginning to grow within him, 'Let's have some fun, Suzie, love, let's have some fuckin fun.'

Suzie placed her hand over her dad's, rubbing his tanned skin, 'Once you kill him, we *are* going to South America as you promised, aren't we?' She asked, meeting his eyes with a wishful look.

'You'll be at your own personal pool sipping a lovely Cachaça cocktail very, very soon. I promise you, sweetheart.'

The van crawled along Broomlands Street as a scouting car passed going in the opposite direction – the driver raising his thumb in affirmation from the steering wheel.

'Pull in here, Fergie. We'll walk the rest of the way and do our own recce before we introduce ourselves.'

'Boss, why don't ye let us sort this? There's nae need for you tae be out here.'

'The thing is, Fergie, I don't get to have fun like this anymore,' he caressed the barrel of the handgun, yet again, 'I miss the fear coming over their eyes when they're about to be stiffed. And this one is long overdue.'

'OK, noted. Remember the pickup point is Canal Street beside the fire station, just five minutes' walk.'

Quinn slid the side door open; and Suzie followed quickly as he walked briskly towards the West End Cross. He pulled the black leather jacket collar tightly around his chin, lowered a baseball cap to just above his eyes and slipped his hands into black leather gloves.

His hand moved to the back of his waist band, reassured that the handgun was in place.

'Time to finish this, Suzie. Once and for all.'

Chapter Thirty-Two

GRACE STOOD RIGID IN the office, her eyes fixed, staring out of the clear windows as she fought to hold back the tears beginning to blur her vision. Tears of anger, frustration and fear all rolled into one as she tried to comprehend the news that the two people who had ruined her family and her future with Dixie were yet again free and certainly not going on trial any time soon. Unless by some miracle the inept Strathclyde Police – who couldn't hold them in the first place somehow managed to recapture them.

'In the name ah Christ. Seriously. How could ye let them get away?' She turned to face Frank and Cal; the now empty glass tucked tightly under her folded arm as her anger took primacy. 'Frank, your bloody gaffer sat in here and told me this wis a high-profile case and everything wis been done to jail them, forever… blah, blah, fuckin blah.'

Cal cut the sound blaring from the television – Freddie Mercury warming his vocal chords to a captivated audience seemed to have lost all relevance.

Frank raised his hand in submission, 'We've fucked up, bigtime. Ah know, Grace, ah know.'

'Ye know whit, Frank? Ye know whit ah've tae say tae they three boys? Tae explain that Mr fuckin Plod couldnae keep ah haud ah the most dangerous criminals they said were oan their watch. Whit, Frank, whit will ah tell them?'

She began pacing the length of the office, her small frame turning and twisting quickly as she reached the flower-patterned wallpaper and her prized pot plants, turning, and repeating like a distraught caged animal.

'Grace, every officer is out there, the now, chasing them down. We'll find them, ah promise ye.'

Grace turned away sharply staring again towards the empty street, drawing her glare off Frank who meekly turned to Cal for support who shrugged his shoulders unable to think of any meaningful contribution that would take the edge off Grace's anger.

A sharp intake of breath could be heard across the office, 'Oh. My. Fuckin. God. Ye won't need tae go looking. They've found you. Fuckin Suzie McGrath is standing across the road,' Grace turned her head quickly as the phone began to ring and Cal and Frank jumped to their feet, rushing to the window.

Cal lifted the receiver, placing it quickly to his ear as he kept his eyes on the row of shops sitting neatly under the grime-stained tenements, the original golden hue of the sandstone hidden by soot and car fumes. The hairdressers and newsagents had closed early to allow the staff to enjoy the day's music extravaganza, while the remaining units had their shutters pulled down a long time ago with no prospect of any new retailers moving in and fulfilling the economic windfall, that the politicians advised was there for the taking.

'Cal Lynch. At last, we get to talk, after all this time. All this time of you trying to finish me and destroy my business.'

Quinn was leaning nonchalantly against the graffitied shutter, the sole of his left foot resting on the metal casing. He held a large mobile phone to his ear, his white teeth prominent against his fading tan as he stared across the road at the lawyer's office. Suzie stood by his side in her prized red woollen jacket, standing upright her legs slightly apart, carrying an air of strength and authority with her posture. Her eyes searched the office searching for Cal, hoping that her memories of how he looked, how he carried himself, were correct and not a figment of her imagination.

Frank frantically pressed his radio as a broken call could be heard coming through intermittently. 'Detective Sergeant Lawrie to base, urgent assistance required at the junction of West Brae and Wellmeadow. Escapees Quinn and McGrath are present, repeat, escapees present.'

Cal's eyes were drawn momentarily to Suzie. She was stunning, as usual, with her slender figure, perfect posture and long black hair framing her model-like features. She had a strange look on her face, he thought, not hateful but demonic which was unnerving.

'I've called the police; they'll be here in minutes,' he answered, attempting to exude confidence.

'No, they won't - they're very busy elsewhere. I want you, out here with me. That's what I want. You've three minutes or I'm coming in after you, and your friends will get it as well,' Quinn rested the handgun on his left thigh, 'and by the way, the phone lines will be dead once I hang up, so don't waste any of your precious time trying to call the polis. Three minutes, Lynch.' He handed the phone to Suzie who placed it inside her long coat.

Cal ran immediately to his office emerging with an unused baseball bat. He looked at Grace, then Frank, 'I need to go out there, you both stay here. Lock the door.'

'With a baseball bat, whit ye gonnae dae, swat away live rounds? Ye fuckin stupid? Did you know they were coming here?' Frank shouted, his instinct, again, telling him that Cal wasn't sharing everything, that his warped plans had now put them all in danger. He walked the room, trying to think of a remedy to their predicament, not waiting for a response to his question.

Cal glanced at the office clock, seven fifteen. He stared at the television, captivated for what seemed like an eternity as Queen singing; We Are the Champions, enthralled a thankful audience.

'Cal, fuckin snap out of it,' Frank shouted.

'You need to stay here. This is my fight, not yours. It ends now with me and him,' Cal replied, realising that the culmination of three decades of thoughts, unanswered questions and planning had come down to what would happen once the three minutes were up.

A raw brutality that he couldn't influence with his sophisticated tongue or charm awaited him.

Grace sat in silence unable to comprehend what was unfolding, everything seemed to have slowed down, to have become surreal. Her first thought was to run across Wellmeadow Street and ragdoll Suzie McGrath as she had dreamed of doing, but her motherly instinct told her that she had to find a way to escape, to ensure that her boys were not left alone in a world as cruel as this one. The back entrance would have been an option if it wasn't blocked by building rubble from the refit. She'd hide in the back office and pray she wouldn't be found.

'Right, I've got a plan,' Frank announced, pointing with his defunct radio, 'Cal, you get ready to run.'

* * *

Frank purposefully stepped out of the office, cursing the creak of the door as he went, and made his way to the middle of the road. He held his police warrant card aloft, facing Quinn and Suzie as both began to make their way towards him.

'Strathclyde Police, lay down your weapon. Armed officers have you surrounded. This can end with no one getting hurt.'

Quinn began to move quicker, the pistol in his right hand by his side. Suzie walked behind him, striding as if on a Paris catwalk, her hands in her jacket pockets wrapping the garment around her body despite the hazy sun warming the early evening.

'Now, Cal,' Frank called over his shoulder as Cal exited the office and ran at full speed up West Brae. Still in his fitted suit trousers he had at least found an old pair of trainers in the office that he hoped would provide him with enough momentum to get over the steep hill, past the Porridge Bowl, down past the back of Woolworths, turn right into the town centre and make his way safely to Mill Street Police Station – just as Frank had hastily set out. He would raise the alarm and back-up would be sent to the West End immediately.

Quinn raised the Glock and fired off two rounds the sound echoing around the tall buildings and filling the eerie silence. Frank let out a cry as the bullets smashed into the left side of his body piercing his shoulder and hip and forcing him to involuntarily spin and crash onto the road.

Quinn took aim at Cal as he momentarily stopped considering to return to help his friend. The bullet hit the tarmac behind him the black bitumen taking on a new role as shrapnel, the fragments exploding into his leg and shoulder. He turned and took off again the adrenaline pumping through his body masking the pain now emanating from his wounds.

Quinn sprinted past the police officer writhing in agony, his eyes firmly on Cal, 'Finish him off, I'll be back in a minute.'

Suzie strolled slowly towards Frank who was now lying on his back and trying to push himself towards the office doorway with the heel of the one leg still moving. He placed his right hand across his body attempting to stem the blood pouring from his shoulder; and darkening his faded clothes.

Grace ran quickly from the office as Suzie removed the small handgun from her pocket and wrapped her manicured hand around it. Grace froze and closed her eyes tightly as Suzie, smiling broadly, pointed the silver pistol at Frank's head and pulled the trigger. She opened them quickly as Suzie pressed the trigger again and again with no success. With anger overtaking her fear, Grace flew at the woman throwing her to the ground and dragging her by her hair across the road. With every ounce of strength in her body she smashed her against the office wall, the sound of her skull coming into contact with the black tiles giving her confidence to attack her further with an increased viciousness. Wrapping both hands around her loose hair she pulled it out to the roots and brought her right foot as hard as she could onto her face. Suzie was now unconscious and not resisting or mounting any sort of defence.

'Ya fuckin evil witch, fuckin die,' Grace screamed as she grabbed her head and smashed it repeatedly into the concrete path.

She had envisioned this moment many times through her tears while she lay, alone, in the darkness, wishing Dixie was lying snoring beside her filling the room with a mixed aroma of cigarette smoke, paint and sawdust.

Suzie's eyes began to swell, the cracking of her high cheekbones competing with Grace's screams. Her looks were ruined forever, or, at least, it would take a sizable chunk of her ill-gotten wealth to recreate her previously beautiful features as her dark blood began to flow freely down the steep West Brae into the gutter.

'Die, ya fuckin witch.'

'Grace, that's enough, stop,' Frank yelled, attempting to lift his head off the road.

'Mum, stop. Now.'

Grace looked up, her eyes bulging, her skin pale as Terence walked towards her, stopping short of the pavement, and glancing between her and the injured Lawrie in disbelief.

'Go home, Son. She's dying today, hell fuckin mend her.'

'Mum, ye cannae dae that.'

'Course ah can, right now ah can.'

'Ye cannae, Mum, ah'm going tae be a priest. Ah cannae have a mother in the jail for murder.'

Grace wrapped Suzie's long hair tightly around her hand, holding her limp head off the ground. She stared intently at her son, trying to comprehend what he had announced.

'In the name ah Christ.'

'Well, aye. That's the idea.'

'But how, what bout Berlin? A priest…'

'Aye, Mum, look we can talk later. Just let her go, please. Ah think Mr Lawrie needs our help.'

Grace dropped Suzie's head unceremoniously the bloodied skin on the side of her face scraping across the path. She ran quickly to Frank who attempted to smile to ease her worry as she leant over him, her eyes quickly glancing all over his wounded body. 'Where's the gun, Grace?'

'Shit, ah don't know,' she scanned the pavement, 'there, it's there.'

'Kick it, slowly, over beside me, Grace. Place ma warrant card on ma chest, armed police will be here soon, somebody must have reported all the shots going off.'

'Fucksake. Frank, where are you hit?'

'Here, Grace, press here,' he pointed at his shoulder. She removed her bloodstained Live Aid t-shirt and wrapping it tightly pressed inside his coat against his shoulder as Frank let out a painful groan.

'Fucksake, Frank.'

'You'll need tae stop that swearing with the young yin here going intae the priesthood.'

She smiled as she looked up at Terence, feeling a sense of pride, 'We'll talk, if we survive this.'

'Of course, Mum. Mr Lawrie, ah'll go and phone the polis.' Terence ran to the nearest phone box his mind racing with what he had witnessed, as well as feeling relief that he had finally shared the news of his calling with the one person he craved complete endorsement from.

'Grace, ah don't know if this is a good time or no, but if we survive this. Ah mean, if that mad bastard doesnae come down that hill after doin Cal in and kill me. Would ye, would ye like tae, like...'

'Spit it oot, Frank.'

'Would ye like tae go to the pictures wan night or go out for a meal. With me...like.'

'Ah'd love tae. But ah don't dae pushin wheelchairs, mate, so ye better get fit.'

Shots could be heard in the distance as she continued to put pressure on the wound, hoping to curtail the flow of blood from his body. Frank began to feel very tired.

'Shit, we better move ye if he comes down here.'

'Ah cannae move, ma legs are fuckin numb. Promise me, Grace, if ye see him running down that hill you'll bolt for home. Promise me.'

Grace looked over at Suzie lying prostrate on the pavement, her body crumpled, motionless, her face smashed beyond recognition. If Quinn sees her in that condition, she'd be dead also, no questions asked, she thought. The boys left alone.

'Aye, Frank, ah will, ah'll run,' she replied, as sirens could be heard wailing in the distance, drawing ever closer.

* * *

Cal attempted to concentrate on his breathing, deep belly breathing which he knew would increase the flow of oxygen-rich blood to his leg muscles and stave off fatigue as he pushed his body up the steep hill. He had run the hill many a time as he worked on his fitness and stamina, determined never to be vulnerable again.

The iconic Porridge Bowl to the left was his marker, his training timer. He knew if he was beyond the iconic landmark in under a minute with the relatively flat roadway ahead of him; he could generate more speed, gain momentum, and be out of Quinn's line of sight and make it to the other end of the town, and guaranteed safety.

The baroque up-turned bowl, covering the large atrium, came into his full view as a further two shots rang out. Cal fell to the ground, letting out a painful groan, as a bullet pierced the back of his leg and cleanly exited his muscular thigh. A sadistic laugh could be heard from behind him as Quinn drew ever nearer.

Cal raised himself quickly and limped forward clutching his thigh. Unable to run, he stumbled on, trying to push his good leg harder, taking long strides. He knew stopping would be signing his own death warrant, but he also realised he wouldn't outrun him, the distance and the ascent were too challenging with blood pouring from his wound. He needed an out.

Cal heard the wind chimes from an adjacent garden, the white wall he had previously rested on weeks before was close to him as he dragged himself towards the house. He sought sanctuary as he fell through the patio doors and attempted to close them behind him as he stumbled into the small living room.

Making his way to a panelled pine door at the rear of the room, collapsing onto the floor as his leg wound tore further open with every bend of his knee, the pain unbearable. He was fully conscious and aware of what was happening around him and what could be coming his way. He knew he couldn't do anything about it.

Quinn had slowed down on the hill, catching his breath, and scanning the area for Cal's hiding place. The trail of blood along the gravel path leading to Cal's smudged fingerprints, marking the white glossed wood of the doorframe had him heartlessly laughing again. Checking the magazine of his Glock he kicked in the front door and rushed into the room.

'Come out, come out, wherever you are,' he whispered, his eyes darting around the room and fixing on the red stains which were congealing on the worn cream carpet. He reached the back of the couch and found his target sitting against the wall his injured leg outstretched a dark blue tie wrapped around his thigh as a tourniquet.

Cal looked up, grimacing at his predicament and the inevitability of what was coming next.

'There you are, Cal. Were you no good at hide-n-seek when you were wee in the Gorbals.? Or did you not have anyone to play with cause yer daddy was pan breed? It's great to meet you in person at last. Shame it'll just be for a wee while.'

Cal looked up, dejected, submitting to his fate. Everything had been in vain with his father's killer winning, yet again.

'One day, Jimmy, in this life or the next, you'll get your comeuppance,' he said, looking up and finally eyeing the man who had shaped his thinking, his purpose, his very being for the majority of his life.

Quinn ran the barrel of his Glock along Cal's smooth chin, 'I really don't have time to talk, but I will, if you want to like, before I kill you.'

'You've nothing to tell me that I don't know already, Jimmy. You're evil, you blooded yourself on my old man. Got the thirst for it, the love of it. You've nothing for me.'

Quinn recalled the stabbing of Cal's father. His victims both shared the same fear in their eyes, a certain acceptance, though Peter Turner had at least tried to save himself, tried to escape. Neither of them seemed to have it in them to beg for their life. They were too proud.

'Your dad put up a better fight than you. He'll be disappointed by your lack of effort; bet he's looking down all sad.'

'Get on with it.'

'As you wish, Cal,' Quinn straightened his arm as he lowered the pistol inches above Cal's forehead. 'It's death before revenge for you.'

A loud, dull thud exploded sending Quinn flying into the iron fireplace, his head now resting amongst the hearth's ashes. The dust rose around his shoulders as another blow landed on the back of his neck, the wooden shaft of the weapon breaking on impact.

'That wis ma best spade, ya fucker,' the tall figure announced, as he launched his boot into Quinn's body followed by repeated heavy blows with his right fist.

'You took your time,' Cal groaned from behind the couch.

'Aye, it's good tae see you too, Cal,' the ponytailed figure responded, bending to examine Cal's gaping wound, 'That wisnae in the script ye gave me.'

'I know, Ger, best laid plans; and all that, eh?'

Stretching out his thick, tattooed forearm he helped Cal to his feet, 'Good to see ye, pal.' He wrapped his powerful arms around him, hugging him tightly.

'You're looking well, Ger, and as mad as ever I see. Where were you hiding?'

'Haha, ah wis bored shitless waiting for all this tae kick-aff, so ah built a false wall, see?' He pointed to a space beside a wooden dresser and the front door, beaming proudly as he presented his handy work.

Cal glanced as the body on the floor let out a drowsy groan. Ger turned quickly and grabbing Quinn's arms, roughly tied them behind his back wrapping the thick rope around his wrists several times. Hauling Quinn's body off the fireplace he leaned him against the bright floral seat.

Cal hunched himself over the couch to take the pressure off his wound as he watched his collaborator at work, once again mesmerised by the brute strength he displayed, 'Well, is she here?'

Ger returned slowly from the kitchen guiding a small female. 'Here she is, Cal,' he stood aside as the grey-haired woman smiled nervously, reached out and hugged Cal.

'God, Son, are ye OK?' She looked down at his bloodied leg and pulled him tightly towards her.

'I'm fine, Mum. I'm fine.'

Ger moved quickly across the room, closing the curtains as the noise of sirens could be heard drawing nearer. Lifting Jimmy by the hair and sitting him upright he placed the Glock into Cal's hand. 'We need to do this now.'

Cal ushered his mother towards Jimmy her feet shuffling small steps, her eyes wide and fixed on the limp body in front of her.

'Is it him that…' she asked in a low, edgy voice, looking towards her son, '… killed your dad?'

'Definitely, Mum. It's him.'

Jimmy began to stir. Coughing, he cleared his mouth of blood, his eyes partially opening. Ger pulled his hair tightly, 'We don't have long, folks. Is this happening?' he asked assertively, the sound of sirens becoming more prominent and bouncing off the high walls opposite the house.

Cal placed his arm reassuringly around his mum's thin shoulders, nudging her closer to the kneeling figure in front of them. 'Mum, just as we practised, remember? Press it tight into his chest so

299

the residue will be found on his clothes. It'll be finished in seconds. After all these years, Mum. Over,' he whispered.

Previously researching causes of death in medical journals relating to wounds inflicted, at close proximity, in combat by firearms Cal learned that the survival rate from cardiac tamponade was virtually zero. The fatal shot would also sow the seeds of a struggle and his frantic attempts to avoid execution from a murdering madman.

Jimmy stirred, his eyes slowly focusing on the figures above him. 'Well, if it's not yourself, Cathy. I've not seen you for a while,' he let out a loud laugh, blood spraying over the room as he noticed the handgun being lowered, shakily, to his chest, 'I dare you, Cathy. Why don't you tell your son first about…'

The bullet exploded into his body forcing him violently back onto the chair before falling forward limp onto the carpet, his head slipping over his knees, his face dropping and resting on its side, his eyes cold and wide. Ger pressed his fingers into Jimmy's neck for a few seconds then nodded towards Cal.

'It's over Mum, finally over.'

Cathy covered her mouth and nose as the smell of the sulphur caught in her throat. Ger removed the gun carefully from her hand and guided her back to the kitchen. 'No, a great whiff, is it? It's like rotten eggs. Go and sit in the back of the van, Cathy, I'll drive ye out of here in a minute.' He closed the door behind him as blue lights could be seen flashing through the edges of the thick living room curtains.

This was going better than Cal had assiduously planned. He knew Jimmy would have felt threatened, his authority being challenged by the trial and an insignificant lawyer who wanted to take him on. He had to show the Police and, importantly the Russo, that he was still completely in charge and running the criminal empire. He wouldn't give up the opportunity to make an example of Cal and anyone else who stood in his way.

The information Cal had been fed had been spot on – when they would break out, how Jimmy would come to finish him off. He was not privy to who the source was, but he was assured that the detail was correct and that he would be targeted. The presence of Grace and Frank had complicated matters somewhat. The guns being fired in public together with his injuries would reinforce the scene that would greet the armed police and influence the investigating officers.

'Right, Cal, ah'll drive yer mother straight tae London. Before that, this needs tae look like an accident. He wis trying tae kill you, remember – the gun went off. That's what ye tell them when they interview you, OK?'

'Got it, Ger.'

He smashed a right hook into Cal's ribs who doubled over leaning on Ger's shoulder. Two further punches landed on his jaw and temple, bursting open his eye socket, and knocking him unconscious. Ger positioned his body, face down, across from Jimmy, wrapping the Glock pistol around Cal's fingers and then placing it next to Jimmy's hand.

Rushed footsteps could be heard coming across the gravel garden pathway, hurriedly approaching the house then slowing. Ger tiptoed from the scene and headed to the back entrance. Smiling he murmured, 'I really enjoyed that, Cal. See ye later, my friend. It's always good tae catch up.' Lifting his tobacco tin and Zippo he closed the door behind him.

Chapter Thirty-Three

CAL WAS ROUSED BY the sound of a member of staff humming an unintelligible tune as the squeaking wheels of the food trolley was pushed towards his bed, the aroma of his hospital breakfast stirring his senses awake.

His head was thumping, and his left hand continuously throbbed as the needle feeding him pain relief sat uncomfortably deep in his vein. Peering over the bandages covering his right eye he glanced across the room. An armed guard, standing motionless, was visible through the glass door. The other three hospital beds in the room were unoccupied adding to the eeriness. His looked at his breakfast of scrambled eggs and soggy toast, he sighed at the condition of the egg, it looked as if it had received a bigger doing than the one, he had received some ten days previous. He insisted on feeding himself, hoping to regain his independence as soon as possible. To get out of hospital, as soon as possible.

Turning his head, he noticed the door opening and a tall figure hobbling towards him, working two crutches, blowing hard with every movement.

'Ah'm getting better wae these things, Cal. Ah'm doing the stairs the morra. Then ah reckon ah'll be out.'

'You're doing great, Frank. What's the surgeon saying about your injuries?'

'Well, ah'm fucked to go back on the tools, the nine-mill bullet disintegrated the top of ma pelvis. So no more operational service for me. They'll try and stick me on a desk job. They can fuck right off with that, pal. Ah'll take ma money – retire early, ah think, if they don't let me stay mobile.'

'I'm sorry. I really didn't think it would turn out like this. You saved my life, again, and now you'll be giving up the job you love. I don't know what to say.'

Frank released a painful groan as he lowered himself into the plastic chair next to Cal's bed, helping himself to the grapes sitting in a bowl on an adjacent bedside table.

'You got grapes as well then?' he smiled, 'Ah think me taking two bullets for you makes me a hero, young man, and…that gets me a date with the lovely Grace.' He grinned, flicking a grape in the air, and catching it in his open mouth.

'A silver lining, Frank. She never mentioned that when she was in. The only thing she talked about was Terence becoming the first ever Scottish pope.'

Glancing towards the door the police officer pulled the chair closer to the bed, 'Have you given a full statement yet?'

'I have but I'll need to go over it again. I can't recall what I said, to be honest, due to the amount of drugs I was given,' Cal responded picking up the *Daily Record* which was still covering the incident on the front cover with four pages of *exclusives* contained within it, 'I see we're still hogging the headlines.'

Frank brought his head closer to Cal's ear, scanning the empty room. 'There's been four of the top brass suspended. It's been a fuck up from start tae finish. They're up tae their necks in corruption, it's smashed wide open. Rumour has it they would have seen it out if the two cops hadn't been killed in the line of duty; and the West End of Paisley turned into the gunfight at the O.K. fuckin Corral.'

Cal flicked through the pages of the paper looking for any reference to his mother. Ger Johnson was pictured in a smart three-piece, tweed, suit his hair tied neatly back in a tight ponytail, beard shaved off, standing, arms folded, looking shocked, outside his now destroyed front door at Oakshaw. He lamented at how much it would cost for him to repair the damage and thanked God that he had been away fishing in the Lake District for the weekend when chaos and death had erupted around his treasured property. He would be selling up, he was quoted – he loved the quiet life, but Paisley wasn't safe anymore. Cal smiled inwardly, knowing Ger he would have loved being the focus of the national press.

* * *

Growing up in the Gorbals, Gerald Johnson, had a fearsome reputation for violence and a love of inflicting pain on those who crossed his path. Bullies and big mouths, who picked out their victims due to the fact they were clearly weaker than them, were his favourite. He took great satisfaction in their embarrassment and witnessing them cry and snivel for mercy. Seeing a damp spot emerge on their trousers, as they wet themselves in anticipation of what was coming, always proved to be a match winner.

Ger grew up across the cold concrete landing on the tenth floor of Queen Elizabeth Square from his younger, neighbour Cal. Like his friend he was insular and a bit of a loner finding it difficult to mix with his peers, which wasn't helped by his fierce temper and quick fists. He'd prevented Cal from being beaten up on several occasions, and they both spent a sizeable amount of their time in the sanctuary of the library in Norfolk Street. Ger reading adventure comics and Cal with his head sunk into yet another book.

He'd a fondness for Peter who was always handing him some change if he met him on the stairs, knowing that his own parents had very little to spare for any treats. Not long after his murder and Cal moving away, his own life had spiralled out of control with exclusion from school and his days spent walking the streets drinking cheap wine, until he was old enough to get a job labouring on the new estates being built across Glasgow.

He still returned to the library of an evening for some solitude due to the constant threat of violence at home. It was there he was given a letter, addressed to him, from Cal, swearing him to secrecy, and providing him with his address in Camden. They had stayed in touch ever since.

His brutality didn't come from his gene pool, he wasn't born like this, he would be relieved to discover in later life through therapy, but a natural survival mode that had developed due to the harsh conditions he was raised in, with an old man who took great pleasure in inflicting pain on his three sons and his timid, nervous wreck of a wife.

He admired Peter; he showed him, by his displays of affection and his general persona, that there were dads who did it differently, who loved their family and were not afraid to show it despite the harsh, unforgiving, society they found themselves in.

Prior to leaving home Ger had ensured the family bully would hurt no more as he caved in his skull with an iron frying pan on the stairs leading to their flat. He had waited for him to return home from one of the very few jobs; he had actually managed to hold down for more than a couple of weeks. It was a Tuesday evening, the only day he came straight home, his dry day due to a lack of funds for booze. He wanted to get him sober so there would be no dubiety, no blurred memories of what had occurred. The attack had rendered him disabled, with speech loss and a dependence on his wife to look after him. It also left him with a look of guilt in his eyes that stayed with him until he succumbed to his injuries ten years later, guilt of the hurt he had inflicted on his family which were only realised by the actions of his son.

Etched in Ger's memory was a small boy, his face ashen white, being guided by his distraught mother as the police escorted them from the flat to a place unknown. The image of his friend staring as he raised his hand at the bedroom window to wave goodbye had never left him.

He joined the army when he reached eighteen, the recruiting sergeant at a promotional stand in the local shopping centre noticing the rawness and fantastic build that was developing on the young man who had a rough outlook on life.

Despite being the most proficient cadet during training and with two years under his belt with his battalion things began to unravel and didn't work out as the recruiting officer had planned. A dishonourable discharge came after a spell in the Military Corrective Training Centre in Colchester, for insubordination, common assault, and the breaking of a corporal's jaw.

A career as a mercenary beckoned with action in Angola and Sri Lanka which only ended when he embarked on a lucrative period displaying his skills, and soaking up his much needed, adrenaline rush from violence while on the bare-knuckle fighting circuit in the back streets of Morocco.

He was famous for adopting the Irish stand down technique, never moving round the makeshift ring but instead standing, feet fixed to the canvas, trading blows until his opponent eventually capitulated or was knocked out cold.

His lucrative fighting days ended abruptly when an illegal bout in the Moroccan city of Er-Rich resulted in a pitched battle with local police, one that he didn't, this time, win. He woke up in the notorious Tazmamart Prison deep in the Atlas Mountains of Morocco, a hellhole that had been covertly set up to hold political prisoners.

He was confined to a small single person cell with no exercise or human contact. The only exception being the sound screams as inmates succumbed to torture or of the trolleys, the wheels bouncing on the rough surface, as dead inmates were pushed down the humid corridor to the makeshift graveyard.

Ger was wise enough to keep his head down to avoid any confrontation with the guards that could encircle him. His foreign status was his saving grace, that and the trusted Moroccan friend who contacted Cal in London, setting the wheels in motion to bring about his eventual release.

A further five years were spent providing security at nightclubs across Ibiza, taking drugs and partying, which cooled his temper.

The loyalty shown by his childhood friend remained with him, how he was saved from certain death in Morocco, how he was always there to bail him out when he repeatedly made an arse of things.

He had packed up his small possessions and left Ibiza and headed for the slightly less sunny climate of Paisley as soon as the cryptic message had come through.

Setting up the house in Oakshaw, as instructed, he enjoyed the months pottering about and awaiting the action to begin. He kept his head down, adopted an indifferent persona with the neighbours or made a scene when instructed to do so.

The wind chimes were his own personal touch and a wee nod to Cal, as they had hung similar from their balconies on Queen Elizabeth Square, the swirling winds around the high rises providing the ammunition to work the pipes continuously.

* * *

'Any word on Suzie? The papers said she was found unconscious,' Cal asked, his eyes still fixed on the sensational headlines in front of him.

Frank laughed, holding his side as his movements triggered the sharp pain to return, 'Ye should have seen it. Grace knocked the complete fuckin shit out of her. If it wasn't for the boy, she'd be deid. She's lying up in the Southern General Hospital, her jaw's wired up, a lung punctured by one of her ribs and eight of her gleaming teeth were found on the street. Oh, and a fractured skull, ah forgot that. She's away forever now, nae danger once the trial is sorted.'

'Such a shame she survived,' Cal replied.

Closing the paper to ensure his undivided attention, Lawrie edged even closer to the bed, his eyes still on the glass door. 'Cal, ah need the full story, nae bullshit. How did ye know they would come looking for ye?'

Cal pushed his shoulders back against the propped-up pillows, rubbing the back of his head against the iron frame of the bed. How much could he share? Lawrie had nearly died protecting him. Surely, he could provide some information to put his mind at rest with what had played out in front of him. He thought of his mother, how she had repeatedly told him; during the planning – *tell no one nothing, not a thing. No matter how much you think they need to know, tell them nothing.*

'OK, Frank, I'll be honest with you. I knew Father Dan was a loose link that they would target, that's why when Ronnie Sanders turned up, I paid him to follow him and to get close to the henchmen who would be looking to take him out. I thought once your lot had arrested them that it would shut all of this down - the house of cards you spoke about. The time you cornered me at the Vatican about my visit to Greenock Prison? You were right, I didn't need to go there. I had arranged it just that morning. I needed to see where they would be held, needed to have it clear in my mind, to be reassured, that they couldn't or wouldn't escape. Little did I know they would use their corrupt police and prison service contacts to do just that. I never thought they would target young Terence in Berlin. Maybe then, we all should have realised how determined they were, how ruthless they could be. It may have saved Nicki if I paid a bit more attention to everything that was going on around us.'

'Ah knew that visit was a pile ah pish. But why come after you, why no just jump on a plane or a boat, get tae fuck away? Why the need tae come for you?'

'I can't figure that out either, Frank. The only thing I can think of is that Quinn thought he was so powerful that there was no way he wouldn't get away with killing me and then being prevented to depart unhindered. He wanted to send out a message about how much the crime gang were in control – nobody capable of challenging them. From what the papers are saying, the syndicate shut down the town to let him in.'

'How ye managed to fight him off with a busted leg, that's brave, ma friend. He must have really fuckin hated ye. Ah told ye, before you and Nicki exposed him to the general public, he was operating under the radar. That riled him, being outed. Ah think he wanted ye tae pay for that.'

Cal lowered his chin, the last few months running quickly through his mind, 'Nicki certainly paid for it.' He sighed and shook his head hoping that now, at last, his life could really begin in earnest having finally extinguished the one person that had dominated his thinking and dictated every decision he had made for years. Every thought, every exam, every court case taken on, won, or lost, each career decision was aimed at achieving revenge.

'Speaking of Nicki, my mate at the Met has been in touch. That was one of the reasons ah was calling over tae see ye that day, then all the shit hit the fan and ah forgot all bout it. He gave me more information on the two London killings.'

'And?'

'You'll no like this, Cal.'

'Frank,' he sighed, waving his hand impatiently for the information.

'Ah asked him to check again all the evidence boxed up for the murders. He went through it thoroughly, checked their employee lists, invoices, bank statements, police records, any dodgy dealings, the lot. He found nothing.'

'And?'

'Apart from the one thing, Cal, a link to both victims. They didn't move in similar circles their businesses were not connected; they were just successful,' Lawrie stared directly at Cal not wanting to miss any reaction to his forthcoming revelation, 'Their address book's both contained one identical entry – Cathy Lynch. She worked as a bookkeeper for both of them. Your mum was paid cash in hand, that's why it wasn't immediately obvious. The pattern seems the same; your mum stopped working for them when they were both churning out large amounts of money, and within three weeks they were shot, executed. And, not that ah need tae remind ye Cal, with the same gun that took Nicki out.'

Frank watched as Cal's skin drained, turning pale, with only the yellowing bruising around his jawline remaining in place. He stayed silent; studying Cal's exposed eye which now seemed devoid of emotion, becoming colder and more distant with each passing second. His body slumped in the bed losing all tautness, as if he had resigned himself to something, accepted it.

'When are you getting out of here?'

'The morra, ah hope. Why?' Frank replied.

Cal slowly turned the pages of the paper folding it at a black and white photograph of Nicki staring up at him proudly with her bright smile and high cheekbones prominent underneath the Metropolitan Police hat.

An eager crime reporter was posing a series of questions about the mysterious death of one of the Met's top serious crime officers in a car crash, immediately after breaking the seal on the country's biggest crime syndicate. Exposing the Russo, revealing their connections across a whole spectrum of industries and the highest echelons of the establishment. Was the accident linked to the ongoing investigation, which she had led with an unstinting conviction?

Cal's mind was going into overdrive reliving the events of the past twelve months and the decisions he had made. *Who had really made those calls, who was really pulling the strings? Who had fed him lines of information and leads?* He needed answers.

'Tomorrow, I'll sign myself out. We're going to London.'

Chapter Thirty-Four

FRANK LAWRIE CURSED UNDER his breath as he hobbled up the spiral staircase of Camden Tube Station counting the worn steps as he went in an attempt to distract his mind from the pain shooting through his hip. The rusted banister, screwed to the polished white tiled walls provided him with much needed support.

Cal stood patiently waiting for him at the busy entrance looking out across the neighbourhood where he had spent his youth and as an adult, honed his talents in the cities courts and built his confidence and skills.

Back then occasionally he would spend his time daydreaming, lost in his own thoughts, scheming in his head as to how he would put his father's killers away. Now that this was finally done, he was unsure if it had actually been worth it; there was no elation just a feeling of emptiness that consumed him.

'Ninety-six fuckin steps there. They ever thought ah getting lifts down here?'

'Did you make that call, Frank?'

'Aye.'

'You fit to walk? The house isn't that far. I'll take you the scenic route up through the Lock and the Market if you wish. It'll help me clear my head.'

'Fine by me, pal.'

Frank limped to the side of the street avoiding the throng of people moving up and down the wide pavement as he took in the surroundings. He smiled observing the mix of London life going about their business. The noise of the metropolitan high street was in full flow with hawkers selling everything from bangles to the now out-of-date, *Feed the World* T-shirts. Chilled Rastafarians sat in groups listening to Gregory Issacs' latest offering from a silver ghetto blaster, adding to the general din.

Preferring the relative; quiet of Paisley and its familiarity, he had little enthusiasm for busy places, packed cities, though he was content to take them in small doses. The empty shop units covered in flyposting made him feel at home.

His gaffer wasn't amused at his early return to work, though acceded to his request to travel to London, intrigued with what the trip may reveal. Lawrie wanted to remain active fearing that there would be attempts to sideline him from operational work influenced by the unseen forces which went about their corrupt business within his organisation.

Frank had clocked how quiet and reserved Cal was on the flight down to Gatwick, which continued on to the Gatwick Express train into central London. He kept his own counsel, waiting for Cal to open up and reveal the expected outcome of the trip. Going by his previous record everything would have been planned and thought out with very little left to chance. He expected that the conclusion of this meeting would be the same.

* * *

Grace exited the bus at the terminus on Hawk Road, Terence following behind her. She had seldom visited the school unless one of the boys was in bother and she had been summoned by the headteacher for another lecture. She would apologise profusely and vow to get them sorted and in line. She would agree to anything they would suggest to help change behaviours, to ensure that Social Work weren't called – no-one wanted they bastards crawling over their family life.

The headteacher was a smart operator. He was full of external bluster, emphasising repeatedly why rules and discipline had to be followed, while also acutely aware of the challenges faced by families such as the Clarks, raising three boys in a society which was coming apart at the seams due to no fault of their own and something they couldn't influence.

'Mum, why are we up here?' Terence asked, running to catch her up as she reached the large black, rusted gate, 'It's the summer holidays.'

'Ah'm well aware of that, Son. There's an open day on for aw the new families who've moved in just up the road there tae the new estate, to promote the school. That's good of them, isn't it.'

She lifted the black bag over her shoulder, her knuckles still red raw from her violent exploits. 'Ah thought ah could help settle them in. Anyway, are you still set on the priesthood?' she asked, striding quickly along the path, squinting her eyes as the warm, mid-morning, sun shone on their faces.

'Definitely, Mum.'

'It's a big thing, Son. A big commitment. It means you'll no have any weans.' She slowed her pace, turning to catch his eye, 'Whit makes ye want tae dae it?'

'Well, it's a calling, something ah can't avoid, something that's been eating away at me for a long while. It's a bit like our Joseph, isn't it. He wants tae get into politics to wipe out that bastard Thatch…'

'Hey, easy, ye cannae swear now, no when yer gonnae be a holy man.'

'To wipe out that bastard Thatcher. But really, he just wants to help people, make a difference. He just doesn't know it yet. Ah think ah'm just the same, tae help people through God. You and dad must have done something right, eh?'

'Ah wish yer granny was still living. She'd be sending umpteen letters back tae Creeslough in

318

Donegal, bumming about ye. How does it work, dae ye just apply?'

'No, there's different stages. Ah'm in the discernment phase to allow me to assess further my calling, then ah'll fill out the form and speak to the Vocations Director and after that, God willing, it's seminary. And seven years later ah'll be ordained a priest and start my new life,' he smiled in contentment.

Grace stopped on the tarmac path, watching as the janitor applied a coat of white paint to the rusted goalpost, 'Well, ah think just to protect your discernment thingy that you should wait outside while ah go in here.'

The gym hall was a hive of activity as potential new pupils, and their parents were being guided around the various departments. Stands had been set up advocating for all the interesting, challenging; subjects they would undertake over the next four years, at least, once enrolled.

The headteacher stood, suited, towards the rear of the hall; and, wide-eyed, nodded a surprised hello to Grace. She could feel his eyes on the back of her head as she scanned the room for the physics table, spotting it beneath the colourful science sign.

Mr Curran was adorned in his washed-out white coverall as he enthusiastically engaged a large audience, demonstrating the speed of a small wooden car on an elevated track, ticker tape wrapped around his shoulders.

She nudged her way to the front of the group, Curran catching her eye, no doubt observing her far from friendly stance and facial expression.

'So, as we see, the speed of the vehicle against the speed of sound can be calculated by this simple experiment. This will inspire, I feel, in you a desire to explore further analysis of the world around us and...'

'Mr Curran,' Grace stepped forward as the teacher's eyes opened wide beneath large, dark-rimmed, glasses. Sitting down behind the table he adopted a defensive manner, unsure what was coming next. The large room fell into an uneasy silence as Grace raised her voice.

'Ma boy, Stephen Clark, you taught him last term? Kinda.'

'Err, err, Stephen, oh yes, Stephen.'

She lifted the large bin bag to her waist. Placing the weight onto her hip she emptied the contents over the table knocking the display onto the floor.

'Well, you've still tae mark his work. Ah count at least forty-five *Daily Records* he read when you were meant tae be teaching him. Ah didnae know the school did O-Grade crossword, ya lazy prick.' She turned to the audience, some pulling their children closer to them, and smiling at a young boy she added, 'Ah wouldnae take physics if ah was you. And don't listen to him, dream big, young man.'

The headteacher approached the table as the uncomfortable parents began drifting away. Lifting one of the papers from the floor he leaned over the table to Curran who was now sitting in shock. 'Clear this mess up and get to my office. Bring your union rep and these papers. You useless fucker.'

Grace strode confidently from the building, her head high. She may have been too late to support Stephen through school but given everything he had endured she felt she owed it to him to stand up to Curran, to show that his type of behaviour and condescending attitude would be checked, that her children, her type, were worth something.

The boys were beginning to tread their own path in life with Terence finally deciding what he wanted to do, and young Joe determined to have Thatcher in his sights. One of Dixie's pals had managed to get Stephen a joiner's apprenticeship with the council, which he was ecstatic about. Maybe Dixie and herself were an inspiration, of some sort, after all. Once Cal reopened the office, after recent events, she would ask him if she could train as a paralegal, if he would allow it.

Dixie's killers were either dead or half dead and behind bars. Now they could all move on.

Chapter Thirty-Five

CAL WEAVED HIS WAY seamlessly between the crowds, returning to his previous London-resident mode. The wound to his thigh had healed quicker than expected with extraordinarily little muscle damage and luckily no main arteries hit. He walked slow enough to allow Lawrie to stay close, the click of the walking stick clear among the general din of the day-to-day business going on around them.

The crowds eased as the pavements widened alongside the three storey high buildings with a mixture of pubs, shops and houses living in perfect harmony.

He paused at a market stall where the seller had piled bootleg music tapes on milk crates next to homemade tailored suits.

'This isnae aw legal,' Lawrie said, looking around for any local police presence, his eyebrows lowered in disdain.

Cal grinned nodding towards the stallholder who glanced up anticipating a sell, his eyes squinting behind a baseball cap. 'Frank, this guy here will sell you The Cure's new album and it's not due out until next month.'

'I'd huckle him if ah worked here. Every day of the week.'

'Just to send your stress levels wild, down there at Camden Bridge,' Cal smirked, the devilment clear in his eyes, 'they'll provide you with any drug that takes your fancy.'

'Fucksake, does naebody get jailed around here then?'

'Big city with lots of priorities and chasing small time dealers isn't one of them. It'll come your way soon enough, wait and see. You'll be told to focus your time elsewhere.'

'Fuck that, ah'll be retired by then.'

Cal continued on before pausing at a barber's shop, each bright, red, leather seat occupied by an expectant youth, 'That's Syd Strong's. He does the best Flat Top in the whole of London.'

Turning onto Jamestown Road the background noise slowly receding they observed residents relaxing on their front steps, enjoying the warm summer sunshine, while others cleaned their large Victorian sash windows or shared gossip with their neighbours.

Cal sighed as he stopped facing the steps of a large, detached building, his eyes soaking up every inch of the yellow brick visible on the top two floors which contrasted with the light blue painted ground floor facade, surrounded by, ornately designed black railings.

'Three Oval Road, Frank. My old home.'

Frank leaned on a nearby lamppost, taking the weight off his leg. 'Swanky,' he responded, nodding in approval particularly impressed with the fan lights above the black gloss, panelled door, framed with smooth, white, concrete pillars on each side.

Sitting in the centre of the symmetrical terrace the place smelled of money; and, power and certainly not the tough upbringing he thought Cal had experienced on landing in London, under the hastily organised police protection programme.

'That must have cost a few quid. Wish ah had stayed in a gaff like that when ah was growing up. Ah've still got the fear from our ootside bog. Sharing that wae seven other families wis nae fun, ah kin tell ye.'

Cal turned to face him. 'We stayed in a small flat on Camden Road when we got here. Mum bought this when the criminal compensation money came through. The outside is a bit deceptive to be honest, inside it isn't all that great. It needs a lot of work done,' folding his arms across his chest, he leaned on the opposite side of the lamppost, his eyes fixed on the front door, 'I'm not really sure I'm ready for what might happen in there, Frank. I've been thinking about it all the way down here. But it needs to be done.'

'Let's just take it easy, we're no in any rush, pal.'

They slowly climbed the small set of steps, Frank grabbing the railing to haul himself up, and chapped the large brass knocker.

'No key?' Frank asked.

'She doesn't know I'm here.'

* * *

Cathy Lynch inched open the large door and peered tentatively from behind it. Her eyes widened and a large smile spread across her wrinkled features.

'Son, it's you,' she said loudly, surprise in her voice as she embraced him, gently touching his swollen cheek, 'are you OK, why didn't ye tell me ye were coming? Come in, come in.' She stood to the side waving him into the hall.

'I'm fine, Mum. Mum, this is my friend, Frank Lawrie.'

Frank stepped from behind Cal, balancing on his walking stick. 'Nice to finally meet you, Mrs Lynch.'

'You're the policeman that saved him, aren't ye? Ah seen yer picture in the paper.'

'Ah jist happened to be in the area, aye.'

'Thanks, officer. You're now my hero. Come in the pair of ye. Whit ye down here for anyway?'

'We need to clear a couple of things up, Mum.'

Cathy eyed her son with a stern stare as Lawrie moved ahead of them into the narrow hall.

Leading them into the living room she walked slowly towards her light brown seat close to the two-bar electric fire sitting within the bright floral tiling of the hearth.

The room was homely with a patterned carpet, which was almost matched by the colourful curtains framing the bay window. A large brown wall unit dominated one side of the room covered with an array of ornaments including, Scottish terrier dogs, colourful thistles and tartan clad pipers sitting behind the polished glass doors. The tackiness was mixed with a collection of pictures of Cal in just about every stage of his life.

'Please sit down and rest yerself, I'll put the kettle on,' Cathy rose from the seat.

'We need to talk, Mum, sit down. Please,' Cal insisted, not meeting her eye.

Lawrie removed his police notebook from his jacket pocket and gave his pen a shake, 'Mrs Lynch, there's a couple of things ah need to clear up and ah'm hoping ye can assist, OK?'

'Ah'll try, Mr Lawrie, but ah've been out of Scotland for years, so ah don't know what ah could help ye with. Ah widnae know the first thing bout the place now. But go ahead anyway,' Cathy replied, clasping her wrinkled, hands tightly at her waist, a whiteness appearing on her bony knuckles contrasting with thin lines of blue veins stretching toward her wrist.

Lawrie extended out his injured leg with a groan and placed the open notebook on his thigh, 'It's about two individuals you worked for a few years ago. A John Garner and a Bill Patrick? Do those names ring a bell?'

'Ach, Mr Lawrie, ah worked for loads ah folk doon here. Ah kin hardly remember where half of them were never mind who ah worked for.'

'Can ye remember reading bout their murders in the papers? We believe they were killed for not agreeing to launder money for a crime gang called, the Russo. You ever heard of that gang, heard that name mentioned anywhere or by anyone?'

'Cal, what's this about?' She asked turning to her son her eyebrows lowering.

'Best you answer everything, Mum. Anything you know.'

He was unsure how this would play out, how much would be revealed. If the meticulous planning and decisive moments that led to ending Jimmy Junior Quinn's life at Oakshaw were to be exposed, then so be it. He was exhausted by the whole affair.

'Ah haven't a clue what yer talking about, Mr Lawrie.'

'The gun used to kill both of these men was also used to kill a police officer, Nicki Henshaw.'

The room fell silent, only the noise of cars and buses passing the window on the street outside interrupted the uneasy quiet.

'Sadly, it wasn't only a dedicated officer who was killed, Cathy. Nicki was also carrying your unborn grandchild.'

Cathy glanced immediately at Cal, a sadness in her eyes, 'Pregnant, Son? Ye never said.'

Cal remained rigid, non-committal.

She whispered, 'I don't know anything about money, guns, nothing,' Cathy stared at the floral carpet, continually raising her eyes towards her son.

'Ah think you do, Cathy. We carried out investigations at other places where you were known tae have worked. We know there are a further eight businesses across London who have either been mysteriously closed down, burnt out or are currently being chased by our fraud colleagues due to suspected money laundering. It's no really a coincidence, is it? You were more than a bookkeeper. Ah think you were sent in to suss out these companies, ones doing well with high turnovers, you would then recommend these to the Russo. To hide their money.'

'Ach away. Ye have fanciful ideas, Mr Lawrie,' She responded rising and moving towards the large bay window, running her fingers over the sash window ledge, and tidying the net curtain.

Cal glanced at Lawrie noting that his friend had withheld details from him, just as he had done to him previously. Only sharing what he wanted him to know. He looked at the pictures proudly adorning the wall unit. Pictures of him as the dux of his private college, her beaming proudly as he graduated at the bar and the framed newspaper cutting of him receiving the Jean Crowe Pro Bono Award for his unstinting work with those most in need.

'Mum, how did you pay for me to go to a private school and cover all the fees for my lawyer training?'

Cathy stared out of the window motionless, her arms folded tightly across her chest.

Cal moved towards the wall unit lifting up pictures, his eyes on them as he spoke, 'I don't think bookkeepers get paid that much, Mum. You always worked, of course you did. But this place must have cost a few pounds, my school fees, you, and me surviving down here with the cost of everything. You're not telling me something. You need to tell me what you know.'

Cathy continued to stare out the window letting out a weary sigh, 'He wouldnae leave me alone, Son. Gave me no peace, not a minute's fuckin peace.' There was a different tone to her voice it was lower, a determination even relief within it.

Cal moved towards her; Lawrie stopped him signalling for him to say nothing.

'See, ah went out with him on a few dates. Granted he was a fair bit older than me. Auld enough to be ma faither to be honest, and ah was a daft wee lassie. Fuckin stupid, no half wise. Ah wis being spoiled, taken tae fancy restaurants and treated like royalty, him throwing about his money. Ah loved it. Me or ma family didnae have two coins tae rub together so tae have this, aw this attention it wis heid turning. Ah didnae really know he was a small-time gangster, beating people up, protection money, robberies, and that. When ah found out how bad ah character his wis, ah ended it. Told him it was over. But he widnae give me any peace.'

'Who, Mum?'

'Then ah met yer dad, and he was everything he wisnae. Yer dad wis kind, considerate, mature above his years. A bit of a dreamer, aye. Jist as skint as me but he wanted the best fur us. He had big plans. But he still widnae leave me alone. If only he would have accepted it. Ah suppose he wisnae used tae somebody saying no tae him. No being scared of him. Certainly no from a wummin.'

'Who are you speaking about, Cathy. Who wouldnae accept it?' Lawrie looked over at Cal, shrugging his shoulders in confusion.

'Jimmy Quinn, ah wis seeing him for a while. No for long, but long enough for him tae feel ah wis his possession. He wis raging when ah called it aff, he'd lost face, ye see. Ah didnae think it wis a big deal but he kept pestering me, begging me tae take him back. Then he threatened me, telt me what he'd dae tae ma family. Unbeknownst tae me, he would sit at home getting steaming and cursing yer dad upside down when he heard we got married,' she turned slowly, a whiteness shrouding her wrinkled face, 'his mad boy, Jimmy Junior. He wis a wee skitter, only a teenager himself. He killed Peter just tae make his da happy.'

'Wait …he killed dad and you; you knew all of this?'

'Jimmy Quinn knew ma heart was broken. When we were moved down here, he would send money through an accountant he used in London. Ah don't think the guilt ever left him, whit his boy did. He wis trying tae make amends, ah suppose. Or mibbae making sure his boy didnae get jailed for murder.'

Cal lowered his head and ran his manicured fingers through his smooth hair. His mind was racing thinking of all the talks they had had over the years about his father's death. How evil his killers were. How they would get their comeuppance. His mother leading the charge, never letting it go, driving him forward for this to become their mutual obsession. He paced across the small living room, the floorboards below his feet creaking as he went.

'So, you knew he'd done it, but you didn't give a statement, you didn't testify?'

'Son, he ran everything, he scared everyone. Ah'm no fuckin stupid. Your life would've been over if I'd done that. It wis best if we jist moved away, started again. Stayed quiet, hidden. You've got tae see that.'

'So…wait. So, Jimmy Quinn whose mad son killed my father. He paid to put me through school and the bar. They would have known all along who I was when I set up the office in Paisley. In the name of fuck.'

'Don't you dare swear at me.' Cathy scowled.

She shrugged her shoulders, and lowering her voice continued. 'Well, no really, no directly anyway. Ah never stopped working, ye know that.'

Cal collapsed on the couch unable to take it all in as Cathy walked slowly towards him taking his hand as she sat at his side.

'You could've just left it, Son. Ye didn't need tae go tae Scotland. Ye stirred it aw up.'

'They knew from the start, didn't they? Who I was when I set up in Paisley.'

Lawrie leaned forward in his seat tapping his pen on his thigh, attempting to get the evidence he required down on paper. 'Cathy, let me run this by you. Once Jimmy Junior took over the family business and expanded his network, he found out what his old man had been doing and decided to use you to wash money through, legitimate, businesses in London. The Russo sent you to work in companies that were doing well, turning huge profits and where it would be possible to hide a few hundred thousand without it drawing much attention. Your job was to pass on the information. Would that be right?'

'Ye should have just stayed here, Cal, with me. We would've been fine. Ye didnae need tae push it. Ah knew how bad they were, that's why ah tried tae help ye.'

'You would pass on the details of the accounts. Sometimes it would work, other times, well…if they didn't co-operate someone had to die.'

'When Jimmy Junior took over the business and found out about the payments, he went ballistic. He was seriously fuckin unhinged, that boy, said ah had stopped him seeing his daughter growing up cause he had tae move abroad. Anyway, he sent one of his contacts round… ah mind the guy was dressed immaculately but he scared the life oot ah me. He gave me two options; Cal would be killed…he even told me how they would do it, there'd be fuck all left to bury, he said or…,' Cathy took a tissue from her apron pocket, wiping her nose with it she tucked it into the sleeve of her cardigan, 'or go and work at places of their choosing and provide copies of the books to tell them how well they're doin. What the owners were like – that sort of thing. It was either losing ma son or give them some details to keep them away from us. Ah didnae know they would kill people, honest ah didnae,' she pleaded, her eyes set squarely on her son.

Cal thought of all the information that his mother had passed up the line – a rogue London lawyer had shared the detail on how Jimmy Junior planned to escape from custody, she said. Everything would kick off as soon as he would be moved for trial. How he had to be ready in case they came looking for him, she said. Get Ger Johnson onboard to protect you, she said. He removed his hand from hers and went and stood beside the fireplace, arms folded tightly across his muscular chest.

He stared at the floor his mind quickly going over the events of the past few months. Slowly he raised his head, looked at Lawrie for what seemed like an eternity then, fixing his glare on his mother, he spoke in a low, controlled voice.

'You were the only one I told. You were the only one who knew,' he pointed his finger at her, shaking his head.

'Knew what, Son?'

'I told you about our running at Strathclyde Park on a Sunday. You even laughed when I mentioned that Nicki hated it but enjoyed spending time with me so would come along anyway. You were the only one who knew. I told you on the phone. You set her up. I can't believe it; you had her killed.'

Cathy stiffened her back, removing the tissue from her sleeve she fiddled with it, lowering her eyes to follow her fidgeting.

'She wis getting too close, Son. Asking too many questions. She had Jimmy Junior in her sights, it was only a matter of time. She would've figured it out, put us aw in the jail.'

'You had her killed, didn't you, because in your warped, sad, controlling head she was taking me away from you.'

Cathy softened her eyes, 'Me and you were doin fine, Son. Can we no go back tae that? Back tae how it wis before ye went up tae that godforsaken place. Jimmy Junior can't hurt us anymore.'

'You worked for Dad's murderers then killed his unborn grandchild with a bullet through Nicki's head,' letting out a sarcastic laugh Cal ran his palms over his face several times attempting, in some way to erase what he was seeing and hearing, 'And what you don't get? They left evidence at all of the three executions that would lead to a direct link to you, to make sure you were implicated.'

Cal looked over at Lawrie now wide-eyed, 'When are they due?'

Lawrie took a quick glance at his watch then stretched his neck to look out of the window as the two police cars came to a halt outside Three Oval Road, 'Just arrived. Do ye want some time alone?'

He looked down at his mother, 'That won't be necessary.'

A look of fear was coming over her as it dawned on her that her life had completely unravelled and the one thing that she loved, had sought to shield and was supremely proud of, had disowned her in front of her eyes.

'Tell them everything, Mum, it might help you.'

Cal opened the front door and two uniformed officers entered. He heard the muffled sound of her rights being read to her in the living room. The officers returned guiding her down the hall, her coat over her hands hiding the handcuffs. She stopped at the door and looked at her son, trying to connect with him. He stood, stiff, holding the polished brass handle, his eyes looking at her with complete loathing as tears streamed down his face.

'Don't hate me, Son. It was done tae protect ye, all of it.'

Cal closed the door slowly and collapsed on the worn stairs dropping his head to his knees he clasped his hands tightly around his head hoping this was all a dream.

Lawrie placed a firm hand on his shoulder, 'Ah'm going to the Met, pal, then ah'll be heading back up the road. Ah need tae update the gaffers straightaway and finish ma report. You staying down here?'

Cal sat up and took a deep breath while wiping his face with his silk handkerchief. He shook his head, his smooth jawline tightening. Slowly he walked the length of the narrow hall and lifted a small, framed picture from the wall under the stairs. Rubbing his hands over the photograph he thought of how innocent they looked, how blissfully happy and contented his father appeared outside the chapel on their wedding day – a whole life of dreams ahead of him.

'There's nothing left for me here. I've a business to run. Once your colleagues are finished pulling this place apart, I'll visit Nicki's grave, then I'll be back up behind you. Up home.'

Cal reached out and shook Lawrie's outstretched hand as the tears flowed again down his cheeks.

'Nicki…Nicki…a letter arrived at the office just days after she was killed. I picked it up when I came back from being, you know, off. It was her handwriting on the envelope. I was shaking when I opened it. It didn't say much, just, "use this if something goes wrong." It's a list of names, individuals, from across the country and their direct connection with the Russo. She was so close. She must have had a gut feeling, a sense, that they wouldn't let her finish what she had started. They couldn't risk it. I suppose if it wasn't through my mother, they would have got her by some other means.'

'OK, Cal. I'll call in when yer back at work we can talk it over then. Let's try and get our lives back to normal, eh?

'There is no normal, Frank. My *normal* from here on in will be to smash the Russo, to wipe them out wherever they exist. They will have no understanding of what's been unleashed, what's coming their way. If they're in every area of public and business life? Then I'll be at their back. For my dad, for Nicki, and the baby. This is now my life's work.'

Other books by the Author

Black Is The Colour

Authors Notes

The satirical poem, Don Juan, written by Lord Byron, coined the phrase, "truth is stranger than fiction." This novel is clearly a work of fiction.

Certain locations in Paisley, London and Berlin will be well known to some and are still prominent almost forty years on from 1985 when the novel is set.

The John Neilson School, known locally as the Porridge Bowl, has been refurbished and the iconic structure still dominates the landscape overlooking the West End of Paisley. The Buddies Bar, aka The Vatican, is well worth a visit.

The Philharmonie Berlin has been the musical heart of Berlin since 1963. Situated at the periphery of West Berlin when it first opened, it is now part of the new urban centre after the fall of the Berlin Wall. Its unusual tent-like shape and distinctive bright golden colour make it a must-see landmark, both inside and out.

The Hutchesontown C tower blocks in Glasgow's Gorbals were officially opened on the 30th of June 1960. The design was partly inspired by Le Corbusier's giant maisonette blocks in Marseille. I would assume the climate in the South of France, with cool, mild winters, moderate rainfall, and hot, mostly dry summers was slightly different from those experienced in the West of Scotland. The blocks were demolished in 1993.

The Renfrewshire World was a free paper distributed throughout Paisley in the 1980's. Much to their relief, teenagers Caroline O'Hara and the author, were unceremoniously sacked for alleged non delivery of this local rag. They both still adore the Pogues.

Kison the Bastard was a very much-loved family pet, and I'm reliably informed that it tended to be over enthusiastic with anything that moved.

As a result of the Live Aid concerts staged in July 1985 in London and Philadelphia an estimated £150 million for famine relief had been raised and set in motion similar campaigns over the next four decades. Many of the artists who gave up their time to perform have subsequently went on to have very successful careers within the music industry.

I wanted to include the story of Berliner, Michael Bittner, and used some creative licence. A year after the book is set Michael, aged twenty-five, attempted to escape at the border grounds in Glienicke/Nordbahn. His relocation application had previously been refused. He was shot dead on 24th November 1986 as he climbed the last outer wall to reach the West.

The Girrmann Group was one of the first and most influential groups helping people escape from East Berlin during the Cold War. It was formed by students at the Eichkamp International student hostel of the Free University of West Berlin. Their original purpose was focussed on students, but the program later expanded to helping anybody who had hopes of escaping. The group managed to set up an evolving network to help thousands of East Berliners. It is estimated that in 1961 alone the group assisted over 5,000 people safely escape.

Markus Wolf was head of the Main Directorate for Reconnaissance, the foreign intelligence division of East Germany's Ministry for State Security – the Stasi. He was the Stasi's number two for 34 years.

The Russo is a multi-conglomerate crime syndicate which operates across Scotland and Europe. All fiction, honest.

Acknowledgements

I have a huge debt of gratitude to Jacqueline Dalrymple for patiently and diligently proofreading, over several months, an early draft of the novel and offering advice and insights as I developed the story. I hope you like the final result, thank you.

Thanks again to Colm Donnelly for designing the cover and amending it on multiple occasions as my mind continued to flip.

Thanks to my good friend, Mark Meehan, for his patience and enthusiasm and for posing like a true professional as we took numerous pictures to capture *the* one which made the cover.

To everyone who shared their laughs and sometimes tears through their stories. I'm eternally grateful that you allowed me to apply certain tweaks and weave them into the book.

To Karen Holmes for your continued advice and positive reinforcement.

Thanks to Gwen and PublishNation for all your support.

A teacher, many years ago, in St Mary's Primary School, Paisley, told me one day that I had a talent for writing and encouraged me to keep working at it. I'm sure she inspired many, many other pupils – thank you, Miss Mulligan.

Not forgetting big Tony Davidson who saved my life in 1985 – thanks Tanya.

And Cara-Marie, again…it's your turn.